Seven Fleurs de Lis

On a German Coat of Arms?

Clark Munger

Clark W Munger — Green Valley, AZ
ISBN: 978-0-578-45587-7
Library of Congress Control Number: Pending
Title: *Seven Fleurs de Lis on a German Coat of Arms?*
Author: Clark Munger
Digital distribution | 2019
Paperback Edition, 2019

Publishing assistance by New Book Authors

Dedication

To my son, Matthew, and my daughter, Michelle, and to my grandson, Gabriel.

With special appreciation to my wonderful wife, Cindy, for her patience and encouragement in this new adventure.

Acknowledgements

Developmental edit assistance by Historical Editorial

CHAPTER I
Sixteen 1356 AD

"Opa," I said, gently interrupting my grandfather as he wrote. "We are Germans, aren't we?"

The old man put down his pen and rubbed his eyes. "You are German, Erik. Both your parents are German and you were born in the city of Lubeck, in Germany. Why do you ask?"

"Last week my tutor told me about the fleur de lis. He said it's French."

"Yes, it is. Some say it represents the lily, the flower of Christ. Others believe it's the iris and represents the King of France. It's used for many purposes and in many places, not only in France."

"Why does a German coat of arms have seven fleurs de lis?"

The old man smiled at me with a gentleness that filled me with warmth. I felt I'd asked a worthy question. He was, in my opinion, a stern old man. I was too young to understand the depth of his love but I felt it. He moved his chair back from his writing desk, turned it towards me and leaned forward. "That's a long story. How old are you now, Enkel?"

He often used my name, Erik, and the affectionate term for grandson, Enkel, interchangeably. I'd been given his name when I was born and felt a closeness to him I couldn't otherwise explain.

"Sixteen." I was baffled he would ask. After all, I had not been permitted to study in the old man's apartments until I was sixteen and my birthday had been several months before.

Between my morning lessons and our midday meal I was now permitted in his apartments to use his large table to prepare for my lessons. With his supervision I could inspect his small collection of manuscripts and maps. He kept a few interesting, even mysterious, objects from his early life there, too. In the early afternoon I had another hour of lessons, then I was free to join my friends for horseback riding, fencing, archery and wrestling. After dinner it was too dark to read or do much of anything.

The old man nodded and motioned for me to be seated in the chair across from him. When I complied, he pointed to our family coat of arms.

"You're asking about our coat of arms, aren't you?"

"Yes," I replied with a nod. A large, carved and painted, wooden coat of arms hung on the north wall of his apartments but nowhere else in our home.

Not taking his eyes off the coat of arms he rubbed his chin, then looked down at me. Taking a deep breath he said, "It's an excellent question with a very long answer. Your father and I knew there would come a time you would ask and he told me I was to explain it to you. But you must promise me and him that in time you will tell your own grandsons and ask them to make the same promise."

It seemed a strange thing to ask of me and an empty promise for a boy of sixteen to make. The thought, at that age, that I might someday have children or a grandchild seemed almost beyond comprehension. But I nodded. Out of respect I would promise the old man anything he asked and I was curious what would he tell me if I made the promise.

"Do you promise?"

"Yes, I promise. But why doesn't my father tell me?"

"Because he will tell your sons. That's the way he and I decided it should be done. Each man should tell his grandsons and ask them to make the same promise."

"Will Hans be told when he's sixteen?" I was concerned my younger brother might not have to wait as long as I had.

"Yes, he will. Your father and I decided sixteen was the right age. So I must ask that you promise not to tell your brother or discuss this with him until your father gives you permission. Your brother is not yet ready but you must never make him feel he isn't. If you do then we will not continue until he is sixteen and then you both will learn at the same time. Do you understand?"

With a frown I nodded. That was not sufficient for the old gentleman and he sat, silent and unsmiling, waiting for my answer.

"Yes, I understand and I promise." Now I had made two solemn promises and felt overwhelmed but I also realized I had been invited into a realm of special knowledge; I had passed into a new stage of life. I sat up straighter in my chair.

He smiled and coughed or maybe it was his laugh, I was often unsure which it was. "Then I'll tell you. To understand our coat of arms you must understand the world we lived in when I was your age and how it has changed. The old orders have been replaced by a new order. It was not an easy change for Europe or for our family. Our coat of arms honors our family's part in that change.

"My father was a skilled blacksmith and taught me a great deal of those skills. Of course he didn't own the tools. That was not permitted. He worked for and at the sufferance of his lord and kept only what his lord permitted. My father wanted something better for me but there were few choices. Everyone worked for the lord who owned the land or for the Church.

"When I was sixteen, my mother died giving birth to twins, their fourth and fifth children. The twins died, too. They died without names. My father's grief was such that he didn't know what to name them.

"Their first child had died, too. From a fever, my father told me, when the child was about four. I don't remember his name. Their third child was very frail, sickly, and died young, about three. I don't know what he died of. His name was William.

"I didn't know it then but I think my father gave up when my mother died. When my mother and the twins died our village priest said something that made my father believe God was unhappy with him but neither my father nor the priest knew why. After that my father told me I should join the Church or become a monk. If I were closer to God then bad things would not happen to me. Maybe I wouldn't suffer the losses he had."

"Where did you live?"

"Oh, it was in a small village in Normandy, a day south of Le Havre."

"You're French?" I was more than a little disappointed by the idea.

"I was then but I'm German now," he replied with a smile. "Besides, Normans didn't really consider themselves French. Normans descended from the Norsemen, Vikings from Denmark and the Baltic countries."

I was somewhat consoled but said nothing.

"As I said, my father was a blacksmith. He frequently did work for an order of warrior monks who wore the red cross. The monks frequently passed through our village on the way to their different commanderies. If a horse threw a shoe or they needed a smithy to repair tack they would stop at my father's forge. Not long after my mother died five monks stopped on their way to Le Havre. One of their horses had thrown a shoe and needed to be shod. That's when he asked them to take me in, to become a monk in their order. He told them I'd already turned sixteen and he'd taught me something of smithing. They could see that I was strong and pretty good with horses.

"I didn't want to become a priest so becoming a warrior monk seemed the right thing to do to please both God and my father. If that's what my father thought best for me, then it was right. As you know, we we're taught in church to honor our father and mother and serve God.

"Three weeks later when the same five monks stopped by my father's forge on their way back to their Commandry at Arville they agreed to take me with them. It didn't take me long to get ready. I had little enough to pack and they explained I would be provided everything I needed. So after a quick lunch my father waved good-bye to me as I set out on foot, following the five monks, to join their Order. I had no idea what a monk was but it was what my father said I should do. It was as simple as that.

"You don't just become a monk right away, you know. You go through years of learning and then they decide if you are qualified and suited to the Order. But during those years you work very hard and don't have much contact outside the Order. It's a simple life but it's not for everyone."

Opa leaned back in his chair, lost in thought, then sighed and smiled again.

"Sorry, I was thinking of my father and mother. I think of them more often lately. I was very young when my mother died but I remember her eyes. Is it the same with you?"

I nodded. I, too, had lost my mother and I, too, remembered the softness of her eyes.

"What did you do? It sounds like an apprenticeship?"

"Yes, it was a kind of apprenticeship. The first year I did whatever I was told to do. Mostly," he said with a laugh, "I mucked out the stables, groomed, fed and watered the horses, cleaned tack, did a little smithing, and helped repair and clean weapons and equipment. It was simple work and I learned to be happy with simple things. Eat, sleep, do your work well without complaint, and honor God's commandments. It's a simple path to happiness and peace of mind."

"Where did you live?"

"In the stable, in a small room next to the horses and the smithy's forge."

"But where was that?"

"Oh, it was at the Commandry of Arville."

"What was the Order, the monks' Order?"

"Then it was known as the Poor Fellow-Soldiers of Christ and of the Temple of Solomon but most people simply knew it as the Knights Templar."

"You were a knight?" I was astonished. I just didn't expect the old man had ever been young or strong enough to be a knight.

"Well, knights came from wealthy families. Eventually I became a sergeant and took the same vows as the Knights. Like the knights the sergeants fought on horseback. Only our uniform was different.

"It took years, five to be exact, before I had grown enough and learned enough to be accepted in the Order. After that first year I'd grown several inches and put on weight. I was well fed and with all the work it was all muscle. At the end of that first year, the summer of 1298, when I turned seventeen, I became a squire to a knight. His name was Alleric. It was his duty to train me and teach me. He was half again my age, very big and very smart. He was like an older brother. I was permitted to move into the dormitory with the other young men who hoped to join the Order. I studied and learned to use weapons, but I still worked in the stables helping the smithies."

"What did you study?"

"Latin, mostly the Bible. Mathematics, geography and I learned to write, too. Not much different than what you study. Alleric was our tutor."

"What weapons did you learn?" I asked, with an excitement anyone my age would feel regarding weapons and war.

"Everything. Both knights and sergeants had to be familiar with all weapons. Even the weapons our enemies might use. On the battlefield you never know what weapons you may be faced with or what will be available to you. And we lifted weights and we ran and wrestled."

"Even catapults?" I asked wide-eyed.

"Oh, yes. We learned to build and shoot catapults, trebuchets. And we jousted on horseback, too."

"Did it hurt?"

"Yes, it hurt! Falling from a horse or getting knocked off your horse by an opponent's lance hurts. For training we used an oak sword and an oak club for a mace or ax. But getting hit by an oak broad sword or club, even in full armor, hurts. But that's just part of it. I never minded it that much, it made me feel stronger. I could get hit or take a fall and get back up to fight. I never felt stronger."

I leaned forward. "Everyone says the Templars found a great treasure under the Dome of the Rock."

Opa chuckled, or coughed. "Years later I heard such rumors in France and in Cyprus. Some said the Templars even found the Holy Grail. When I asked Brother Matthew about the rumors he explained the history of the Temple and assured me the Templars had found neither wealth nor the Grail.

"When you think about it that wasn't shocking. Three decades after Christ was crucified the Romans sacked the city and destroyed the old Jewish Temple. The Romans built a temple to Jupiter on the Temple ruins. Almost six hundred years later the Muslims captured the city and built the first Islamic shrine on the same site. That temple collapsed and a few years after that the Dome of the Rock was built over the ruins.

"All that happened before the Templars arrived. The rumors don't say where this supposed treasure came from. Any treasure, including the Grail, whether owned by the Jews or the Romans or the Muslims, would have been found and removed before the city was taken from them."

"Brother Matthew was certain the Jews would not have let the treasure fall into the hands of the Romans, and the Romans would not have let the Muslims have it. The Muslim leaders were not about to leave such a treasure behind when the Crusaders took the city.

"There was no treasure in or beneath the Dome of the Rock when the Templars took it a thousand years after Christ was crucified. Any treasure that might have once been there was gone.

"Brother Matthew was certain the Grail used at the Last Supper was owned by Joseph of Arimathea, a wealthy Jew, and would not have been stored in the Jewish Temple. After all, Jesus and all his followers were not held in high regard by the Jewish priests who guarded the Temple."

"Did your father come to see you?"

"No, the first year I was not allowed to have visitors or leave the commandry. Just before that year was up, Alleric came to see me one Sunday evening after Vespers. He told me my father had died. After I left home that day with the monks I never saw my father again."

8

The old man sadly shook his head. "The last I saw him he was waving good-bye. I think he knew we would not meet again in this life."

I wanted to say something that might ease my grandfather's pain but couldn't find the words.

"That's why I never feared battle or death. It made me stronger and fearless. I knew that if, when, I died I would see my mother and father again and my siblings, if I kept God's commandments."

"Did you like your apprenticeship?"

"Yes, I did. Very much. It was a simple life and I enjoyed the comradeship, they were the brothers I never had. I also enjoyed learning. I learned to read and write Latin but I was far better at mathematics.

"My father was an excellent smithy and an intelligent man but he could not read, write nor do mathematics. He had never traveled more than a day from his forge and knew very little of what was happening in Europe. It wasn't that he was lazy or not able. He was obligated to serve his lord and wasn't a free man.

"I didn't have to worry about food or shelter and I was always busy, surrounded by my brothers, my friends. I had no use or need for money. I always slept well and was rarely sick.

"I felt I had a purpose. I would become one of Christ's warriors to open the Holy Lands to Christian pilgrims and protect them on their journey. I felt clean, protected from sin by the Order and by God. I felt sheltered from the kind of loss my father had suffered. I also felt very close to my parents. I was doing what they wanted me to do.

"One of the happiest days of my life was the day Alleric told me I had been accepted into the Order and would be initiated on the next Sabbath. I prayed I would be permitted to join in another crusade to the Holy Land.

"When that Sunday came Matthew presided over the initiation and administered the oath. I was issued my chainmail, helmet, shield emblazoned with red cross, black tunic with red cross, brown mantel and hood, two handed sword, mace and misericordes, two horses, a saddle and tack. It was everything I needed to carry out my duty. I felt blessed."

"What's a misericordes?"

"It's a knife. It has a long, thin, narrow, double-edged blade. Very deadly weapon. I still have it. It's on the mantel above the fireplace. "

"What happened at the initiation?"

"I swore a solemn oath to God and the Order, an oath of poverty, obedience and chastity."

"When did you become a Templar?"

"In 1302 when I was twenty-one."

"Did you go to the Holy Land?"

"Unfortunately, no. After the Templars and other Crusaders were driven out of the Holy Land at the battle of Acre the Templars set up new bases on the island of Cyprus. Not long after our initiation twenty of us, all new Templars, led by Alleric sailed to Rome, then to Cyprus. Except for a few exploratory raids on the mainland, that was as close as I got to the Holy Land.

"There was a great deal of talk of another Crusade. Philip, the King of France, wanted to restructure the three Orders into one with him as their commander to retake the Holy Land. Several other kings argued they should lead the Crusade. Each wanted to be in control but none of them really wanted to leave his kingdom and fight in the deserts of the Holy Land.

"Our Grand Master de Molay, Pope Clement, and King Philip tried to form a new alliance with the Mongol leader,

Ghazan, who controlled Persia and was moving south and west into Syria. Our hopes of a new crusade and the power struggles between Phillip and the other kings ended with the death of Ghazan. When he died there was no possibility of a Christian-Mongol alliance and without an alliance there was no possibility of another Crusade.

"The Templars were trained as warriors to protect Christians in the Holy Land but we were also bankers and managed properties all over France. We had ships, both cogs and galleys, and were involved in trade along the northern coast of the Mediterranean from Gibraltar to Cyprus, even up the Atlantic coast as far as England and Scotland.

"I was assigned to keep business records for our supplies and shipments. Later I handled banking for travelers and merchants throughout the Mediterranean. Templars helped spread the new Arabic numbering system and double-entry bookkeeping through Europe.

"During those years I learned not just how to sail our ships but to navigate at sea using a compass and to use sea maps. The best maps had compass bearings marked on them. That doesn't sound remarkable now but at the time both compasses and sea maps were new. Sea maps with compass bearings were very rare. The Templars didn't invent them but were among the first to widely use them. The world was changing very rapidly. It seemed every year there were new inventions and discoveries and the Templars were quick to make use of them."

I don't recall how long we had been talking but I remember I was getting restless trying to absorb all this information and began to fidget. The old man could see it and leaned back in his chair and reached for his incense, burner and candle. "Enkel, I'm tired and I talk too much. You are polite to listen to an old man. If you don't mind I'm going to sit awhile then take my nap. We'll talk more, another day."

That evening I told my father what had happened and I was surprised at his smile as he hugged me and told me how proud he was that I wanted to know about our family coat of arms. Clearly there was something important in what the old man had to say about it.

In the morning, before my tutor could begin the day's lessons I asked him if he had heard of the Knights Templar. He was usually quite animated while teaching but he surprised me. He gave me a quizzical look, then answered in a monotone, as if he were reading from a manuscript.

"The Knights Templar were an order of warrior monks founded in 1119. The Order was officially known as the Poor Fellow Soldiers of Christ and of the Temple of Solomon and sanctioned by the Holy Catholic church in 1129 to protect Christian pilgrims to the Holy Land. It was disbanded by Pope Clement V and King Philip IV of France in 1312. All Templars were killed, arrested or disappeared in 1307. There are no Knights Templar still living."

There was an awkward pause. "Why do you ask?"

He didn't wait for my answer. That was peculiar because he had a habit of teaching by asking me questions and evaluating my answers. Instead, he immediately started his lesson for the day. I'm sure it was a valuable lesson that morning, it always was, but I don't think I heard a word of it after he told me that all the Knights Templar were dead.

After my lessons I ran up the stairs to the old man's apartments on the second floor but the heavy wooden double doors were closed. I debated whether to knock or not. I was certain he was at home but I was afraid I would interrupt his work. Finally, I knocked. After all within that room was a

Templar but my tutor had just told me there were no living Templars.

No sooner had I knocked twice when the doors opened and the old man stood before me smiling, then waved me in and pointed to my chair.

"Come in Enkel! Please sit down. I'm so happy you decided to come back. I was afraid I had bored you. Maybe just a little?"

"No, I wasn't bored. It's a lot to learn all at one time."

When we'd settled in to our chairs I said, "This morning my tutor told me that all the Knights Templar are dead."

"He did, did he? Well, it shows he doesn't know everything. But then no one really does."

It took him several minutes to light his burner but it gave me time to study the old man. I'd never really looked at him before. He had always been there as long as I could remember; a kind of stern but friendly, moving, talking fixture in what I had always thought of as my father's home, my home. It had never occurred to me that he had a life before my own or outside my home.

I respected him because my father, clearly, respected him. Suddenly he had become interesting, a relic that my tutor said should be dead but obviously wasn't. I'd seen colored drawings of Knights Templar but try as I might I just couldn't envision the old man as a warrior knight in Templar armor sitting on a mighty charger, lance in hand, Templar banner flying in the wind.

When satisfied he had it right, he smiled at the burner then at me, rubbed his shoulders into the cushion tied to the back of his chair and began, "Yesterday I explained that Alleric and the rest of us had been in Cyprus with little hope of reopening the Holy Land.

"Alleric and the rest of us were unexpectedly ordered back to France in early 1307 with four vessels, two cogs and two galleys. They were supply ships really but we also used them to transport knights and special passengers. We returned by the long route, first to the Commandry at Hyeres where we picked up crates and five brothers, then through the Straits of Gibraltar, up the coast of Spain and Portugal to France and the harbor at La Rochelle. It was a long, difficult voyage but we arrived safely in late July.

He paused long enough for me to ask, "What were the other Templars like?" I hoped that by explaining who they were I would learn more about who he had been.

"Oh, the ones I trained with were great friends. My closest friends were Dieter and Jehan. During Philip's dispute with Edward I, he was known as "Longshanks, Philip confiscated the land of a noble in Gascony who Philip thought was helping Longshanks. After taking the land Philip removed Dieter's family and the other tenant farmers to make room for people loyal to him. Dieter and his brother, Alfred, became Templars rather than join Philip's army.

"Jehan's family farmed the land of a Norman baron with too little fertile land to feed all his people. Jehan was the oldest son and left when he was old enough to fend for himself. The local bishop refused to take him into the priesthood. Jehan wasn't too disappointed about that. The Templars seemed a better choice. There weren't many choices in life for Jehan.

"Alleric was a great knight and friend, strong and quick, both physically and mentally. Unlike me he had been born into a wealthy noble family but he never made that a consideration. In fact, I think he respected the fact that I had not been. Wilhelm was second-in-command of Alleric's men.

"In Cyprus, I worked for an older brother, Matthew. He was in charge of our financial matters in Cyprus. As I told you, I was pretty good at mathematics so it was a logical assignment.

"Over the years Templars created a clever way to protect pilgrims' money on their journey to the Holy Lands. Before starting his journey a pilgrim would deposit funds with the Templars, in any of the Templar commanderies. In return he would be given a coded receipt. Along the way a pilgrim could stop at any Templar fort or location and the cost of lodging, food, whatever goods were needed, would be deducted from the receipt. It was all done in a secret code. If the pilgrim was robbed no one else could use the receipt so in dangerous lands it was safer to carry a Templar receipt than gold or silver coins.

"Didn't you have time for fun?"

"Well, not really. We were very busy and when you've taken a vow of poverty and chastity, well, we just didn't have time."

It sounded like a difficult, lonely life to me. "What were the other men like, those who had just been initiated with you?"

"They were other young men, like Dieter, Alfred and Jehan, who were looking for a life of purpose, dedicated to a life of purpose, to serve God and our Lord."

"You haven't told me why there are seven fleurs de lis on our coat of arms."

"I know. It's a long answer and we've hardly started. If I gave you a short answer it wouldn't make sense. To understand the coat of arms' significance you must first understand how Europe has changed. It wasn't like it is today. If it were, I'd be a blacksmith like my father or a Templar like I once was and we wouldn't live in Lubeck and we wouldn't be involved in the Hansa and the Baltic trade. All those changes are represented in our coat of arms."

For a moment my attention shifted to the coat of arms but as I studied it I couldn't see how it represented any changes.

"What happened when you arrived in La Rochelle?"

"Ah! Yes. La Rochelle. Well, under Matthew's leadership all four of our ships arrived safely in late July, 1307. Our Grand Master, de Molay, wanted all of us in La Rochelle but no one knew why. He was in Paris where he had been summoned by both Pope Clement V and King Philip IV. At the time I didn't know why they had summoned him to Paris or why de Molay wanted us in La Rochelle. I didn't learn why until much later.

"Upon our arrival in La Rochelle, sealed orders from the Grand Master required Brother Matthew join him in Paris as soon as possible. So he left early the morning after our arrival. There were already eight Templar ships in the harbor when we arrive and while Brother Matthew was in Paris four more Templar ships, two galleys and two cogs, anchored in La Rochelle's harbor.

"It took ten days to travel overland from La Rochelle to Paris and another ten to return. When Brother Matthew returned from Paris almost a month later, it was late August, he looked very tired. I remember he immediately retired to the Templar chapel, alone without even a priest or a brother Templar, for several hours. When he came out he said nothing of his meeting in Paris but simply ordered Alleric and the other captains to keep their ships provisioned and their crews, and all Templar knights and sergeants ready for a long sea voyage on short notice. No one was to say anything of the preparations to anyone outside the Order.

"During the balance of August and through September rumors were common, most were unbelievable. Most disturbing were rumors that King Philip owed vast sums to the Templars. We didn't know why he owed the debt. If the rumor were true it might explain why he summoned de

Molay to Paris and it would be a very serious matter. The year before he'd ordered expulsion of the French Jews, mostly because he owed them a great deal of money.

"Clement feared the King. Fear wasn't a strong enough word; he was terrified of him. Two preceding Popes, Boniface and Benedict, had died under mysterious circumstances. There was speculation Philip had ordered one of his advisors, a man named de Nogaret, to murder them. Clement lived in Pointers where the King could get to him, not in Rome where he might be safe.

"Pope Clement and King Philip wanted to merge the Templars with the Knights Hospitallers and the Teutonic Knights to break the Templars' power. Each had his private reasons but in public they both said it was because a single combined order of warrior monks under the control of King Philip would have more success against the Mamluks."

I interrupted, "What's a Mamluk, Opa? I've never heard of a Mamluk. Is it an animal?"

I hadn't either and couldn't believe any animal, no matter where it came from, or how terrible it might be could stand up to the Templars.

The old man nodded. "A good question, Enkel. But it needs time to answer it and I think we've used our time for today. We're covered a great deal. I'd like you to continue your studies and learn what you can of the Crusades. We'll talk again in six months, if you're still interested."

It was a long six months. At times I asked questions about the coat of arms or the Templars but neither my father nor my grandfather would respond. The closer it came to that date the more I tried to learn on my own but I found few people knew much about the Templars, except that Templars fought in the crusades and had all been murdered by the French king.

None of the priests I asked wanted to talk about the Templars. One gave me the same summary my tutor had, almost word for word and in the same dry monotone. The others claimed they didn't know anything about the Templars. It was as if the priests resented that the Templars had ever existed.

I tried a different approach. I decided to go to the Lubeck headquarters of the Teutonic Knights. It was a risky move as the Teutonic Knights and the Hansas were at times given to disputes. I did not tell either my father or my grandfather but it seemed to me a logical move. Both Orders had fought in the Holy Lands, had been officially sanctioned by the Holy Church, and had as part of their charge the protection of the Holy Lands and pilgrims. Certainly they might know something of the Templars.

I had the good fortune to meet a knight, a man older than my father, closer in age to Opa. I didn't tell him who I was or why I was there. I just told him I was Erik and I was interested in his Order and the Crusades. We talked for over an hour that first time mostly of the history of the Crusades and the wars between Islam and Christianity. Nothing was said of the Hansas or Baltic commerce. He encouraged me to return if I had more questions. I was certain I would so I made a special effort to be respectful. He did not ask my last name and I did not ask his. He called me Erik and I called him "sir."

I talked with him three or four times in the following months. He never asked who I was or why I was curious. If we saw each other on the street or in the market, which was not often, we just nodded politely but didn't speak. I didn't learn his name until later.

The anticipated date finally arrived and I waited impatiently all that day but neither Opa nor my father said a word of the Templars or the coat of arms. At dinner that evening I summoned my courage and asked, "Will you tell me more about the coat of arms?"

My father smiled as Opa said, "Tomorrow, after your lessons."

The next day after my tutor concluded the day's lessons I ran up the stairs, three at a time, and knocked on the double doors to Opa's apartments. Either I knocked very loudly or he was waiting because the doors opened immediately. I remember it was a cold, blustery day and he had a fire in his fireplace.

"Come in Enkel." He waived me in and pointed to my chair which had been moved from the writing table so it sat across from his large cushioned chair. "I have so looked forward to this day and very pleased you're still interested. How are your studies?"

"Good, I guess. I like mathematics and history but not Latin."

"Is that all you've been studying?"

"No, I've been studying the Crusades and the Templars, and the Mamluks, too."

"Ah, what have you learned?"

"Mamluks were Muslim warriors," I responded as I sat up a little straighter.

"Yes they were. And excellent warriors too. With very capable leaders. Do you know who any of their leaders were?"

"Yes, Saladin the Great."

"He was one. A very able leader during the Third Crusade. And Sultan Khalil led the siege of Acre, the last Templar stronghold in the Holy Land. But what made Mamluks great warriors in battle was their belief in life after death. Especially if they died in battle against the Infidels. Do you know what an infidel is?"

Yes, that's what Muslims call people who aren't followers of Islam."

"And what is Islam?"

I frowned. The questions were beginning to seem endless and I feared I might run out of answers. I answered but in a rote monotone I reserved for my lessons. "Islam is a religion. Followers say it is the one true faith and Mohammed its only true prophet."

"Excellent, you've been learning history."

His unexpected compliment renewed my enthusiasm and I said, "Vikings believed in life after death, too. If they died in battle they believed they would join Odin in Valhalla."

"Yes, they did. And you know Christians also believe in life after death if you follow and believe in Christ. The Templars believed they would go to heaven if they died in battle.

"Christians and our ancestors, the pagan Vikings, also believed in a final battle. A battle between good and evil some say. Vikings called it Ragnarok. Christians call it Armageddon. I'm sure Islam has such a belief but I don't know what they call it."

"What else have you learned?"

"I've learned about the Muslims and the Crusades and the Iberian Reconquista. Do you want to hear what I've learned?"

The old man nodded and sat back in his chair.

"Mohammed lived in the five hundreds. Some say he was born in 570. His followers believe he was the one true prophet of God and his followers spread from Arabia through North Africa and as far as India. They even crossed to Andalusia, then to Spain and Portugal and north into France. Charles Martel, he was called Charles the Hammer, stopped the Muslims at Tours. He was Charlemagne's grandfather.

"When Muslims conquered lands they killed anyone who would not convert to Islam and they killed any Muslim who wanted to convert to any other religion. Churches and synagogues or temples were destroyed and mosques were built over them, like the Temple of Solomon, it's now the Dome of the Rock in Jerusalem. They formed a caliphate and captured the Holy Lands."

"Why did you refer to the Temple of Solomon?"

"Because the Templars used the Dome of the Rock as their fortress in Jerusalem. The Dome was built on top of the old Jewish Temple of Solomon. That's how the Templars got their name."

"When did the Crusades start?'

"The first one was thirty years after William conquered England. He defeated Harold, the English king."

"When did the Crusades end?"

"Well, Acre fell in 1291. There weren't any after that."

"You mentioned William. Where did he come from?"

"France."

"What part of France?"

"Normandy." At the same time I said it I recalled that's where he'd been born. "Did your family, our family, fight with William?"

"I don't know, they might have."

"Where did the Normans come from? Why are they called Normans and why were their lands in France called Normandy?"

"My tutor says Normans were called that because it means men from the north, northmen."

"Your tutor is correct. The Normans or Norsemen were Vikings from the north."

He leaned back and smiled. "So if I came from Normandy, am I a Frenchman or a Viking? And was England conquered by Frenchmen or Vikings?"

I guess I looked confused but at the same time I was also proud that I had Viking ancestors.

"Enkel, the more you learn, the more you will find that our world has a history that has led us to the present and will lead you to the future. The Viking raids against the Christian lands were brutal, a scourge greater than the plagues we've suffered. The raids began in the seven hundreds and ended about three hundred years later. The old Viking pagan religion ended about the same time, when Iceland decided to convert to Christianity. I think there's a connection.

"Perhaps the Viking raids brought our family to France from somewhere far to the north but I don't know when or where they came from.

"The Crusades lasted almost two hundred years. But unlike the Viking raids, the conflict between Christianity and Islam has not ended. It may not end during your lifetime. It may not end until one of the two religions ceases to have moral authority."

He stoked the fire, then settled back into his chair. "I didn't know it at the time but I learned later that on October 7 of 1307 Brother Matthew and the other Templar leaders in La Rochelle received a coded message from the Grand Master. All sixteen of the Templar ships in La Rochelle were to sail not later than the morning of Thursday, October 12th. Beginning on the ninth of October and every day thereafter one of the four fleets sailed from La Rochelle harbor. Each fleet had four ships.

"The rumor on the docks was the ships were provisioning Templar outposts or carrying on our usual trade but only the captains of those ships knew their true destinations. It was all very secretive. Even we didn't understand what was happening.

"Our four Templar ships were the last to leave La Rochelle harbor with Matthew in charge. We were fully loaded and sailed with the tide on the 12th. Once at sea and out of sight of land we replaced our sails bearing the Templar cross with plain sails without insignia.

"Much later I learned that on September 14th the King had sent sealed orders to his forces throughout France that the Templars were to be arrested at dawn on Friday, the 13th of October. If they resisted they were to be killed. Somehow word of it had reached the Grand Master.

"I don't know what cargo the other three fleets carried. Our four ships were loaded with food, wine and beer, business records, tools, weapons, and a very little gold and silver."

"Where did the other ships go?" I asked.

"Years later I learned the first fleet to leave, it had four galleys, went to Portugal. The third fleet, two cogs and two galleys, went to Scotland.

"The mystery was, and still is, what happened to the second fleet to leave. It had four cogs. I've heard different reports. Some say they went to Iceland, others say Sicily or Cyprus. All that is possible but doubtful. We would have heard from them if that were the case. There was a terrible storm in the Atlantic the day after the second fleet left La Rochelle harbor. Some believe all four ships were lost at sea."

"They just disappeared?"

"Yes, but there's another possibility. I'm certain your tutor has told you of Iceland and Greenland. Has he told you of Gudrid Thorbjarnardottir?"

"I remember something about her, in the Greenland Saga and Erik the Red's saga. She was from Iceland."

"According to those sagas there are lands far to the west of Greenland. Vikings found those lands and tried to settle them. They called it Vinland but no one really knows where Vinland is. Sometime around the year one thousand Gudrid gave birth to a child in Vinland, a son she named Snorri. Later she traveled to Norway and then south to Rome. Some reports say she became a nun and returned to Iceland where she died."

I simply nodded. The sagas were, I thought, part history and part fiction, like Beowolf.

"Well," he continued, "some think the storm blew the ships west to Vinland and they never returned."

"Did all the other Templars escape?"

"No, King Philip carried out his plan and arrested the Grand Master, Jacques De Molay, and the other leaders at dawn on Friday, October 13th in the Templar Enclos just outside of Paris. In France over a hundred Templars were arrested. No one knows exactly how many. The King's records weren't accurate and many records were later destroyed. Templars who didn't surrender or who tried to escape were murdered. But no one knows how many.

"People thought all the Templars were either imprisoned or murdered that terrible day and that's what Philip wanted people to believe. But that's not correct. A great many Templars were not in France at the time of the arrests and many, most really, who were in France escaped. The Teutonic Knights and the Knights Hospitallers, even a few Catholic churches in southern France, gave sanctuary to many Templars even though Philip threatened anyone who helped us.

"Philip wasn't popular with some of the barons either. Remember the Templars managed a great many of the barons' properties. Templars were trusted by those barons, more than they trusted the king who had confiscated many of their lands. Many of the barons secretly helped Templars escape.

"What the king found were empty warehouses, no ships, no gold, no silver, and no records. He did have our Grand Master, over a hundred brothers, and our lands in France. He also took control of lands that were managed by Templars but owned by barons who, in Philip's opinion, were sympathetic to Templars, Jews or the Italian Pope."

"Where did your four ships go?"

"North. We went north and that led us here to Lubeck. "

"What happened then?"

"Enkel, we have many more years to cover before I can answer all your questions. This will make more sense as you get older and we should wait before we go on."

"Wait? For how long?"

"Until you're seventeen. Until then I would like you to learn more about the Templars.

It was a disappointment. I'd waited almost a year to learn of our family coat of arms, only to be told I had to wait a few more months.

CHAPTER II:
Seventeen 1357 AD

On my seventeenth birthday my father, grandfather and I had a special dinner. Our cook, Herr Koch, as I was told to address him, prepared a roast of beef with pudding and we had my favorite wheat beer. According to my father it was a very expensive beer for a seventeen-year- old.

As we finished I opened subject that had occupied my thoughts the past months. "I'm seventeen now. Will I learn more of our coat of arms?"

Opa announced with enthusiasm. "Yes, you've done well with your studies. Even your tutor agrees and he has very high standards. You've also become an accomplished horseman and an excellent archer. Last month I saw you take that duck in flight. That was a difficult shot."

After dinner Opa and I settled in before the fireplace in his apartments and I waited for him to light his incense. When he had his burner going to his satisfaction he pushed his shoulders into the cushion on the back of his favorite chair. "Last time we talked you asked what happened to Matthew's four ships and I told you they went north under plain sail."

Over the next few months we met one or two evenings each week. I'll relate what Opa told me of the events after the initial arrest of the Templars.

At the time we left La Rochelle harbor on the morning of the 12th none of us, except Matthew, had any reason to expect the arrests on the 13th. · After leaving La Rochelle harbor our fleet of four ships sailed due west, with Matthew in charge, into the Atlantic until out of sight of land, then changed to plain sail and tacked north. Alleric commanded one of the four ships and Wilhelm was in charge of another. I was with Alleric's ship, a cog.

We crossed the Channel to the mouth of the river Plym but we didn't stay long. We sailed up to Portsmouth. During our short stay in Portsmouth we met eleven Templars who had escaped to England. That was when we first heard of the arrests on the 13th. They had been on their way back to their commandery when they learned Philip's troops were arresting Templars. After making their way to a fishing village they hired a fisherman to take them across the channel. From what they told us it was clear those Templars not already in custody or dead were scattered throughout France, disorganized and without leadership. No one knew what had happened to de Molay and the other leaders in Paris but Philip's agents were arresting or murdering all Templars not taken on October 13th.

The new English king was unpredictable and Matthew did not feel it was safe to stay in England so we sailed up the Channel to Moray Firth in the north of Scotland where Templars held property. There we found safety and time to plan.

Before we sailed from Scotland we burned all our Templar insignia. It was a sad time but we had no choice, we had to disappear. As I watched the fire consume our sails, flags, banners, tunics, robes, and anything else with the Templar's Red Cross I felt a crushing loss and a greater anger than I had ever experienced. All that I had trained for since my parents' death was taken from me on the day, Friday the 13th of October, when Philip arrested the Templars.

My father had believed that if I became a warrior monk for Christ I might be spared from terrible loss. I had been in Christ's service and had been true to my oaths but on that terrible day I believed the purpose of my life had been taken. The Templars were respected and trusted by all Christians yet for some reason unknown to me we'd become fugitives from our king, and abandoned by our pope. I could not understand what was happening and neither Matthew nor Alleric could say what would become of the Templars.

Our Templar brothers in Scotland provided us with charts of the coast of the lowlands and northwestern Germany, even a few of western Denmark, and we crossed the Channel to a small settlement north of Bremen on the Weser river. Crossing the Channel is dangerous any time but never worse that December. It was a terrible time.

No one in Bremen knew we were Templars. That was a secret we would never disclose, not in Bremen, not in Visby, not anywhere. I didn't know it then but our future began in Bremen, in Matthew's meetings with the Bremen merchants.

Unlike most towns in northern Europe, Bremen was a free town. We knew of such cities; Italy had several free cities and all were prosperous trading centers. Each had been granted special rights by the Church and the aristocracy. Those rights limited a prince's, even a king's, ability to interfere with the city's trade or levy excessive taxes. A few Baltic cities had been granted similar status and several formed alliances, informal and limited to two or three cities in each alliance, to protect their trading rights. As a result a prosperous trade in valuable goods from as far as England, France, the Mediterranean countries, and Russia had developed in those towns.

Matthew learned that the independent towns in the Baltic needed fighting men. Svear pirates from the Baltic's north coast were a constant threat to trade ships throughout the Baltic and to the coastal towns along the Baltic's southern coast. Groups of merchants banded together and frequently fought the pirates together but there were few trained men-at-arms and fewer men capable of leading them. The merchants desperately needed men who could effectively protect their trade ships and their towns.

Rumors of King Philip's continued pursuit of Templars with Clement's blessing or at least his willing cooperation, made it impossible for us to settle in Bremen or anywhere else within Philip's or Clement's influence. So we sailed north from Bremen around Denmark and east into the Baltic Sea to the Hansa town of Visby on the island of Gotland. It was as far as we could get from Philip and Clement.

We desperately needed funds so Matthew arranged with two Bremen merchants to ship wool, tools, salt, and iron ore to Gotland. In the bargain he received charts of the Baltic.

By the time our four ships arrived in Visby in late March, Matthew had the basic plan worked out. First, we would hire out to protect trading ships in the Baltic, then establish our own shipping routes in the Baltic. It was logical. We had dependable, trained men who knew how to fight and men who knew how to lead them. And we had four sound ships that could carry cargo and experienced crews and captains to man them. If we were successful we would then establish our banking system between several of the Baltic towns.

We'd turned a profit on the goods from Bremen and with those funds Matthew arranged for dock and harbor space for our ships as well as accommodations for all of us. Not long after we arrived in Visby Matthew met with several prominent merchants and agreed, for a significant fee, to deal with a group of particularly violent svear pirates operating from Oland, an island along the eastern coast of Sweden. The merchants thought us foolish, they didn't know we were Templars, but they were desperate and willing to let us take the risk. The financial risk to the merchants was low, payment was due only after we disposed of the pirates known as the Black Boars.

Alleric waited for a stormy, overcast day with a steady wind from the northeast, then with myself, Dieter, Alfred, Jehan and sixteen other Templars who'd been with him in Cypress, sailed south and west out of Visby in one of our cogs disguised as a Visby cargo ship. It would have been a foolish course for a single merchant ship, it would take us close to Oland.

Wilhelm followed upwind of us in his galley with twenty trained and armed Templars. With a gray sky, a gray sea, a low free board, gray hull, and gray sail it was almost impossible to see Wilhelm's ship even if you were looking for it

Low, dark clouds and a light, cold rain made a sun bearing impossible. In such weather it was impossible to distinguish sea from sky or make out land. Even dead reckoning would be impossible. Alleric knew where we were, he had a compass and a sea map. His course was part of our deception to lure the Oland pirates into the open sea.

The pirates, always in search of easy prey, would believe we were a lone merchant ship out of Visby, loaded with valuable trade goods, and carrying a crew of ten or twelve men, all lightly armed and untrained in their use. We were for all appearances, an unlucky ship with an unfortunate captain, probably young and inexperienced, who had lost his bearings in the foul weather and wandered close enough to Oland's coast to be seen by the island's svear pirates. If the pirates were deceived they couldn't be faulted, it was a reasonable conclusion.

Sometime after mid-day, in the cog's crow's nest directly above me, our lookout cried out and gestured wildly at a galley that suddenly appeared out of a nearby squall. Alleric, dressed in the clothing of a prosperous Visby merchant, stood on the cog's aft castle grimly starring at the fast approaching galley flying a well-known svear pennant, red and bearing a large, black, white-tusked boar.

The rest of us stayed out of sight and silent below our cog's high sides. Dieter and I took turns watching the galley through the small hole we'd bored in the cog's side. I could see fifteen oars on the galleys port side, indicating a crew of fifty or more. As I willed the galley forward I realized I wanted the coming fight. I wanted to take out my anger on the pirates.

As the pirate galley closed on us I looked over at Dieter and nodded. Dieter was a hand taller and a little heavier than I was and all muscle. He returned the nod and I think I saw him grin beneath his helmet. I could have been mistaken. He was, after all, a man of God.

Through the bored hole I could see a giant of a man standing in the approaching galley's bow. With a dark red beard, chainmail shirt, and scrubbed iron nose-helmet he was grinning as he pointed his short, curved sword at Alleric.

Alleric shook his fist at the man and in the guise of loudly, cursing the approaching pirates in Latin and French kept us informed how our trap was developing. We knew what he was saying, what he was doing. He was telling us Red Beard was their leader, kill him first.

Red Beard pointed his sword at Alleric and laughed. Whether he intended humor or not I don't know but I almost burst out laughing. Maybe it was just nerves.

The pirates began to beat on their shields with swords, ax, pikes and spears and took up their ancient Viking war chant, *"Tyr!, Tyr!, Tyr*! It was the name of their god of war. Other than our lookout above and Alleric no one on our ship made a sound. My heart pounded as I gripped my crossbow and I had to fight back the temptation to stand up and put an arrow through Red Bead's chest.

A grappling hook thrown by someone in the galley wrapped around our mast and caught tight. We'd been expecting that, counting on it and no one tried to cut the rope. The pirates pulled their galley hull to hull with our cog and prepared to board. We'd been expecting, counting on, that, too.

Our cog's freeboard, the height from the sea to our ship's railings, was a man's height above the galley's railings so we had the advantage. The pirates could not see us hidden behind the cog's sides. When our trap was sprung we would be able to look down on the pirate's galley and the pirates had to use both hands as they tried to board us.

Red Beard yelled something I couldn't understand then started to climb the side of our ship. Dieter was a good man with a short pike, very quick, very strong but Red Beard found that out too late in his ugly, violent life. As Red Beard hoisted himself over the oak sides of our cog and was certain of victory, Dieter rammed his pike beneath Red Beard's unprotected chin up into his brains and through his skull until a forearm length of pike removed his fine metal helm, throwing helmet and Red Beard back into his ship, pumping his life's blood over his crew as they tried to follow him.

It occurred to me this was their bloody baptism, a suitable preparation for their imminent journey into Hell or Valhalla. At that moment I really didn't care which.

As Red Beard's crew recoiled from their leader's brains and blood all twenty of us stood and took up our own battle cry, *"Deus Vult!"* I recall the ferocity of it. I believe all of us gave voice to our anger and frustration in that moment.

Our war cry made it clear we were Templars, a fact we did not want to disclose to the world. But the pirates would not live to tell our secret.

For a precious moment the pirates were stopped cold in shock at their leader's unexpected, sudden death and the sight of armed men on what they thought was an unarmed merchant ship.

I put a bolt from my crossbow, an ignoble weapon for knight to knight combat but very effective in the cramped quarters of ship to ship warfare, into the man I thought might be next in command of the pirates. Apparently I was right as the remaining, now leaderless, pirates stumbled over themselves in a futile effort to use their oars to push their galley away from us. Their grappling hook line, intended to prevent us from escaping the pirate's trap, prevented the svear pirates from escaping ours. In their confused panic none of them thought to cut the line.

Wilhelm had the weather gage on the pirates and, shipping his oars, the sail was enough to bring Wilhelm's galley along the pirate's starboard side, their blind and exposed side. The first the pirates knew of his presence was when the bow of Wilhelm's galley sheared off their starboard oars and the almost simultaneous arrival of Wilhelm's grappling hook as it wound around the pirate galley's mast and caught. The pirates were trapped between Alleric's cog and Wilhelm's galley; escape was impossible, the outcome inevitable.

From the cog's high deck and aft castle we had a clear shot at the pirates with our crossbows; they had nowhere to hide. In desperation or frustration a few jumped overboard in their iron and leather armor, and drown. Templar bolts from both Alleric's cog and Wilhelm's galley cut down the remaining pirates.

In recognition that Dieter had killed Red Beard, Alleric gave Dieter the honor of sailing the svear galley back to Visby. He picked a crew of ten, including Jehan and me, to man the galley. It didn't take us long to throw the bodies over the side but even with the rain it took several hours to wash away the blood and gore.

The weather hadn't cleared by the time we returned to Visby so the harbor lookouts in their stone watch towers could not see there were three returning ships. The first reaction by the lookouts as Alleric's cog, followed at a distance by Wilhelm's galley, sailed out of a dark squall was indifference. They'd recognized both ships. When a third ship, a svear galley flying the Black Boar banner, broke through the blowing rain and spray the outlooks sounded the alarm of an imminent attack.

Alleric had planned our return to make an impression on the people of Visby. As the trumpets blared a warning Dieter dropped the Black Boar banner and raised the flag of Visby. Alleric and Wilhelm luffed their sails and backed their oars to let Dieter and the svear galley lead the way into the harbor. The trumpets changed their tattoo from alarm to celebration.

The people of Visby knew we'd left with two ships and were returning with a third, a svear galley. As the galley slid to a stop along the wharf the townspeople pushed their way aboard to examine our collection of fine swear swords, well-crafted axes, chainmail, helmets, shields, and several banners recognized and feared by Baltic merchants. The conclusion was obvious, we'd eliminated the Oland pirates known as the Black Boars.

With our victory so complete, we'd not lost a man and none had been injured, the people of Visby looked on us in a new light. The value of such fighting men in the Baltic couldn't be ignored. And our own morale improved. Since the October arrests in France we'd been fugitives, hunted men under a death sentence. We were trained as knights to open the Holy Lands and protect pilgrims and merchants. We weren't in the Holy Lands but we were protecting a peaceful people and their trade. It was a purpose we were familiar with.

Shortly after our arrival in Visby, Matthew, Alleric and Wilhelm had agreed with the Visby merchants to take on the Baltic pirates. We'd won a clear victory, an apparently easy victory. And we now had a fifth ship, an excellent svear galley suited for attacking other pirates in the islands and fjords throughout the Baltic. For coastal and island work the galley was superior to the cog. With its shallow draft a galley could navigate in shallow waters where a cog or hulk could not, and it could be rowed if the wind wasn't favorable.

Several merchant ships from other Baltic towns were in Visby harbor when we returned that first time. The following morning a Rostock merchant, Herr Keller, negotiated with Matthew for one of our ships and twenty armed men to escort three of his ships on his return voyage to his home port. Apparently he had a very valuable cargo and our services cost less than insurance, or he had family with him on the ship, that wasn't unusual. Whatever his reason he had a healthy fear of Baltic pirates.

Matthew assigned Alleric and his crew to protect Keller's convoy. Dieter and I were fortunate to join the first of our new Templar ventures. Other than a few minor storms it was an easy voyage. The convoy visited Riga and Gdansk on its way to Rostock. In each town Keller introduced Alleric to his friends and told other merchants and town authorities of our miraculous victory over the Black Boar pirates. In the following months several Baltic merchants hired us to protect their own convoys and in each town including the foremost

Baltic city, Lubeck, Alleric met with town leaders and merchants to introduce our escort services.

A Lubeck merchant, Herr de Vries, hired us to escort two of his ships. Both carried valuable cargoes from Denmark to be delivered in Gdansk and were to return to Lubeck with Russian furs. On the return voyage we were attacked by two svear galleys. We were able to ram and sink one galley and destroy the other's steering oar. It was a close battle, not as one sided as our first. We killed an unknown number of the pirates but three Templars died in the battle.

Herr de Vries knew he would have lost his ships, their valuable cargo and most probably his life had he not hired us. When we returned to Lubeck, de Vries and his investors hosted Alleric and his crew for a celebration dinner in a prosperous Lubeck tavern. That was the first time I was personally introduced to Herr de Vries, the man who would become my father-in-law.

Throughout Europe there were rumors and questions regarding the Templars and what had happened to them after the arrests. Since our arrival in Visby, merchants in the Baltic towns speculated as to where Matthew's ships and crews had come from. No one asked but after our victories over the svear pirates most of the Baltic merchants believed or at least suspected we were Templars. It was well-known that Templars were hunted men and Philip had a bounty on them but the merchants understood the value of trained, disciplined men-at-arms to protect Baltic commerce so nothing was said.

In those months we learned more of the Hansa towns and the rivalries and jealousies between towns and groups of merchants. Matthew saw opportunities where others saw problems. The Templars were able to act as intermediaries between competing factions and provided a common vision of the Baltic commercial possibilities.

Our numbers increased as word quietly spread through Europe that Templars could find refuge in the Baltic. It was not unusual that when one of our ships stopped in a European harbor one or two escaped Templars would make themselves known through secret signs and words, and be taken aboard. With each man we learned more of Philip's inquisition, torture and trials.

We learned that in the weeks following the arrests Philip tortured more than one hundred thirty Templars before putting them on trial for heresy. Our Grand Master and the others had admitted their guilt. The Pope, however, seemed less interested in the prosecution and during the trials told the King he did not favor the Templar's arrest. Sometime later that year De Molay disavowed his confession.

It was all sketchy information, fact mixed with rumors and speculation. Some rumors said the Grand Master had already been executed. Others said he was alive but put him in half-dozen different castle donjons.

Such news, as bad as it was, was a relief in some respects. Apparently the King had captured less than one hundred fifty Templars in all of France. Still it was a terrible number and it included most of our leaders. Although aware of the King's secret order to arrest Templars de Molay and the other leaders had decided to stay in France rather than escape. Most troubling to me was there were no rumors or news of resistance by the Templars at the time of the arrests. No one knew why de Molay and the others hadn't escaped or why there had been no armed resistance to the arrests.

While on escort duty in Emden harbor I met one fugitive Templar. One evening Brother Hans, dressed in rags and looking as though he hadn't eaten in days, appeared at the docks. I was standing night watch as he shuffled out of the evening shadows, then stood quietly, patiently, at each ship's gangplank and made the Templar sign of distress. When he stopped at our gangplank we took him aboard.

Over a hot meal, his first since his escape, Brother Hans explained he had been in eastern France, near Besancon on the Daubs river, managing the estate of a baron when word reached him that King Philip was arresting Templars. The baron was on a pilgrimage but with God's grace and the help of the baron's family Hans made a harrowing escape into Switzerland. Traveling at night on the trails along the Daubs and hiding from the King's agents during the day it took four nights to make the journey. Eventually he made his way to Germany and to Emden.

Upon our return to Visby after escort duty I learned three more Templars had reached our safety. For the most part they had no new information except that thirty-eight of our brethren had died in the Corbel during tortures leading up to their trials. We were to hear a great deal more of Corbel and the Bishop of Sens, Bishop Marigny.

Several weeks after our fourth escort voyage, Alleric asked Dieter, Hans and me to join him for dinner. When we arrived that evening he asked us to sit down, he said he had something to tell us.

Alleric got right to the point. "We've all heard rumors of what's happening in Paris. By the time news reaches Gotland it's several weeks old and we have no idea of either the source or its reliability. Last week another Templar reached Lubeck. He told us there were rumors Clement has pardoned De Molay and the others. But as far as we know Philip has not released them, and the trials continue.

"Before Matthew, Wilhelm and I settle on plans for the Templar's future in the Baltic we must know what's become of our Grand Master and other leaders. The last information we have is that they're being held somewhere in Paris but no one has actually seen them."

"I'll go," Dieter said.

I looked at Dieter, then at Alleric. "So will I."

Hans smiled and nodded his intention to join us.

"Thank you," Dieter said. "Tomorrow you'll begin your preparations. You'll leave as soon as we settle on a plan."

In the following days we asked our brothers who had escaped France what they'd seen or heard regarding Philip's search for Templars. Most told us the King's agents thought all Templars who were in France had either been arrested or murdered, or had already escaped the country. So there was little reason to continue the search.

His own men weren't diligent so Philip had resorted to a bounty for anyone who brought him a Templar. Philip didn't ask how they got their man and didn't care if the Templar was alive or dead. Local authorities were not permitted to interfere with their work. Bounty hunters were diligent and violent and roamed the European ports and rivers, all the likely avenues Templars would use to escape France.

The three of us understood the risks. If we were arrested terrible tortures, imprisonment, and death would follow. We also knew if we weren't successful then our imprisoned brethren would suffer the same fate.

Le Havre's busy harbor and the Seine's constant traffic between Le Havre and Paris were the best avenues for our search. Rouen, with its busy barge traffic and market, was conveniently between the two cities. Getting to Le Havre wouldn't be difficult. Its port was used by ships from the south of Spain to the northern Baltic states, and from England and Scotland. How best to get from Le Havre to Paris was the question. Overland was out of the question, it was slow and risky.

We needed plausible explanations why we were in various locations at the times we were there, where were we going and why, where we'd been and why. We must have explanations that would satisfy curious minds and not raise questions, alarm or suspicion.

The solution we settled on was that the three of us would jump ship in Le Havre and meld with the harbor people, always a mixture of foreigners and languages and therefore unlikely to draw attention to ourselves. Then we'd make our way up the Seine in a small boat to Rouen and Paris.

Each of us was fluent in French and Latin, and had a passable use of north German. Language shouldn't be a problem. Strangers wandering through an unfamiliar city or countryside would always raise questions. But if we spoke a language the local people understood, questions might be convincingly answered and we might avoid difficulties.

We might need to exchange messages with Matthew or Alleric and a well-known tavern, La Grande Baleine, in Le Havre harbor seemed the safest location. On the ninth and twenty-third of each month a merchant ship captained by a Templar would be anchored in Le Havre harbor. With Vesper bells a sailor, a brother Templar, from the ship would visit the tavern, order a tankard of ale and take his time enjoying his drink.

Sailors usually carried their own tankard, frequently elaborately carved, both because it was unsavory to share unwashed tankards and to prevent a tavern keeper from pouring a short measure of ale or wine.

The tankard wouldn't be unusual, oak carved with one or more fleurs de lis. Fleurs de lis were commonly used as decorations by ordinary seamen, especially those from Rouen, its coat of arms had three, or Le Havre, its arms had two.

He would wear an eye patch over his left eye. That wasn't terribly unusual either but would make his identification easier in a busy tavern filled with sailors from all over western Europe.

Our own tankards would be ordinary oak, without carvings.

At Vesper bells one of us would enter the tavern and, if a man fitting the description was there, sit down, take a look at the man's tankard, and ask, "Are you a son of Rollo."

The correct response would be, "I am but I am no son of Odin." With that response he would draw the Christian fish in some ale intentionally spilled on the table. Our response would be to draw another Christian fish at right angles to the first. The result roughly resembled a fleur de lis.

If any detail were omitted the two men would each have a drink, talk about the weather, and eventually leave, separately.

If a written message was to be conveyed the one with the message would admire the other's knife and ask to examine it. The other would ask to see his knife and in the process the two men would agree to exchange knives.

Templar armorers crafted a seaman's knife for each of us. They were not identical and each was a wonderfully balanced tool any sailor would find useful in his trade. None were remarkable in appearance but the haft of each could be opened and a written message inserted. The metal pommel screwed into and out of the haft and was also attached to the guard by what appeared to be two metal decorations affixed to the haft. A particular, deliberate procedure was required to remove and to re-secure the pommel and haft. It would not happen by mistake or accident.

We believed de Molay and other Templars were being held somewhere in Paris but Paris was a big city. Those brothers most familiar with Paris believed there were no less than nine possible locations where Templars might be imprisoned. We had information about three of them. As to the other locations we had almost nothing that might prove helpful.

The Concierge on the Isle de la Cite had three donjons, the Tour de Cesar, the ancient Grosse Tour in the center, and the unnamed tower in the northwest corner of the complex. All three had been used as prisons. It also had the Tour de Argent where Philip housed and protected his wealth.

Within the old walls of Paris and close to the Seine were three more possible locations, the Louvre fortress on the Seine's north bank, the Tour du Coin adjacent to it, and the Tour de Nesle on the south bank across from the Tour de Coin.

We had a great deal of information on the other three possible locations, all were within the walls of the Enclos du Temple, our own fortress. Many of our brothers had served in our Paris Enclos over the years and knew it well. It was north of Paris, outside the old city walls, and far from the Seine. Within its crenellated curtain walls were a jail, the older three story Tour de Cesar, and the newer Tour du Temple.

Philip and Nogaret also knew the Enclos well. The year before the arrests Phillip sought refuge in the Templar Enclos when his life was threatened by an armed mob after the he devalued French coinage by two-thirds and tripled rents. De Molay took Philip into his own personal residence within the Enclos. It was in the Grand Master's same residence, the Villeneuve du Temple, where De Molay and the others were arrested.

The most difficult problem was how to locate de Molay once we reached Paris. There were many different suggestions but really only one plan fit the realities, the three of us would use our judgment when we got there. After all, we didn't know for certain de Molay and the others were in Paris and if they were they may not all be in the same location. We'd have to see what we found and what we encountered.

Our own ships might be known in France so in Kiel, a Hansa city, we arranged for a trusted local merchant to purchase a cog for us. Wilhelm was our ship's captain but to reduce our link with Visby our crew consisted of sailors from England, Scotland and the low countries. All were men who had no love for Philip.

We also purchased an old, double keeled ship's skiff, ostensibly as our cog's boat. The skiff, about twenty-four feet in length with single mast and lateen sail, was large enough for the three of us with our gear and small enough to be rowed if necessary, two could row with the third at the tiller. The forward third was decked and a canvas awning could be rigged over the cockpit to provide shelter from bad weather. It would be cramped but we could all sleep aboard the skiff if necessary.

Several of our brethren, talented carpenters and cabinetmakers, modified the boat while preserving its weathered appearance. Hidden compartments contained three crossbows, several dozen bolts, three misericordes, clothes of various descriptions, three leather bags of a variety of jetons from several countries, and a dozen bags of coins, including gold Florins, the most accepted currency in Europe. We planned to find work to support ourselves and blend with the public while we searched for de Molay but we had sufficient resources to get us to and from Paris, and bribe a few officials along the way if necessary.

From Kiel we sailed to the Moray Firth in Scotland, then down England's east coast to Portsmouth. When weather permitted we crossed the Channel to Le Havre. Our ship remained in Le Havre long enough to sell the trade goods and not at sale prices. We must make a reasonable profit to cover the costs of our mission and avoid raising questions.

In Le Havre our captain purchased a new skiff and our old, modified skiff was tied alongside our cog. The night before our ship was to leave Le Havre the three of us were assigned to the night watch and before dawn the next morning we slipped over the side and rowed off in our skiff. As far as the crew knew we'd simply jumped ship and stolen the ship's old skiff.

To our relief no one in the busy Seine river traffic took the slightest interest in us. For all outward appearances we were nothing more than three common men of the sea, looking more French than English or Flemish, in loose fitting canvas pants ending just above the ankle, woolen jersey with rough leather jerkin, wool caps and soft well-worn leather boots. Our clothes were old, and bleached by sun and salt. In our canvas sea bags we carried the normal seaman's gear and a mixture of small coins, French, English, Flemish and German.

Each of us carried our personal knife and either a belaying pin or marlinspike, all typical tools for men of the sea but very useful for other purposes too. The point of Dieter's oak marlinspike was a little sharper than most and, unlike any other I'd seen, midway down the shaft was a slight bulge that would prevent the user's hand from slipping down the shaft. He kept it in a leather sheath sewn to his right boot and partially covered by his pant leg. Hans preferred, as did I, an ordinary oak belaying pin slipped through a belt loop.

We sailed our skiff east up the Seine with the strong belief we were carrying out God's will. Knowing the cog and crew would leave Le Havre harbor with the tide we felt very far from our brethren but took comfort in our faith that our Lord would guide and direct us.

The morning breeze held and when the tide began to ebb in early afternoon we were well east of the harbor. We'd been on watch all night so we made camp in a forest grove along the river's north bank and slept.

CHAPTER III:
The Seine

Before venturing deeper into the heart of Philip's kingdom we needed to test our story. We had to know the three of us were believable. The countryside along the Seine was thick with men who would cut your throat for a tankard of ale but we were confident we were able to deal with them. More dangerous, in our minds, were bounty hunters and curious people, people whose loyalty to the King or fear of strangers who didn't seem to quite fit their appearances might bring forces we couldn't contend with.

In larger towns curious people might be turned away by a frown, a threatening stare or a harsh word. Everyone was a stranger in a large town and few asked questions; even fewer wanted contact with the authorities. County inns and taverns along the river, however, were full of inquisitive people, people who knew their neighbors and were quick to see a stranger as a threat.

One of the country taverns along the Seine seemed an appropriate test. If people were suspicious we would return to Le Havre as fast as possible and sign on one of the many ships headed north to Amsterdam, west to England, or south to Portugal and Spain. On the other hand if we were accepted as common sailors off to see the world we would continue on to Rouen and Paris.

The Seine flows gently in wide loops through lush meadows, thick forests and farm lands. Between Le Havre and Paris barge traffic on the river was regular but not heavy.

Barges carried people and hauled produce, animals and goods to and from market towns up and down the river. Every dozen miles or so there were docks for loading and unloading. Farmers brought their goods to the docks for transport and nearby there were usually taverns and an occasional inn.

Tides had little influence so far from the coast and the current wasn't strong so even the light morning breeze carried us up river with no more effort that trimming the sail and manning the tiller. About half way between Le Havre and Rouen, as the river finished its swing north and turned south, we saw a tavern on the river's north bank and a short, wide dock suitable for both river barges and our small boat.

Two roads, one from the northwest, the other from the northeast, converged on the dock with the tavern set between the two. The countryside east of Le Havre was full of small farming communities. Apparently this was where local farmers loaded their produce onto river barges for transport to either Le Havre or Rouen. We judged it a suitable place to stop for an ale and a bite to eat, listen to the local gossip, and judge people's reaction to the three of us.

A faded sign above the door seemed peaceful enough, a winged angel over a sheaf of wheat. Below someone had carved and painted a name known to all Normans, "St. Adela," the sainted daughter of William himself. In my mind it was a good omen.

Smoke drifted from the tavern's chimney and the smell of hot food surrounded us. We must have looked a hard bunch but Dieter, always cheerful, outgoing and hungry, offered to see if it was safe for us and satisfy anyone in the tavern we weren't dangerous. Hans and I waited beneath a huge old elm shading both the tavern's west side and a dirt track between two oak pins marking a quoits court, frequently used by the look of it. Dieter was gone only a moment before he reappeared at the door and with a grin, waived us in.

The tavern was clean, floor swept, windows open, cut flowers decorated each table. It had a cheerful, bright, welcoming feel to it.

The tavern was empty except for the keeper himself and he was all smiles at the sight of us, apparently happy to have our business. He was typical of what everyone pictured a keeper would be, fat, bald, cheerful and wearing an apron over his loose, rumpled leggings and plain tan shirt. It struck me the keeper was as clean and cheerful as his establishment.

We chose a table near an unshuttered window with a view of the river and our skiff then each ordered ale and a meat pie with dark rye bread.

"That'll be seven deniers," the innkeeper said with a smile. It was more as a question than a fact. Apparently he had some concern regarding our ability or willingness to pay.

When I nodded and placed a dozen, a sou's worth, on the table the innkeeper grinned, deftly swept seven into his left hand, turned and hurried back to his bar.

When the innkeeper delivered our ale Dieter said, "Sir, please pour yourself an ale and join us. We've been traveling too long and need conversation with someone other than ourselves."

The innkeeper poured himself a tankard of ale, pulled a stool to our table, sat down and with a polite, unassuming smile pocketed another denier. Whether the additional denier was for the tankard of ale he was drinking or for the pleasure of his company he didn't say.

"We've never been to your crossing, who's lord of this region?"

"Depends who you're talking to, and whether you're paying taxes or asking for help," he responded with a good natured chuckle. Then with a sideward look at Dieter he took a drink of his ale and added, "And what brings three deep-water sailors to Saint Adela?"

"We've left the sea," I responded with conviction. "Our captain, a cheap English bastard, no son of our William I swear, shorted us on our pay. So we decided to seek fair employment in Rouen, or perhaps even in Paris. Do you know of work hereabouts?"

The claim of affiliation with William, Norman conqueror of England, and general disparagement of our English captain seemed to work for he grinned and responded, "Left the sea, eh. Couldn't find another ship in all of Le Havre? Well, there are men along the Seine who find work lifting the burdens of wealthy travelers. Is that your line?"

"No, no, we're honest men," Hans responded with a smile and a chuckle that seemed to prove his point.

"Well, you've the look of men who've been to sea, no doubt of that," the innkeeper said with a tilt of his head and a smile.

Still I wondered if he really believed us.

He was about to say something but stopped as the tavern door opened, took another quick drink of ale, rose from the stool, and started towards the door. He'd gotten half way when two young men shuffled in, looked around and stopped to look us over. The way they stared at the three of us looked more like an invitation for us to leave than any fear or curiosity about us.

I estimated both to be in their very early twenties or younger, probably brothers by the look of them. Average height but heavier than most men their height, and strong. Farmers, I concluded.

The keeper grinned as he said, "Hello boys, good to see you. Come in we have visitors, men from Le Havre on their way to Paris."

His greeting was met with a nod and polite smile then the two men returned their attention to the three of us.

"Is that your skiff at the dock?" the slightly older of the two asked, giving the three of us a hard look. "We've got a load that needs to get to Rouen, today. And that little thing tied to the dock isn't big enough to take a cow much less our goods but it'll block the barge when it tries to tie up."

"Sorry, *frère*," I responded with a smile as I rose. "I'll move it right away."

Hans immediately picked up, "Have an ale on us, while you wait for the barge."

Before any one answered Dieter cleared room at our table and pulled around two more stools.

The two young farmers looked at each other, nodded and sat down as the innkeeper went for two more tankards.

The mood quickly changed. The innkeeper would sell several more tankards of his excellent ale, our skiff would no longer interfere with river commerce, two thirsty farmers got a free drink for their inconvenience, and we didn't have a fight on our hands.

As I walked out the tavern's door I saw a two wheeled ox cart stopped near the dock. After moving our skiff, I tied it up to a tree where it would not interfere with the river barge and we could keep an eye on it from the tavern, I walked slowly by the cart to examine its contents. From what I could see there was a mixture of firewood, a half dozen or so bushels of apples, several baskets of a variety of vegetables, a clay pot of what I thought might be honey, and three young pigs in wooden cages. The cart itself and the two oxen pulling it were in excellent condition.

As I approached the cart I heard a low, but unmistakable, growl and stepped back. In the shade of the cart lay a large dog, a mixed breed shepherd. I stepped back to a safe distance, knelt down and examined the animal. It stopped growling when I stepped back. The dog was not threatening, it hadn't gotten up, but I had the distinct impression it didn't want me too close to the cart.

By the time I returned the two farmers were each eating a plowman's lunch to go with their ale, the innkeeper had collected the last of my deniers from the table, and the conversation seemed friendly, cheerful really.

As I took a drink of ale, still cold, and a bite of meat pie, still hot, Dieter introduced me to the two brothers, Gaidar and Ulf. Both men nodded and grinned but didn't stop eating.

"Nice cart of goods you've got," I said.

The brothers nodded but didn't stop eating.

"Nice dog, too," I said and got the same response.

I turned to the keeper. "When is the barge due here?"

"Soon, within an hour, more or less," he responded with a shrug.

I looked out the open window as another ox cart pulled up next to Gaidar and Ulf's.

The keeper, Dieter introduced him as Gaspard, looked out the window. "It's Pierre and his son, Hugo."

Gaspard turned to Gaidar. "Say, didn't I hear you've been spending time with Pierre's daughter. There's no bad blood between you and Pierre, is there?"

Gaidar stopped chewing long enough to respond. "None at all. We're to be married soon."

Dieter redirected the conversation back to the Rouen barge. "How long does it take the barge to reach Rouen?"

Ulf looked up from his food. "Depends on the tide, the current and the wind. Half day or so. Why?"

"We're headed that way, I thought we might follow the barge. Do you sell your goods to the barge owner?"

Gaidar shook his head and frowned as if it was a dumb question. "No, we'll load it and go with the barge. We pay the bargeman. Our father will get our cart later today. He usually comes with us but was delayed and we didn't want to miss today's barge. After we sell our goods Ulf and I will walk home, tomorrow or the next day."

"You just leave your cart and oxen here?" Hans asked.

Ulf nodded, laughed. "Sure, it's safe here. Besides our dog won't let anyone take it. He isn't one to mix with. Even if they did they'd never get out of our valley. Oxen don't move fast and everyone knows that's our cart and oxen. One of our neighbors would stop the thief. And the punishment for theft is harsh in these regions."

Gaidar stopped eating long enough to say, "Why don't you follow the barge. We'll show you the town after we sell our goods. It won't take long, a day at most. We know the market and the people know us."

It sounded like an excellent idea. Ulf and Gaidar were apparently well-known both around Saint Adela and in the Rouen market place. If we were with the two of them it was less likely anyone would question the three of us. Just being with them would eliminate questions.

The three of us looked at each other, then nodded. "Sure," Hans responded. "We've never been to Rouen. You could show us around."

Pierre followed by Hugo came through the doorway, smiling broadly, and yelled to Gaspard, "Has the Rouen barge been here? Are we too late?"

Gaspard yelled back, "No but it should be here soon. Get your cart down to the dock then come on back. I'll have a tankard of perry and some fresh baked rye bread for you, and some excellent cheese, too."

As Hugo ran to move their cart, Pierre yelled back at Gaspard, "Hugo will take care of the cart and oxen. Pour us both a tankard. And fill the tankards this time you old scoundrel. And we'll take something to eat, too. I miss your lovely wife's cooking. Her perry is the finest. You don't deserve such a woman."

Guidar whispered to the three of us, "Pierre is deaf as a tree. But he has a good heart."

"That's because you're going to marry his daughter," Ulf responded.

Gaspard pulled another table next to ours and added two more stools, then left to pour two more tankards. It dawned on me that someone other than Gaspard had prepared our food. He'd simply disappeared around the corner, into the kitchen I'd assumed, and returned a little later with the food.

"How's my lovely sister?" Pierre yelled at Gaspard.

Before Gaspard could respond a voice from the kitchen yelled, "I'm still well brother but you're still deaf. I can hear you from here. I'll have your food ready in a moment. Sit down. Have a tankard."

As Pierre pulled up a stool and sat down next to Gaspard the voice from the kitchen added, "And we have paying guests so don't yell, you'll scare them."

Pierre added a nod to his grin and nudged Gaspard with his elbow as if there were some secret joke.

"Hello son," Pierre said with a smile and nod to Guidar, who responded with a smile,

"And to you, father of my wife to be."

A woman I decided must be Gaspard's wife and Pierre's sister appeared out of the kitchen with platters of food for Pierre and Hugo. Pierre paid with a flourish. "Hello, dear sister. You look beautiful today."

She did, too. A little younger than Gaspard but still with a woman's form that was emphasized by her apron. Neatly dressed and her bright blue eyes had a smile all their own. She'd removed the tie that held her hair and her thick, reddish blonde hair fell below her shoulders. I found I could not help but return her warm, happy smile.

Ulf looked at her, perhaps a little too long. She just smiled back like she would at a little boy or a puppy.

She turned to the three of us, all three of us were a little taken aback by her, and announced with a smile, "I'm Michelle, Gaspard's wife."

My impression was that Pierre had been correct, Gaspard was a lucky man.

Before getting up Gaspard looked at our three empty tankards with an unspoken but obvious question in mind. Dieter nodded and placed three more deniers on the table. Gaspard swept up the three coins, gathered our three empty tankards along with his own, then rose to replenish all four. I gathered he did not expect us to pay for his.

"So where are you three from?" Michelle asked as Gaspard filled our tankards.

"The sea," I replied.

Dieter added, "We're all Normans by birth. Me? Well, small farm near Bayeux. A family with too many children and not enough land so I set to sea. We've been ship mates over the years."

Everything Dieter said was true, at least as far as it went. After Philip had taken his family's holdings in Gascony they were fortunate to find work on a small farm near Bayeux. He and his brother had little choice but to become soldiers or priests, so they became Templars. And we had certainly been ship mates but not for an English captain.

Pierre turned to me. "And you, are you Norman, too?"

"Yes. My father was a smithy on the road between Rouen and Alencon. He died when I was seventeen. He was the last of my family so I went to sea, out of Le Havre."

Pierre looked at me a long, sad moment. "A smithy, eh. We could use another in these parts."

His attention shifted to Hans who responded before Pierre had a chance to ask.

"I'm from Calais. Always liked the sea better than the plow. We found ourselves mates again on our last ship, the one with the English captain." Hans added a frown when it came to mention of the captain. "We thought we'd revisit the land of our births at least until our money ran out or we found good work, maybe in Rouen, maybe in Paris."

"Then you're at the right tavern. We're all good Normans here about." Michelle said with a bright smile. "You saw our dear Saint Adela above our door. Gaspard carved it shortly after we opened our tavern and our son, Luc, carved her name. Our parish priest showed Luc what letters to use but he carved it himself."

I felt a great sense of relief. Apparently, we'd established ourselves as fellow Normans.

Gaspard returned with four full-to-the-brim tankards, smiled and sat down. "Oh, you'll find work in Rouen if you want it. Trade is good in Rouen and it gets better as you get closer to Paris."

Gaspard took a long drink, then added, "The barges up and down the Seine are expensive but dependable. Fortunately our farmers get excellent prices. When they have a surplus."

"Don't you usually have surplus?" I asked.

"They've been hard to come by since the weather's turned colder. Crops are poor. And that means fewer animals, pigs, chickens, sheep, goats survive the winters. Used to be a surplus every year and land owners got wealthy as their tenants had more children and families cleared more land to grow more crops."

He took a drink and shook his head. "But with more children born each year there were more mouths to feed. Then the weather turned colder. Now every coupl'a years the crops fail. Nothing like when I was Ulf's age. Now people go hungry and animals starve."

"And your, our, king? Is he a good king?" Hans asked without making eye contact.

Between bites Dieter said, "We've been at sea so long, out of the country, up and down the coast from the low lands to Portugal and from the south of England to Scotland with that cheap English bastard, and a few others like him. So we didn't hear much."

Gaspard rubbed his beard. "I can imagine. I don't know why a man would go to sea, away from his family. Well, our king, Philip, is called Philip la Bel. But I don't know why. Maybe because women find he's handsome. God knows he's been hard on the Jews, threw them out over a year ago, took their property, too. And the fight with those Flemish nobles. That cost him plenty. We hear he needs money. Fortunately he doesn't bother us much. Mostly because we don't have much to give him."

"But the clergy and their Popes haven't fared as well," Pierre added with a hearty laugh. "Being Pope is dangerous work and Philip's been after a share of their lands and income for years."

Michelle added, "Well, from what I've heard he's been after both the church and the Templars. He called a States General against the old Italian Pope, that was some time ago. But earlier this year he called it again in Poitier and again in Tours against the Templars. Our good king wanted the three estates to join in his condemnation and bless his arrests. I guess he got what he wanted."

I looked out the window as a barge pulled up to the dock.

Guidar must have seen it too. He jumped up, pointed to the barge and with a mouth full of food exclaimed, "Here it is boys, let's get our goods aboard."

Waiving his tankard towards the three of us, Ulf said, "Guidar and I are taking our produce to Rouen this afternoon. These three men are going too, in the skiff tied up near the dock. Perhaps Hugo will join us?"

Pierre looked at us, then at the three young men, men soon to be related by marriage. "Well, I'd planned to go with Hugo myself. But, it is a long walk home."

He took a deep breath and slowly exhaled. "Maybe it's time Hugo went without me. He can handle the sales now. It'll give him experience. Sure, the three of you young lads need some time in Rouen. If the three of you promise to stay together, take care of each other, and return safely together."

He paused again as he looked at Gaidar. "Hugo will help your brother keep you out of trouble, away from all those pretty girls in Rouen. I don't want my lovely daughter's wedding plans spoiled."

Pierre looked at his sister. "Where's your boy? I haven't seen Luc."

Michelle smiled. "He's in Rouen for the fair. Two days ago he took six casks of cider, three of apple and three of perry, both excellent. He's sold it all by now and I expect he's looking for adventure. He's young and healthy."

She turned to the three boys. "Find Luc. He'll help sell your goods and the four of you come back together. Hugo and Ulf, you can have fun, then get to the cathedral. Say your prayers, light a few candles."

Michelle paused a moment as she looked at each of the young men. "See the priest if you have something to confess."

She turned to Guidar with a knowing smile and a nod. "But you, Guidar, you stay out of trouble. You and your pretty Elsie will be married soon."

Her smile and slight nod at the thought said it all. And Guidar's grin made it evident he had nothing but Elsie on his mind.

Although the barge to Rouen was a little late there was room for the three lads and the contents of both ox carts, and time to reach Rouen before dark. It was a quiet, sunny day with an easy breeze in our favor. As the bargemen pushed away from the dock and started up river using both oars and sails the three young men waived good-by to Pierre and Gaspard standing on the dock. The two brothers-in-law stood arm-in-arm, grinning, each with a tankard in hand. We waited for the barge to take its lead then hoisted our sail to catch the breeze and followed.

With our stop at Saint Adela we'd learned very little of the King or the Pope and nothing of the Templars' fate but we hadn't aroused suspicions or encountered questions that might prove difficult. The three of us agreed we seemed to have passed a test of sorts, our first. Our story had held. We'd been accepted as just another part of life on the Seine, nothing unusual, nothing to be concerned with.

From Saint Adela tavern it isn't far by road to Rouen, and shorter as the crow flies. The Seine meanders through the river's wide valley making it a longer but much easier journey by barge, and there were two other stops in between. A dozen or so crowded docks, a large open market square, and several inns and taverns along the river's north bank marked the Rouen landings.

With the sun hardly more than a hand above the western horizon, the barge carrying our three young friends and their goods pulled alongside one of Rouen's docks. Before leaving Visby we'd heard rumors that several Templars had been tortured and tried in Rouen castle's donjon. This was our opportunity to learn what had actually happened, and separate fact from rumor.

People's general temperament and spirit comes through in the way they buy and sell in the market and the way they drink and eat in taverns. So after finding slip for our skiff we made ourselves useful helping the boys unload their goods. No one paid attention to us. The boys appreciated the help and it was an opportunity to observe without seeming to be too curious. There was always some reason to stop, adjust a load, look around, rearrange your goods, take our time doing it and listen to what people are saying. Later the three of us sat quietly in one of the many crowded, noisy taverns along the river and enjoyed a tankard of ale.

We heard a great deal about Rouen and what was on everyone's mind. That evening we heard nothing but the excitement typical of a market fair. If the good people of Rouen had thoughts of their King or Pope we heard nothing of it. Certainly the plight of the imprisoned Templars was not a topic of discussion. Perhaps the people of Rouen had little interest in the Templars.

The following morning Hans, Dieter and I wandered the streets of Rouen to get a feel of the town. All Normans would be expected to visit the grand cathedral Notre Dame de Rouen where the heart of Richard Coeur de Lion, great grandson of William, is entombed. The great Rollo had been baptized and entombed in the same cathedral. We made the cathedral our first stop.

Later, in need of something to eat, we walked the streets around the Rouen castle. We hoped to find a tavern frequented by men employed in the castle and a talkative innkeeper who had a talkative jailor as a regular customer.

Down a narrow cobbled street, just north of Rouen's tower, we found a fair sized inn. Above it were two overhanging stories, the second probably the owner's residence, and the third perhaps lodging for wealthy travelers. Above the tavern's door hung a brightly painted wooden sign or coat of arms with a red border in the shape of a shield, bearing two black, crossed, war maces above three wavy, blue lines. We hoped the owner had once crossed a sea as a man-of-arms, perhaps as part of the Crusades.

Dieter and I were greeted by a tall young man with a cheerful smile, fifteen or sixteen years old, I thought.

"In town for our fair?" he asked.

The coat of arms couldn't have been his. He probably hadn't been born when Acre fell in ninety-one.

"Mmm," I said with a nod as my eyes adjusted to the dark room. Even with the windows open the overhanging story allowed little sunlight in. In the back was a long bar and behind that several casks, ale, cider and wine, by the look of them. Six tables, each with four stools and two candles, filled the room.

To our right at the far end of the room two middle aged couples stopped long enough to look us over then resumed eating. Out-of-town merchants by the look of them, well-dressed but not wealthy, certainly not nobility. Probably in town for the fair and to visit the cathedral.

"What's your mid-day fare?" Dieter asked.

"A generous portion of fresh bacon, wonderful dark rye, hot from the oven, with a tankard of cold ale, wine or cider, pear or apple. All fresh," the young man replied with a grin.

"And a boiled egg if you wish but it costs more."

"Ah!" Dieter responded with a smile. He was a big man, required frequent feeding and had eaten only a large bowl of barley porridge with a thick slice of day old bread earlier that morning. "And the fare for such fare?" he asked and then laughed at his pun.

The young man was quick witted. He grinned and chuckled politely. "Three deniers, sir, for each of you. The egg is another denier."

Dieter ordered the egg in addition to the regular fare with apple cider. I just ordered the regular and ale. Dieter and I each put our tankards on the table and carefully counted out the coins. It was our effort to show we were neither spendthrift sailors nor wealthy.

The young man nodded and picked up the coins and our tankards, "Thank you, gentlemen. I'll have it out for you right away. Would you like your drinks now?"

We nodded.

The two couples finished their food and left by the back stairs. Up to their rooms, I guessed. When the young man returned with our tankards Dieter said with a grin, "And what name are you called by, young man?"

"Andre."

"Andre, Andre. A sound name," Dieter said with a firm nod. "Tell me, Andre, about the arms above your door."

"My father's great uncle, God rest his soul, fought in the Crusades. His brother, my father's grandfather, stayed here in Rouen, to run our family's inn, this very inn. When he heard his brother had been killed in battle he made the sign now hanging above our door. We paint it each year."

"Which battle?" Dieter asked.

"Mansourah. In Egypt. 1250. At least that's what I've been told."

Dieter nodded. "The ill-fated seventh Crusade. Louis IX made mistakes, God rest his soul."

"Was he part of an Order?" I asked as I examined my tankard.

Andre frowned. "He was part of Louis' army. An ax man, I suppose."

The way he answered, I wasn't sure. There might be more to this.

Dieter didn't look at the lad, he just examined his tankard and its contents, "I've heard there were Templars on that Crusade. All were lost."

Dieter paused then added, "Excellent cider, Andre, excellent."

"And Hospitallers, too," I added to give Andre an acceptable alternative to the Templars.

Andre just frowned, "Templars aren't popular around here. Your food will be ready, I'll get it."

As Andre left, Dieter and I looked at each other with a slight shrug. Both of us felt there was more to the story. Few families could or would add arms such as the one above the tavern if a lost man were a common soldier. Besides it wasn't two axes on the sign, it was two maces. We knew mounted horsemen, knights or sergeants, not foot soldiers, used maces.

When Andre returned with our food he was smiling. "I don't know much about all that. Perhaps my father could tell you more. Would you like to talk with him?"

I nodded as I took in the marvelous aroma of steaming food. "We've been to the cathedral this morning, seen Richard's tomb. Might be interesting to hear more of the Crusades, eh Dieter. Where's your father?"

"Oh, he'll be out shortly. He's training our new cook."

Trade Andre's smile for a frown and Andre was the very image of his father, Henri. Henri pulled up a chair and sat down at our table. "Welcome to our tavern. Andre tells me you're new here. I see by your clothes you've been to sea."

"Mmm," I added with a nod. "We left Le Havre several days ago, unhappy with our captain's wages. So we decided to ship up river to Rouen, maybe even to Paris. Find work for a while. Eventually, when we run out of money and can't find work, we'll go back to Le Havre and the sea."

It was Henri's turn. "Oh," he replied as he nodded without losing his frown. "Andre says you've been to our cathedral and Richard's tomb. Too bad you couldn't have seen Our Lady's chapel, beautiful but it was taken down several years ago. Still, it is beautiful. Something every traveler should see don't you agree?"

"Yes," I replied. "I'm from a small village south of here, not far from Angers. My father was a smithy. When he died I went to sea but I always wanted to see Rouen's cathedral and the tombs of Richard and Rollo. My father shod a lot of horses for people traveling to and from Rouen. Many were Templars so I heard a great many stories of Rouen, and of Richard and the Crusades. I always wanted to visit his tomb here. And I'm curious about the sign, the arms, above your door."

"Andre says the Templars aren't popular now," Dieter said.

"Times change," Henri said. "Seems both Philip and the Pope had a falling out with the Templars. Caught seven or eight of them in their commandry here in Rouen. Put them on trial later, after they, uh, admitted to the charges." He ever so slightly rolled his eyes as he said "admitted."

"What happened to them?" Dieter asked.

"I don't really know but one of the castle clerks frequently comes in for a tankard after work. He says they were taken to Paris after they were encouraged to admit their sins. No blood you understand. They wanted to confess their sins to save their immortal souls. Inquisition laws, as everyone knows, prohibit shedding of blood and inquisitors are men of justice and very careful to follow the law.

"I guess they're all somewhere in Paris awaiting trial. The clerk didn't say where in Paris but the rumors are they're being held at Philip's palace on the Isle de la Cite."

"Is the clerk a member of the clergy?" Dieter asked.

"No, I think he's more of a jailer but he calls himself a clerk. He's clever. Says he can read and do numbers so maybe he really is a clerk. He wears the King's uniform but he has a bad limp so I think he's done with wars."

"And the arms above your door?" I asked.

"There was a time a family was proud to say a son or brother fought in the Crusades, even those who fought as Templars," Henri said with a firmness that left no doubt in our minds regarding his view of the Templars.

With that Hans entered the tavern. We'd planed for him to walk twice around the castle complex, wait in the shadows down the street and watch for any unusual activity, then join us.

Hans looked around the room as his eyes adjusted to the poor light, settled on us, and walked to our table. "I got lost. Just lucky I found you." He handed his tankard to Andre and pointed at me. "Apple cider if you have it, and a bite to eat. Whatever he had."

Dieter and I nodded towards our own tankards and at the same time. Both of us said, "Me, too."

Henri smiled."If you're in town long you might see the clerk one of these evenings. He comes in two or three times a week for a tankard, sometimes two." Henri chuckled, "He might enjoy someone other than me and Andre to talk with. Especially if you're buying."

"Does he drink a lot?" I asked, hoping the man might talk a great deal if he did.

"No, not really. I've never seen him have more than two."

"What time?" I asked.

"Oh, shortly after Vesper bells. If you'll excuse me now I'll make sure the new cook tends to his work."

We spent the afternoon helping Hugo, Ulf and Guidar. It was easy work, all three knew their business, had customers they knew from previous trips, and seemed to have a great many friends their own age willing to help. By the time the market closed with the Vespers bells most of their goods had been sold. Gaspard and Michelle's son Luc had found them and was anxious to show them Rouen's night life before the curfew bell rang. That didn't leave them much time, maybe two hours if the bell ringers were slow, so we offered to watch their goods and gear while they joined the revelry that accompanies every market fair.

To say they enjoyed themselves would not give their celebrations credit. Not long after the curfew bells chimed we saw them at the far side of the market slowly making their way, singing and dancing with three girls, each with a tankard of something. At first we laughed at the sight. Guidar was drunk but alone. The other boys each had a girl in tow. Guidar was headed towards their spot in the market but the girls seemed to be leading the other three boys into the trees along the Seine.

Dieter and I had the same thought, the girls were up to no good but what their game was we couldn't tell. The Baltic cities had their share of low life and we'd seen sailors and tradesmen, even experienced merchants, mugged after too much celebration. A little innocent fun in the woods is fine but it wasn't clear that was what this was about.

My two companions seemed as worried as I was. "Hans, stay here. Dieter and I will circle around to the trees and make certain the boys are not in over their heads."

By the time Dieter and I reached the woods Guidar had left his three friends behind and was headed to their goods, and safety. The other three, clearly drunk, were now being guided not too gently into the trees. The closer we got, the plainer it was that these were not young girls, and nothing innocent was happening. We could make out several men waiting in the shadows but it wasn't clear exactly how many.

Hans had seen what was happening and when Guidar was out of trouble Hans joined us. Confident the three of us would be more than a match for whoever was waiting in the shadows we flanked the men hiding in the trees.

As the three women, each with one of the boys in tow, reached the trees one of the four men stepped forward. "Look what we have here," the leader said with a wicked laugh. "Three lads with heavy purses. We must lighten their burden, boys."

The four thieves, probably a little drunk themselves and focused as they were on their intended victims, had neglected to watch their flanks. When the leader spoke Hans clubbed one with his belaying pin and I did the same to another. Both men went down with a groan which the leader mistook for a complaint and turned to see what had happened.

The odds were now three to two in our favor, and we were sober. The third man bolted for the market with the three women close behind leaving the leader alone. He drew a dagger and backed away then turned and followed the others into the darkness.

Shocked by the sudden violence, Luc, Hugo and Ulf began to regain their senses, if not their sobriety. Hugo looked at us and then at the retreating thieves and their female collaborators, shook his head and threw up. Luc and Ulf each sat down with a thump.

"My God they were going to rob us," Luc exclaimed, head in hands.

"Maybe murder us," Ulf added.

Hugo nodded, turned, gagged twice and threw up again.

We left the two unconscious men in the woods and took the boys back to their market space to sleep off their celebrations.

The following morning I walked through the woods. The two men we'd clubbed were gone but in daylight it was clear the location had been used before, probably by the same gang. It was an ideal location for theft and murder. The Seine was not far and a body, unconscious or dead, could easily be hauled to the bank and thrown in the river to be swept down river to Le Havre and the sea.

The boys, suffering severe hangovers, sold the balance of their goods and packed up their gear. With our encouragement they booked passage on one of the west bound river barges rather than risk walking home with their sale proceeds. As we saw them off at the dock it struck me Rouen seemed a little empty without our four young friends. I hoped we'd made friends who might be of help should we need it.

CHAPTER IV:

The Two Maces

At Vespers bells we waited just down the narrow street from Andre's inn for someone who had the look of a jailor. Henri had described him well, medium height, medium weight, brown hair, wearing the standard French military uniform we'd seen entering and leaving the castle, and he walked with a distinct limp. We'd seen half a dozen customers enter the inn, none wearing a uniform and none with a limp. Not long after the bells we saw him, he was the only one who fit the description. We waited long enough for him to order a tankard and settle himself comfortably.

I found the man standing at the bar, tankard in hand, minding his own business. He struck me as a wealthy knight's squire, certainly a soldier. Physically fit, in spite of his limp, he stood straight, shoulders square. He wore a thigh length, tan tunic cut to the elbows over a tan shirt and dark brown trousers. At the waist was a leather belt with purse in front and a standard military dagger on the left. His short, dark brown shoulder cape was neatly tied at the throat and a brown rolled-rim cap came to a point at the forehead. Unlike many in the King's service, his uniform was clean and fit him. His still dark beard was carefully trimmed, shoulder length hair cut and combed.

Andre was attending to a table but I caught his eye and he nodded towards the man. Stepping up to the bar, next to the man and on his right, I put my tankard on the bar, looked to my right then to my left and gave him a perfunctory smile. He returned it.

I stopped as if considering what to order. "How's the ale here?"

"Good," he replied without looking directly at me or changing his expression.

I ordered an ale and while I waited I asked him, "How's the food?"

"Good." This time he looked at me, apparently deciding whether I was worthy of his attention. "Your accent says you're Norman. But you have the look of a man who's been to sea."

"True. I'm a sailor. A couple of my shipmates and I wanted to see Rouen and maybe Paris. Then we'll go back. You from Rouen?"

"I live here. I'm a clerk at the castle."

We chatted a little about the Rouen fair and the cathedral. When Hans and Dieter entered the tavern I waived them over.

"Ask for a table," I called to them, then turned to Milun. "Join us. We've been shipmates but don't know Rouen. Maybe you could tell us what sights to see. Here, see your tankard is almost empty, let us buy you a drink and something to eat for your troubles."

Milun shrugged, looked at his almost empty tankard and nodded. "I guess I could tell you what to see, here and in Paris. I've been to Paris many times."

Andre steered us to a table well away from his other customers. We ordered food and more drinks and I paid for the four of us.

As we ate, Milun loosen up. He'd been in the army since a young man. In his twenty-one, almost twenty-two, years in the army he'd seen a great deal of France and the surrounding lands. Since the end of the Flemish wars he and his officer, that's how he referred to the officer he'd served all those years, worked for the provost at the Rouen castle. The provost,

Milun explained, managed the King's affairs in the Rouen district, collected his revenues and taxes as well as oversaw local military matters. Milun didn't say exactly what it was that he personally did or what his officer did for the provost.

It occurred to me that Henri had overestimated the importance of this man and his knowledge of what went on in the castle. Perhaps his role in the provost's office was insignificant but I doubted that. He was intelligent so perhaps his job was very significant.

That evening we said nothing of Philip, the Church or the Templars. But he did recommend a number of local sights to see and several we should see if we got to Paris.

My impression was that he might know more about the Templars arrested in Rouen than what he'd told Andre and Henri. But he was naturally reserved and would have to get to know us better before he'd trust us. He was a possible source of information we should cultivate.

As we left the tavern Dieter shook Milun's hand. "We're in town for a few more days. The food and ale are good here, I think we'll be back."

Milun nodded with a polite smile. "Excellent. I must work late tomorrow evening but I'll be here two evenings from now. Maybe I'll see you."

The three of us assured him we would meet as he'd suggested.

We hired out as day labor along the river for the next two days, loading and unloading barges for merchants. It was honest work and an opportunity to watch and listen but we saw and heard nothing that might help us. Hans did see two men, both with nasty lumps on the back of the head, hanging around the market but neither man seemed to recognize us so we avoided them. There was no reason to risk problems with the local authorities.

Shortly following Vespers bells we were outside the Two Maces, that's what we'd decided to call Andre's inn, waiting for Milun. He was late but we finally saw him leaving the castle gate closest to the tavern. Even with his distinct limp he made his way down the street faster than I expected.

When Andre took our drink orders Milun surprised us by producing the required deniers for his tankard of ale and dinner.

As Andre left to bring our ale Dieter said, "I don't mean to be rude, just tell me to mind my own business if I offend you. You said you've been in the army for a long time. Is that how you got the limp?"

"I was, and still am, a soldier. The limp, a trebuchet accident broke my leg."

"Wicked instrument in the right hands," I said.

"That it is and a danger to all those near it if one of the crew is careless. I was sergeant in charge of 'Hell Fire,' that's what we named our trebuchet. In the heat of battle one of my men didn't secure the wheel correctly and it released too soon, swung the carriage and I was hit. He was a new man to our squad. The man he'd replaced was killed earlier that morning by a bolt

"Bad luck. How'd you wind up here in Rouen's castle?" I asked.

"Well, in one way I was, am, very lucky. My leg healed and my officer kept me on his staff when he was posted here in Rouen. As I said he works for the provost. He's a good man."

"What does he do for the provost?" Dieter asked as he took a drink.

"We're not a large garrison, so he's in charge of both supplies and prisoners."

I tried not to show it, but I hoped a door had just opened for us. This man might know what happened to the Templars captured in Rouen.

"That must be a very difficult job," Hans said.

"Mmm," Milun answered as he took another drink.

"So you came to Rouen. Ever married?" Hans asked.

"No. Wouldn't mind it but my parents are elderly so I take care of them." He paused then continued with a chuckle, as if the idea were ridiculous. "Try to find a good wife for a soldier with a bad leg and two elderly parents. Good luck."

"Do you work with the local Bishop?" Dieter asked.

"About a wife?"

"No, no. At your work," Dieter replied.

"Only rarely. The King has his jurisdiction and the Bishop has his. They don't overlap much." He took another drink. "Well they do sometimes, like the Templars."

"What happened with the Templars? We've been at sea and don't hear much about such matters. Templars are crusaders, and money handlers, right?" I asked.

"Well, they were. Seems the King and the Templars, and the Pope, got into a dispute of some sort. I'm not really sure why but the King had all of 'em arrested for heresy. Some say they've managed the King's moneys for so long maybe they were taking a little for themselves. Wouldn't be the first time a trusted agent took what wasn't his. That struck me as strange though. If the Templars had taken Philip's funds, then why charge them with heresy?"

"Did the provost work with the church on that?" I asked.

"No, but the Bishop in Paris sent inquisitors to question the Templars arrested in Rouen. The Bishop of Rouen didn't object and the provost doesn't interfere with inquisitors. Besides heresy is an offense against God and the church, so church inquisitors seem to be appropriate, rather than the

King or the provost. If the Templars had taken the King's funds then the church inquisitors wouldn't have been involved."

"Sounds confusing," Hans said.

"Mmm," Milun responded with a nod and took another drink.

"What did the inquisitors do?" Dieter asked.

"Inquisitors don't allow us to be present when they question people. But by the end of the day all seven Templars confessed to the charges."

"What will happen to them?" I asked.

"I don't know. I suppose they'll be tried. They're somewhere in Paris now."

Hans asked, "At Notre Dame?"

Milun laughed, not loud, more of a chuckle. "No, not in Notre Dame. King wouldn't let the Church have 'em. They're in one of the King's towers. He's got several in Paris. What will happen after the trials I don't know. If they repent they'll probably live."

He took another drink. "Either way the Templars are done. Philip's troops have occupied all the Templar properties. He'll never give their lands back."

I was surprised, shocked really, to hear his conclusion. "How many are there, how many were arrested?" I asked.

"Seven here in Rouen. Throughout France? It's hard to say but I've heard less than two hundred. The records are sketchy, maybe intentionally. The men are moved around, it's hard to say."

Nothing more was said of the Templars the rest of the evening. The curfew bell chimed and we finished our tankards. As Milun turned north and we headed back to our skiff I called back to him, "See you tomorrow?"

He laughed and nodded.

We worked the docks again the next day and met Milun for dinner at Two Maces. He was in a good mood, told us his day went well that day, there were no new prisoners.

"What do you do over there?" I asked.

"I keep the prisoner records and account for supplies."

"You can read, and write?"

"Enough to keep the records. But I'm better with numbers. I learned numbers when I was trebuchet sergeant. It's not as easy as it looks. You have to consider the weight of the stone, the distance to the target, and its elevation. Then you must reckon the tension on the line and the number of wheel revolutions required to hit the target, so you don't come up short or overshoot. It's not hard if you're just throwing rocks over a wall and don't care where they land but if you're taking down a castle wall, well, that requires that you hit the same spot on the wall time after time. It's even harder if you're aiming at a keep or a barbican."

He took a drink and I thought he was about to give us a long lesson on calculating trajectory so I interrupted. "You can do calculations?"

"Yes, so my officer finds me useful. I can keep the financial records he needs for the provost."

"You mentioned you've been to Paris many times. What do you do there?"

"Usually escort prisoners. But sometimes just with the provost and my officer, take care of their horses, run errands, organize the records they need, things like that. Why?"

Dieter said, "We've been talking about going up river to Paris. See the city before we return to sea. We hoped you could give us some ideas of where the good taverns are, things like that. Do you know anyone on the Isle who could help us? Someone we might talk to about work?"

Milun nodded. "Jacques Bonet. We were in the army together. He was sergeant in charge of another trebuchet in our battery of three. He works on the Isle de la Cite. He'll know the people at the docks where supplies are brought in for the palace and the troops posted there. But don't play Nine Men's Morris with him. I've never seen him lose."

"How do we find him?"

"Trois Moines tavern, on the Isle's Pont au Change not far from the fortress. He eats dinner there. Food's good. If you see him say hello. And say hello to Greta too. She's a sweetheart."

"Who's Greta?" I asked.

"She works at Trois Moines. She and Jacques are good friends. If you know what I mean."

The three of us nodded. We knew what he meant.

"And Marc Lafevre. Last I was in Paris he was working in Notre Dame. I don't know him as well but Jacques may know how to find him."

"Thanks," I said. "Can we repay you? Maybe bring something from Paris when we come back this way?"

"I really don't need anything, but stop off in Rouen on your way back. We'll have a tankard. And you can tell me about your adventures in Paris and how Jacques and Greta are, if you see them."

The following morning the three of us set off for Paris with a favorable breeze. Each day we took our time, stopping for midday meals and dinners at inns and taverns frequented by the Seine's travelers, merchants and boatmen. We were generous with tankards of ale, perry, cider and wine for those inclined to chat about the events of the day. There weren't many Vespers bells in the countryside to remind people of the hour so dinners frequently lasted until well after sunset.

Three easy days later we stopped for a day in the beautiful countryside near Les Andelys. Normandy and the Chateau Gaillard in Les Andelys had been under English rule a mere hundred years before and many Norman lords had close relatives among England's aristocracy who held lands on both sides of the Channel. More than a few of the Norman aristocracy held secret hopes of once again pledging fealty to the English king rather than to Philip and the House of Capet. Edward would welcome them and the opportunity to reassert an old family claim to the French throne.

It was possible some Templars might be held in the chateau. But we found no one in the town who believed that. Sentiment of the local people was still mixed when it came to Philip. This would not be his first choice to imprison Templars.

By the time we left Les Andelys we were comfortable with our story. No one had challenged our claim to be what we said we were, simple men of the sea. People were usually talkative and cheerful but the closer we got to Paris the less they had to say about the King or the Templars. Along the way we heard a wild combination of fact, rumor, speculation and outright lies. Every kind of prejudice, bias, faith, blind trust, fear and hatred colored individual views.

Most people we met were aware the Templars had confessed after their arrest and a few heard rumors de Molay had retracted his confession. Apparently the Pope had stopped his inquisitors from further examination of the Templars and had pardoned the Templars. The Bishop of Sens, however, supported Philip and continued his prosecution without the Pope's consent.

CHAPTER V
Paris

I was awe struck by Paris and I think Dieter and Hans were too. As we sailed east up the Seine I was overwhelmed by the Louvre fortress on the north bank, the Tour du Coin adjacent to it, the Tour de Nesle on the south bank to our right, and the Isle de la Cite with both the palace fortress known as the Concierge, and Notre Dame.

We'd learned something of these fortresses as part of our preparations but seeing their true dimensions they seemed even more formidable. Certainly I knew the city would have defenses, walls and forts of some dimension, but these were beyond any I'd seen even in the Mediterranean.

Such fortifications confirmed what had been our belief from the start, rescue by the Seine river would be impossible. A surprise assault so far from the sea, so far from any friendly lands, was impossible. Whether an armed assault came by river or land Philip would have several weeks notice. Any direct assault would result in immediate execution of all imprisoned Templars.

The commercial district and markets were located on the Seine's north banks across from the Isle de la Cite, so that's where we landed. We were immediately indistinguishable from the city's laborers, merchants and general population. It occurred to me we were invisible, no one noticed us as we walked the muddy, dirt streets and alley ways of the great city.

I hadn't expected the size of the city or the number of its citizens, or the filth and odor. We heard Paris was home to some two hundred thousand souls but that was just a grand number until I saw the city. The people of Paris were different not only in their number but in their almost universal disregard for other humans. There was a constant competition for space and air to breathe. As I walked through the town it seemed a sport to crowd me out of the way and suck the air from in front of me so that I had no place to stand and no air to breathe that had not already been used a dozen times. Woe to the lame or meek in Paris, they would quickly be swept aside and forgotten.

I'd heard the Isle de la Cite was the soul of Paris. The more I saw of Paris the more I agreed. The island had been a stronghold since Versingetorix fought Caesar before the birth of our Christ. Almost a thousand years later it was Odo's stronghold when the Vikings laid siege to the city. Later French kings built the Cathedral Notre-Dame on the east half of the island and fortified the west half for themselves. The old stone bridge from the south shore to the Isle de la Cite had been washed away earlier in the year but there were several wooden bridges connecting the island to both the river's north and south banks.

The Louvre, the Tour de Coin and the Tour de Nesle were massive. Each seemed a likely location for Philip to keep his special prisoners but each was closed to outsiders, which included anyone not a member of the King's army or his Court. We could tell nothing from the outside and had no idea how we might gain entrance.

The next day we walked the boundaries of the Templar Enclos outside the old city walls. This was where de Molay and the other leaders had been arrested and where many of our brethren might still be held. All we could see behind its crenellated, stone walls rising twenty-five or more feet above us were the tiled roof of the Tour de Temple some five stories above the land, and the third and upper level of Tour de Cesar. I looked at the heavy, oak, iron reinforced gates in the enclosure's west wall, the dozen or more turrets on the massive stone walls surrounding the six or seven acre grounds within and wondered how on that terrible morning, Friday the 13th of October, our brethren had been arrested without a fight. I came to the conclusion de Molay had been betrayed by someone within our Order. One of our own, a Trojan horse of sorts, had opened the gates and delivered him and our Order to his enemies. By whom I did not know.

It didn't make sense. Our Grand Master had known to warn us. A month before the arrests he'd sent word to prepare our ships and leave La Rochelle's harbor before the 13th. Yet Philip's man and our mortal enemy, Guillaume de Nogaret, had walked through the open gates of the Templar fortress, across the courtyard into the Villeneuve du Temple and arrested De Molay and more than a hundred Templars without a weapon being raised in resistance.

The morning after our explorations we found work, day labor loading and unloading river barges. It was hard work and the pay wasn't much but if we were careful it covered our daily expenses. More importantly, we worked with men who knew Paris and the quays, taverns and inns along the Seine, had a keen interest in all rumors and gossip concerning Paris intrigues no matter how bizarre, and liked to talk. A few even had limited access, for purposes of delivering goods and supplies, to a number of locations where Templars might be imprisoned. Everyone had their favorite theory but no one claimed personal knowledge of the Templars' actual location, number or condition. Significantly, no one believed the Templars were held in the Louvre, the Tour de Nesle or the Tour du Coin.

The following week we went in search of Jacques Bonet. Milun had told us Jacques worked in the Concierge but from what we could see its fortress was four or five times as large as the one in Rouen. It was clear one didn't just walk up to one of the gates and ask to see Jacques Bonet. Fortunately, Milun had also said we might find Jacques in the Trois Moines tavern on the Pont au Change connecting the Seine's north bank with the Isle. The three of us had laughed at the tavern's name, the three monks certainly fit the three of us.

The tavern itself was easy enough to find, one need only ask any stranger. In style the outside wasn't much different from the Two Maces, perhaps slightly larger. Hanging from two chains attached to an iron support above the door was an artfully carved and brightly painted wooden sign depicting three rather fat, jolly monks each with a tankard and a smile. Above the tavern were two overlapping stories. Inside, the tavern was much like the Two Maces but perhaps not quite as clean.

We decided to take a chance and each ordered a meat pie and a tankard of ale from a rather dim-witted but pleasant young man. I was surprised when a woman with a cheerful smile brought our ale but I asked her if Greta was working that day.

"Who wants to know?" the woman responded with a dubious look.

"A friend in Rouen told us to say hello to Jacques Bonet and Greta. Said they might be found at the Trois Moines," I answered.

"Well," she said with a cautious smile, "this is the Trois Moines and you've found Greta. Who's your friend and what do you want with Jacques, other than to say hello?"

"Milun, and work if any can be found," I answered.

Greta's face lit up with a smile. "Oh, Milun, that's different. Jacques'll be in shortly after Vespers bell. He's always looking for men who aren't afraid of hard work. And friends of Milun are always welcome in the Trois Moines."

Greta, I guessed, was about Milun's age, maybe mid or late thirties. Her dark blonde hair, blue eyes and quick smile added to her beauty. From her response I had the thought she and Jacques knew each other rather well.

Jacques was prompt. Echoes of the Vespers bell had barely faded when the door opened and a big man, Dieter's height but heavier, more beef than fat, walked in as if he owned the place. He looked to be Milun's age and by all appearances a tough old soldier. I would have guessed he was our man, his uniform was identical to Milun's and worn with the same care and attention.

Greta nodded towards the man, then called, "Aye, Jacques. Some boys from Rouen are here to say hello and buy you dinner and a tankard or two, if you'll swap stories about your little bitch and that handsome rascal, Milun."

Jacques turned and with a huge grin replied, "Milun! From Rouen, eh. Well, for dinner and ale I can tell 'em all about my lovely lady. The only woman I ever loved as much as I love you, Greta."

We made room at our table for Jacques and Greta then asked the dim-witted young man to bring meat pies and ale for both Jacques and Greta and another tankard of ale for each of us.

Greta looked at us with a grin. "That'll be three denier for each of you. Two for dinner and one for the tankard, the first tankard. Another for the second. And six denier for dinner and ale for Jacques and me. That's two more from each of you."

The young man, Greta introduced him as Piers, held out his hand and I counted out eighteen denier. Greta nodded her approval and went to get the pies as Piers left for the ale.

Jacques sat down with a thump, "*Salut, mes amies.* What brings you to my Isle, other than the noble cause of filling my belly and to say hello. You want stories of my dear Princess of Perdition? Well, this is your lucky day, I'm of a mind to tell you."

As Piers set a tankard in front of Jacques he swooped it up and took a long drink.

While Jacques wiped his mouth I said, "Milun told us to look you up. Said you might know of work for three able-bodied men who want to see Paris."

"Milun, uh? Best trebuchet sergeant I ever knew. But don't tell him I said that. I'll deny it and curse you for liars. At three hundred yards he could pick an archer off a tower and leave his empty boots on the rampart. Damn shame that little bastard didn't lock the wheel like Milun told him to. Broke Milun's leg. Hell, could'a taken his leg off. How is he?"

"He's well," I said.

"Thank God! After Milun was injured I beat the crap out of the little bastard and sent him back to the front lines. Two days later he died with an arrow in his skinny belly. I almost felt bad about it."

Jacques looked us over for a moment then asked, "How'd three men of the sea meet Milun?"

Hans answered, "We met him in Rouen, by chance. We grew tired of our cheap English captain. He cheated us on our wages so we decided to see Paris. On the way we stopped in for a tankard at an inn we call the Two Maces."

Jacques took another drink and wiped his chin. "Ah, yes. I know the place, coat of arms over the door with two black maces. Good name, the Two Maces. I like it."

As Greta approached with our food Jacques continued but a little louder. "Yes, the Two Maces. Now that's a great inn! Real tankards not these ladies' cups. And the food, my God the food. They really know how to feed a man."

Greta put our food down and laughed. "Jacques if I gave you a bigger tankard or more food you'd be too fat to get through the door. I'm just looking after your good health."

Jacques grinned. "Yes, my love, I don't know what I'd do without you."

"Well, find these boys work so they come back again. They actually pay for their food and drink, unlike some of our customers."

"Oh love, it was only the one time. I was so smitten with you, I just forgot," Jacques responded with a nod and a smile. "But I'll help 'em if that's what you want."

Jacques turned to us with a grin. "Be here with the sun tomorrow. I'll see what I can do."

Several tankards and a round of Nine Men's Morris later, which Jacques won handily, we parted as fast friends with Jacques and Greta. And we'd heard some wild stories about Jacques' beloved Princess of Perdition. It was as simple as that.

On our walk back across the bridge Dieter said, "God is on our side here. He placed us with the right people. No doubt, He is with us."

I couldn't help but believe Dieter was right. With His help we would find our imprisoned brethren. My hopes had never been higher.

We were waiting in front of Trois Moines before the sun rose and Jacques wasn't late. I wasn't surprised either that he was punctual or that his uniform was clean and worn with pride and purpose.

Jacques grinned as he looked us over, more of an inspection, to be sure we were sober and ready to work.

"Well, my three monks, have you eaten?" he asked with a hearty laugh and a questioning look that left no doubt what the answer had to be.

"Yes, we've eaten and we're ready for duty, er, work," I said.

Jacques grinned at that. "Excellent. Follow me. I don't warrant you'll like your new duties but the wages are fair. Unlike the English captain you spoke of."

He put us to work mucking the fortress stables. But we'd learned how to do that many years ago and we did it well. Well enough that it surprised Jacques when he did his noon inspection. When he made his final inspection just before Vespers bell he grinned and told us to come back the next day. This time he told us to meet him at the fortress' north gate.

We spent two weeks in the stables. He looked in on us twice a day to be sure we were mindful of our duties and each day he paid each of us a fair workman's wage. We got to know the fortress stables well and the yards, too, but not the donjon where Templars might be held. On Saturday at noon, our second at the stables, he stopped for a final inspection of our work before we left. We only worked half a day on Saturdays.

"Do you boys have to work together all the time? At times I could use one or two of you on other duties if you've a mind to do something other than mucking stables and repairing tack."

We all nodded and I spoke up, "That's fine with us. Might be a nice change. What kind of work is it?"

"Weapons repair and maintenance. The irons get rusty if they aren't sharpened and oiled regularly. And oil the oak so it doesn't dry and crack. Nothing more useless than a pike with a dull blade and a broken haft. And once in a while help feed the prisoners. Clean out a cell if a man dies or is moved."

I shrugged. "We could do that if someone shows us what needs to be done."

"Good, then it's settled," Jacques responded. "Monday you'll work in the armory.

The following week Jacques had Dieter and I sharpening swords, pikes and axes while Hans oiled oak and maintained crossbows. That, too, was something we knew how to do well and Jacques let us know he was pleased with our work. Jacques's work kept him busy, he had more than twenty men to train and supervise. With our new duties we were required to work in areas we hadn't been in before and we had the freedom to inspect adjoining parts of the towers and the troop quarters.

Some days we were required to help feed prisoners but as best we could determine there weren't more than twenty. None were Templars. As we worked we rarely spoke to the prisoners but it was easy to assume a secret posture or whisper a secret phrase that any Templar would recognize and respond to. There were no responses.

Jacques put us to work on two of the five trebuchets in the fortress yard. One was his prized Princess of Perdition and he glowed when we showed him our work.

One afternoon he introduced us to his officer, de Martz, the second son of a nobleman. It hadn't been planned. De Martz was crossing the main bailey as the three of us were working on the Princess. Jacques hadn't seen de Martz leave the armory and enter the yard so didn't see his officer's reaction both to our work and to Jacques' pride in his old siege engine.

De Martz watched, expressionless, then cleared his throat, just loud enough for Jacques to hear. Jacques came to attention and saluted.

De Martz smiled. "Good afternoon Sergeant Bonet. Your Princess looks beautiful as ever. Fighting trim, don't you think?"

"Yes she does, sir. May I introduce the three men who have restored her full beauty?"

We climbed down and came to attention as Jacques introduced us. De Martz nodded, "Excellent work men. Sergeant, when these men have finished with your Princess talk with Lieutenant de Roux. See if we can make use of their talents?"

"*Oui*, I'll do that," Jacques said with a smart military salute.

De Roux, a young man eager to please his superior officer, and gratified his sergeant had impressed de Martz, permitted Sergeant Bonet to put us to work anywhere within the Concierge's various towers and jails. The young officer laughed as he explained we would not be allowed in either the palace residence or the new Tour d'Argent where, he explained, the King's wealth was stored.

We could hardly contain our surprise. With such access it might be possible to find the imprisoned Templars or at least determine if our brethren had, at some prior time, been imprisoned within the Concierge.

Over the next week Jacques put us to work cleaning the Salle and cells previously occupied by now deceased prisoners, delivering food to the remaining prisoners, repairing weapons and maintaining the five trebuchets. The soldiers and staff came to see us as just another part of Jacques' work crew and ignored us.

In the course of our work we cleaned the Salle des Gardes built to house the men who actually guarded the King. Within the Salle was a small brig but it was obvious the Templars were not kept there. The unnamed tower in the northwest corner was under construction or repair. If the Templars had been held there at one time we could not tell. The Tour d'Argent's twin, the Tour Cesar on the south wall, had its share of unfortunate occupants but no sign of Templars.

Last of all we cleaned the cells within the Grosse Tour, over thirty-five feet wide at the base with walls over eight feet thick. Its tower rose well above all but the chapel spire. It was a true prison. There were no Templars held within its cold, stone cells when we were there but as I examined one cell I found Templar symbols scratched into the stones in the northeast corner just a foot or so above the floor. My imagination created the vision of a tortured Templar huddled in pain, scratching these very symbols in a search for any strength he could find in remembering the honor and traditions of his Order, resigned to his fate but comforted by his faith that he would find eternal peace for having faithfully served his Lord.

Within the Concierge, were four possible locations for our imprisoned brethren, the Tour Cesar in the center of the north wall, the Tour at the west end of the north wall, the Grosse Tour in the center of the compound, and somewhere within the Salle des Gardes. We'd visited and ruled out all four.

CHAPTER VI
The Enclos

It was time to search elsewhere and the most logical location was the Enclos, the Templar fortress where de Molay had been arrested. We made our excuses to Sergeant Bonet, explained we'd saved our earnings and wanted to see more of Paris and France, then made our way up river.

We found a slip for our boat on the Seine's north bank, up river of Ile Notre Dame. From there we could reach the Enclos du Temple without entering the old city.

The morning after our move we woke to a heavy rain with lightening flashing to the west of us. Huddled beneath the canvas awning covering the boat's cockpit we settled in for a long, restless, uncomfortable day. Wind, rain, lightning and thunder made sleep difficult that night. I was already unsettled with the question of how to gain entry to the Enclos but as our boat rocked in the wind and waves I finally slept, and dreamt of a homeless, blind monk wandering the streets of Paris.

Low clouds and steady, cold drizzle were an inauspicious beginning to our day but the weather matched my mood. I told Hans and Dieter of my strange, troubling dream. Neither seemed particularly interested and listened without comment as they ate cold bread and sausage.

Dieter finished eating and leaned back to stretch his legs in the boat's cramped spaces. "It might work."

"What might work?" I asked.

"A mendicant monk attacked by a thief near the Enclos main gate, somewhere you'll be seen by the guards. That small oak grove about a crossbow shot from the main gate would work well. If they take you in maybe you'll see something that would help us."

"How do we arrange that and what will the two of you do, while I'm being beaten?"

Dieter laughed. "Well, if no one else shows up to attack you, Hans will do the job."

I looked at Dieter to see if he was putting me on but he was serious.

Dieter smiled. "When he's beating you, start yelling. I'll be close by, dressed as another friar and try to stop the attack. Make lots of noise. I'll call for help. The guards may not take pity on a friar and invite him inside the Enclos but I think they'll help if the poor friar is injured in a robbery. If the guards come to our aid, feign injury and I'll ask for help. Maybe they'll take you to the infirmary. I'll come by in the morning to see how you're doing and we'll have a look around, ask a few questions."

"Dominican," I said. "We have tunic, scapular, capuce and cappa."

Dieter thought a long moment. "Black Friars, yes, Black Friars is perfect."

I nodded. "What about Hans?"

"He'll take off. The guards won't have a good look at him so they won't recognize him later. If they don't come to help us, I'll help you off. Then we'll have to come up with another idea."

It didn't seem much of a plan but I didn't see much risk either.

The following day, dressed as Black Friars, Dieter and I found temporary lodging, suitable for friars under an oath of poverty, outside the city walls. Each day after morning bells for the next week Dieter and I made our way by separate routes to the oak grove near the Enclos to pray for a few minutes before going our separate ways. Each evening shortly before Vespers bells we met again in the grove for prayers before leaving by separate routes to meet Hans and then return to our lodging.

Each morning and each evening we waved to the Enclos guards. After a few days our greeting was returned, not just with perfunctory returning waves but with grins. By the end of that first week one or two guards would shout a greeting, "Morning padre" or "Evening padre." We'd become just another part of their daily routine.

Except for the poor most people ignored us. A few gave a slight bow which we answered with the sign of the cross and a smile. People assumed we were what we wore. For all appearances we were about our duties ministering to the poor.

The following week, on a drizzling, cold Saturday morning, we prepared to spring our ruse. Hans was to follow a bow shot behind me as I made my way along the old path through the meadow I'd been using to reach the grove. I tried to look forlorn, in the miserable weather it was easy. Dieter was to be late so when I reached the grove I pretended to look for him, looked at the low, dark clouds, finally pulled the hood over my head, and huddled under an oak to wait for him. I had a clear view of the Enclos' main entry and the guards in their shelters had a clear view of me. I waived to them just to be certain they'd seen me, they waived back.

There was little activity outside the fortress walls until two ox drawn wagons brought provisions of some description to the gate and waited for three guards to come out to inspect their goods. In spite of the bad weather the guards made a thorough examination of the wagons before signaling for the gates to be opened. The fortress commander knew how to keep his men focused on their duty.

Other than the two wagons there was nothing to distract me from the miserable weather and I began to look forward to the coming robbery. I pretended not to see Hans when he appeared at the meadow's edge looking every bit a cutthroat, sometime after we parted that morning he'd collected an old woolen jacket and cap. I chucked to myself, it certainly added to his character.

I tried not to watch Hans as he approached and lost sight of him when he slipped around the grove and out of sight. Suddenly he was at my back. I hadn't heard a thing and was genuinely startled when his hand roughly grasped my shoulder, threw me to the ground and pulled the hood down over my head so I couldn't see. It was a good touch I thought. Not only would it look like a real robbery, but the hood would prevent cuts and bruises as we rolled on the ground.

I screamed and struggled but his grip held me tight. I tried to roll away and screamed for help, loud enough that I was certain the guards would hear. Hans cuffed me in the mouth, hard enough to loosen a tooth and bloody my mouth, and stop my screaming.

I heard Dieter yelling something in Latin. I could tell from his yell that he was running hard. In my confusion I thought he was telling me it wasn't Hans who'd attacked me. I began to fight back but, blinded by the hood, I had no idea where the man was. And the bulky friar's habit made fighting almost impossible.

In the struggle my head hit a rock or I was hit with a rock, I couldn't tell which. I was struck a second time and felt blood run down my forehead. I gasped for air and lost all sense of balance. Through the pain I heard Dieter yelling, coming hard by the sound of it.

I was rolling, stumbling, off balance, pushed, pulled, pounded. I managed to get to all fours then something slammed my head, a bright light, then darkness and silence.

Something held me down, then I was free, floating. I slept, for how long I couldn't tell, then I was dreaming. I lay still trying to catch my breath and stop the spinning world.

Someone pulled my hood back but when I looked around the world was spinning, out of focus. I tried to sit up but couldn't. I gagged and vomited.

A Black Friar was starring down at me saying something I couldn't make sense of. Sitting on the ground next to me was a rough looking man, his head bloody, surrounded by a half-dozen armed men but I couldn't make sense of that either.

I turned to one side, I wanted to throw up but just gagged. The last thing I remember hearing is someone saying, "Get him inside." It made no sense. I had no idea who he was talking about.

I woke with a terrible headache to the smell of chicken broth and warm rye bread in what was clearly an infirmary. My clothing hung on a wooden peg next to my bed. When I carefully touched my head I felt stitches. I didn't feel like moving but I was hungry, a good sign. Eventually, someone noticed I was awake and asked how I felt.

Good question, I thought. The room wasn't spinning and I was hungry but sitting up seemed a bad idea. I just nodded and tried to smile. The effort was painful so I stopped. I must have fallen asleep because when I woke again it was dark. I felt much better and moving wasn't quite as painful.

A stranger in a uniform similar to what Jacques wore was sitting on the bed next to mine. He smiled. "Your brother, the Black Friar, was here this morning and again this afternoon. But you were sleeping so we didn't bother you."

I nodded and lifted myself onto one elbow. "Will he be back?"

The man nodded. "We offered to let him stay here but he said he had duties to attend to and he'd come again in the morning. Are you hungry? The broth is excellent but the rye is cold. Maybe we can warm it for you."

I was able to eat a little. Then slept until morning.

When I woke Dieter, dressed as a Black Friar, was sitting on a three legged stool next to my bed. With his help I was able to sit up. Until then I hadn't noticed how uncomfortable the wooden bed was. Dieter handed me a quarter loaf of rye bread and a small tankard of ale. Both were exquisite.

Dieter looked at me and whispered, "Glad you're feeling better, but don't recover too quickly. We're in the Enclos infirmary. You've been here two days. I've had a look around the chapel and the beautiful, old church. Yesterday I had permission to minister to the men held in Caesar's Tower. I think there're twenty there now but I couldn't be certain. There may be more.

"Three Templars told me there'd been more, including de Molay, but they were moved. To the Tour du Temple they think. That was shortly after the arrests. They think Philip arrested as many as two or three hundred Templars but no one claims to know for certain how many. Most were held here for a time but they don't know where they all are now.

"I've asked to minister to all the prisoners held here. I have permission to minister today but I don't know which tower. I need one more day, two if you can manage it."

I nodded and between bites said, "Won't be difficult. I'm certain I couldn't walk out of here. What happened?"

"The man who assaulted you had been watching us for several days. He saw us handing out alms to the poor and intended to rob you, and me, of the coins intended for the poor."

"What happened to him, where is he?"

"Guards used him for archery practice after they found your coin purse in his jerkin pocket. Didn't take much to figure out what he'd been up to."

I looked at him, blinked several times in disbelief. "They did what?"

"Well, the sergeant of the guards gave him a fifty-fifty chance, on a queek cloth. But his pebble landed on a black square. Bad luck. Still they gave him a fifty pace start for the gate, from the Tour. Poor bastard ran like the wind, zigged and zagged. But he made it less than half way to the gate when the first arrow got him in the thigh. As he started to go down the second arrow got him in the small of the back. The third arrow hit just behind his jaw and went up into his brains. He was dead when he hit the ground."

Dieter gave a grim smile, "The guards don't take kindly to robbing money intended for the poor. I think they would've killed him even if his pebble found a white square."

Three days later Dieter announced I was well enough to leave. With the aid of two guards and my Black Friar brother I made it to the gate where I thanked everyone I could, with genuine gratitude for their care. Dieter and I slowly made our way back to our boat. I was grateful we could now leave Paris.

When we were well out of sight of the Enclos, Hans joined us. "What did you find in the Tour du Temple?" I asked as the three of us slowly made our way along the old city walls.

"There are ten old Templars in the tower, all in bad shape after torture and the awful food. They've been held here since the arrests last October. They believe seventy or more were taken south, they think to Poitiers. More are being held somewhere in or near Paris but they don't know where or how many."

"When?" I asked.

"Over the past few months, the last group just a few weeks ago."

I looked at Dieter, "My God we just missed them. Was de Molay taken to Poitiers?

"De Molay was taken away last year, the end of October just after he confessed to the intellectuals of the Paris University. He wrote a letter to all Templars telling them to confess."

"Where is he now?"

"They don't know. They don't know if he's alive. No one's seen or heard from him since last November."

"What happened after the arrests?" I asked.

"Nogaret announced the written accusations on the fourteenth and the trials began the next day. Over the next few days all were tortured in the Enclos and all confessed. De Molay confessed again the next day to the University of Paris. De Pairraud confessed in November. Apparently the Pope didn't like or agree to the arrests but it sounds like the inquisition continued, both by the King and the bishops Philip controls.

"Torture. Rack and thumbscrew mostly, and starvation. The King and de Nogaret are getting creative, puts a rag over their nose and mouth, then pours water over them until they almost drown. Doesn't leave a mark so the Inquisitors aren't offended. All confessed several days after they were captured."

"Why are the ten men still here?"

"They're all old, probably too weak to travel. The King doesn't really need them, they're just pawns. A dozen died in the last month. Starvation mostly, maybe despair. They told me a hundred and thirty-eight Templars were arrested in the Enclos on the thirteenth.

"In the following weeks another four hundred or maybe as many as another five hundred, maybe as few as two hundred were arrested in Paris and around France. No one really knows how many were arrested or where they are. They're moved around and mixed up so it's likely the same men have been counted more than once."

Hans squinted as if he were thinking out loud. "Did they say how the King was able to make the arrests, here in the Templars' own fortifications? Was there a fight, did the Templars resist?"

Dieter shook his head. "No, and I don't understand it. Two old Templars told me de Molay ordered the men in the Enclos to open the gates and not resist. He knew what was going to happen. All our ships in La Rochelle harbor left by the thirteenth so Matthew must have known. It doesn't make sense. Why wasn't there a fight? De Molay and the others here could have held out until we mounted a counter attack."

CHAPTER VII:
Return to Le Havre

Three long days later with a favorable current but contrary winds we pulled alongside one of Rouen's commercial docks as the sun was setting. We hadn't learned much in Paris and wanted to see Milun, maybe he'd seen or heard something that would help us.

The following day we wandered through town and spent most of our time in the market listening to the latest rumors. Something had happened in Rouen but we couldn't make sense of it. That evening we finished at the Two Maces in hopes Andre or Milun could tell us what had happened.

As I entered I stopped to let my eyes adjust to the darkness. Before I could recognize anyone I heard someone call out, "Well, if it isn't the three sailors. Come in, come in!"

"Andre?" I called back.

"Yes, Erik. Where're your two friends?"

"They'll be right in. Had to stop to make room for some of your excellent ale."

"Take the table over here and tell me about Paris. We've got some excellent pork stew to go with your ale."

"Order us three of the pork stew and three tankards of ale. Make it four of everything and join us if you have time. Seen Milun lately?"

"Hell yes. He'll be in shortly unless I miss my guess. He's been in regularly, with a group from the castle. Tough lookin' bastards but they pay well. He might have information for you. But don't press him while his companions are around."

"Then make it five if he comes alone. He gave us good advice about Paris and he'll want to hear about Greta and Jacques."

Dieter, Hans and Milun came through the door, laughing. Dieter called into the darkness, "Erik, look who we found outside. My God he's thin and dry. He needs food and ale, lots of both!"

"I've already ordered it and Andre says the pork stew is excellent. fatten us up a little."

Milun grinned broadly as he sat down. "Good to see you again. How was Paris, did you see Jacques and Greta?

"Paris, what a city. It's huge!" Dieter responded, then added with a sour look, "And it smells!"

Milun laughed and nodded. "Yes, that it does."

"Jacques and Greta said to say hello," Hans added as he pulled up a stool.

"Jacques put us to work. Good work and fair wages. We met his Princess of Perdition, quite a machine," I said.

"Ahh! The beautiful Princess. Throws a stone farther than any but my own Hell Fire."

Andre delivered five bowls of pork stew and returned with five tankards of ale, then sat down with us but said nothing about the cost of the feast he'd delivered.

"Andre, what's the fare for such a feast?" I asked.

"It's on the house," he said with a smile.

I shook my head. "No, no, you'll never make it as a tavern keep if you do that. Thanks to you we met Milun. And thanks to Milun we met Jacques. And thanks to Jacques we found work and not with some cheap English bastard. De Martz paid us very well. So what's the rate?"

"Well, when you put it that way, fifteen deniers will do it," Andre responded with a grin.

I shelled out the coins from my side pouch and he shoveled them into his apron pocket.

As we finished the stew Dieter asked the question the three of us were thinking, "Had any interesting prisoners since we left?"

Milun nodded, started to take another sip of ale but put the tankard down. With a frown he looked at the four of us. "Yes, we have. We had four Templars here for three days, important ones. De Molay, himself, was here with three others."

"De Molay? What's he like?" was all I could say.

"No, he's just a man. Tall, he must have been quite a knight when he was young. Now he's an old man, polite, quiet. Humble really."

"I felt sorry for him but he seems to have accepted his fate."

"Where'd they take him, and the others?" I asked.

"I heard men talking about Poitiers and Chinon. But I wasn't really able to hear whether they'd been there already or were going there. I did hear the King keeps moving de Molay and the other leaders so it's hard to say where he is now. Some say he's somewhere in Paris, the old Temple Enclos or Corbiel.

"The angels know Philip has plenty of castles and most have donjons suitable for important prisoners. I also heard them talk of Chateau de Gisors, it's about half way between here and Paris. It's got a fine donjon, too."

Dieter asked, "Did you actually talk with the Templars? I heard they'd been tortured, their tongues torn out."

"I talked with him, de Molay. He could talk just fine but he said very little. He and the others looked tired, exhausted really, thin as a sapling."

I shook my head. "Keeps moving 'em, uh? Well, that's got to be difficult for everyone. You, too."

Milun took a drink. "I suppose. But the escorts, the men who do the transferring, have the real problem. They just keep moving from castle to castle and never know from day to day if they'll have to pack up and move again."

Andre started to refill Milun's tankard but Milun politely waived him way.

"Do you know the men who transport him, de Molay, and the others?" I asked.

Milun nodded. "Uh-huh, I served with a couple of them."

"Were they the men you were drinking with?" Andre asked.

Milun shrugged. "As I said, I served with some of 'em. In the Flemish wars."

"De Molay and the others can't ride, can they?" I asked in surprise. "How do they transport them?"

"By cart, they're shackled in a cart. With a dozen or more guards."

"Not by river?" Dieter asked.

"No, they always travel at night so they use the roads. Don't waste any time at it either. They get a message one day and are long gone by the next morning."

Our reunion went on until the curfew bell but nothing more was said of de Molay or the Templars. As Milun left the Two Maces, Andre motioned for the three of us to wait.

"You missed de Molay by less than a week. Milun was in with five or six guards almost every night while de Molay was kept in Rouen. Kept us busy and a few other inns, too. The house up the road, the one with the women, was busy enough."

"Were there just six of them?" I asked.

"No, I think there were at least a dozen, perhaps more, in the escort. That's what they call themselves. All in uniforms so no one will interfere. That's all I saw but maybe there were others. Six of them were here having a late dinner. They'd been to the house up the road but Milun wasn't with them when a rider came in with a note. Orders, I think, because they all left in a hurry. Didn't even finish their tankards. I wondered what was going on so I closed up and watched the castle gates. They and their prisoners were on the road within an hour."

"Why did you take such a risk, you had to know it was dangerous?" Dieter said.

"They didn't like Templars. When they were here the first time one of them asked about the coat of arms over our door, the one with two maces. When I told him my father's great uncle had been in the Crusades they spat on the floor and damned the Templars. Called 'em a bunch of devil worshipers, queers, and worse. You've always been respectful."

He paused, looked me in the eyes, shrugged. "I thought you might want to know."

I wondered if we'd said or done something that directly connected us with the Templars. If Andre had seen it then so might others. But Andre gave no hint, he looked down as he cleared the table. "See you tomorrow?"

Dieter nodded. "See you tomorrow."

Unfortunately, we did not see Milun again before we left two days later.

Our reception in Saint Adela was an open table with all the food and ale we could consume. It seems Luc and the boys had embellished the events of their last evening with us in Rouen. Michelle and Gaspard were certain we'd saved their son's life.

Well into dinner and tankards of ale Dieter turned to Gaspard. "Anyone seen a cart, traveling at night, with a couple of men in it and a dozen or so armed troops as escort?"

Gaspard laughed. "Someone after you boys? You're safe here with us, you know."

"No, no," I responded. "No one's after us. But we've heard rumors of such on the roads between Le Havre and Paris. All very mysterious, no one knows what it's all about."

Gaspard turned to Michelle with a conspiratorial grin. "My dear wife, I know if anyone has seen or heard of such a mystery it's the women of Normandy and it wouldn't be long until you would hear of it. Perhaps some Parisian aristocrat visiting a pretty, young woman of the countryside?"

Michelle chuckled. "Well, I hear a great many things you men are deaf to. But a cart traveling at night with armed guards isn't one of them. Norman women wouldn't let such a mystery go unnoticed."

We arrived in Le Havre on the 20th of September, 1308, too early to meet our contact. So we made use of our time as day laborers around the docks and warehouses, listened to rumors and waited for the 23rd.

On the 23rd as I waited impatiently across a muddy road from Le Grande Baline for the Vespers bell I knew there was little information we could provide to the man with an eye patch and an oak tankard carved with fleurs de lis.

It was a discouraging situation. We could report that de Molay and the other Templar leaders were not within the Concierge or the Enclos but we could not say where they were. We had not been able to inspect the Louvre or the Tour du Coin or the Tour du Nesle but no rumors placed Templars in any of those locations.

I entered the tavern, purchased ale for my tankard and looked around at the customers, a dozen or so seamen. Three were singing shanties in a far corner. All except one of the other customers were with one or two friends. In the corner across the room from the singers a single man sat with a patch over his left eye. My heart beat faster at the sight of a messenger from Gotland, our connection to Alleric and the others. His oak tankard was carved with three fleurs de lis so I sat down, looked closely at the carving and asked if he was a son of Rolo. His response was that he was but was no son of Odin, then he drew the Christian fish and I responded appropriately.

"How's Paris?" he asked without a hint of a smile.

"Well enough but the Concierge is empty and the Enclos has two dozen older residents. He'd been in the Grosse Tour but left in October or November. No one knows where he is now."

"Any rumors?"

"A friend in Rouen reports our friend was there not long ago, just a few weeks. They move frequently without notice. Someone, probably Nogaret, sends written orders by courier and that night the men are moved. By cart escorted by a dozen or more armed men wearing the King's uniform. It's possible they might be at any of a number of castles. Several were mentioned, Gisors, Gaillard and Chinon, even Poitiers. He and a few others could be in the Corbiel outside Paris, a guest of the archbishop of Sens, de Marigny. But we heard nothing more definite."

"Alleric wants the three of you in Emden."

I frowned. "Emden?"

He just shrugged, and gave us the name of a ship where we could sign on as able seamen for the voyage.

Our captain, Captain Schmidt, made it clear that most of the crew were not Templars so we kept to ourselves when not on duty and made a point of getting along with the ship's crew and officers. We signed on as able seamen and were placed on the same watch. Captain Schmidt also had our old skiff brought aboard as a second ship's boat.

While on watch the evening before we reached Emden, Captain Schmidt suggested we try a harbor tavern he was familiar with, the Emsehafen. Excellent food and even better beer, he said.

CHAPTER VIII:
Emden

It rained heavily the day we arrived in Emden's harbor. In the foul weather and the organized, hectic labor of unloading and loading cargo to and from lighters no one paid attention to the three of us when Captain Schmidt ordered we take our skiff and run messages to local merchants. To all appearances it was just part of the ship's harbor routine. We made our way past several dozen anchored ships and far up the Emse river where a helpful dock master directed us to the Emsehafen.

It was easy, almost ordinary. I'd become used to looking and acting like someone, something, I wasn't. I was just another nondescript seaman, seemingly carefree and curious about the world, working the North Sea and Baltic shipping routes with side trips up the Seine. All for personal enjoyment.

Shortly after Vespers bells the three of us entered the Emsehafen. Sitting at a small table in the far corner was a man with patch over his left eye and a wooden tankard carved with fleurs de lis. I was surprised, I'd expected Alleric himself not another mysterious Templar contact. We sat down at a table next to his and ordered dinner and a tankard. The man made no effort to be noticed and I wondered if I'd been mistaken about him, maybe he wasn't our contact.

We decided I should just go to his table, sit down and strike up a conversation with him, put him to the test. To my relief the man passed the test although he was clearly uncomfortable. From time to time he stopped in mid-sentence and without being too obvious about it watched anyone entering the tavern.

Just as we finished establishing our bona fides he finished his ale, looked around the room, picked up his tankard, stood up and quietly said, "Finish your dinners, take your time at it. Turn left when you leave. Two streets north of here there's an inn, the Emdenhaus. It's for wealthy merchants, not ordinary seamen. Walk by it. I'll be waiting farther down the street but do not look for me. I want to see if you're followed.

"Tomorrow night be at the Emdenhaus at Vespers bells. When you enter tell the man you have a message for Master Mannheim. Be careful. Philip has agents looking for us."

I was puzzled by the precautions. So were Hans and Dieter when I told them. We weren't in France and Philip had little support from the people of Emden as far as I knew. But from the way he spoke I had no doubt he believed there was a very real threat to us.

We finished our dinner and left the Emsehafen, turned left and started up the street. We'd made it maybe a dozen yards when the man with a patch, the very man I'd just met in the tavern, came running towards us with two men close behind. Our contact had just passed us and, although he hadn't said a word, when the two pursuers reached us I tripped one. As he went down I clubbed him with my belaying pin. Dieter apparently had the same thought as the second pursuer was face down in the mud.

Our contact stopped, turned around and leaned over, I thought to catch his breath. But it was clear when he did that he'd been injured and was bleeding badly. Hans caught him as he started to fall, and helped him sit down next to the two men who, moments before, were pursuing him.

"Philip's men or bounty hunters. They were hiding in the shadows up the street. Tried to take me into custody. When I fought back one of them tried to kill me, knifed me in the arm.

They must have been following me or you. So they know at least one of us is a Templar."

As Hans tended to the man's wounded left forearm I asked, "Is there somewhere safe for you?"

The man nodded. "I'll be fine but first we've got to eliminate these two. Can't have them tell anyone what they saw."

With that the man pulled a dagger from his boot sheath and slit both their throats, then added without emotion, "Rob them. We want this to look like the work of harbor cut-throats."

I was stunned to watch such a cold, deliberate murder. From the way he went about it I had the impression this wasn't his first time. But if what he'd said was true, and I had no doubt of that, then only moments before they'd tried to murder him.

He nodded his thanks and said, "Make your appointment tomorrow. Don't be late. Leave now and be careful. Philip may have more than these two watching the harbor."

With difficulty he got to his feet, slowly walked into the shadows of a nearby alley and disappeared.

We took his advice and left, taking a circuitous route back to our boat to be certain we weren't followed.

The following evening as Emden's cathedral rang the Vespers bells we walked into Emdenhaus. We'd cleaned up, still sailors but in clean clothes all of a kind, with hair pulled back and tied. We looked like the crew of a wealthy Flemish captain's gig.

The doorman, dressed in a tan, finely woven, woolen long coat, polished black belt and boots, and stylish hat, looked at us as if we were lost or stupid, then asked what we wanted.

I knuckled my forehead with a slight bow. "We've a message for Master Mannheim. If you please."

The doorman looked at our shoes and, apparently satisfied we didn't track mud from the street, nodded. "Follow me." The clear but unspoken part of his instruction was, "And for God's sake don't touch anything."

We silently followed him single file down a long, wide hall decorated with a variety of tapestries, mostly hunting and religious scenes. It struck me as a very quiet place, a refuge for the wealthy. Somewhere a small, brass, table bell rang twice. After several turns into connecting hallways we approached heavy, oak, double doors at the end of the hall. Our guide stopped and knocked three times on the right door. I saw an eye appear in the door's peephole and a moment later the door opened into a dimly lit room.

I could tell the room was large, in the soft light it looked cavernous. A voice I was certain I recognized said, "Thank you Fritz. Gentlemen please come in. Fritz, we'll have some of that excellent wine and ale, then dinner."

Fritz nodded. "Very good sir." Then he closed and barred the two oak doors from the inside, turned and disappeared behind a door off to our left.

As soon as the door closed another servant, dressed identically to Fritz, began lighting the room's many candles. I hadn't seen the man when we entered. He must have been somewhere in the room's shadows.

No one said a word as the servant went about his task and I took the opportunity to examine the room. Heavy, dark beams supported its high vaulted ceiling. The room was large enough to comfortably provide for a dinner table with bench seating for six, and at the far end as many cushioned stools in an arc before a stone, walk-in fireplace.

Large, expensive by the look of them, tapestries depicting hunting scenes and ships at sea hung from three walls giving the room a quiet, warm, safe feeling. The walnut dinner table was set for six with pewter plates and metal goblets for wine or ale.

Fritz's counterpart finished setting the kindling afire, then added a small log as the fire grew. When satisfied with his work he left by the same door Fritz had used.

I was right, the voice belonged to Alleric. Standing with him by the fireplace were Wilhelm and a well-dressed gentleman who looked vaguely familiar. When I saw the man's left arm wrapped in cloth and held in a sling it struck me. He was our contact from the prior evening. Without the eye patch and sailor's rough attire I would not have known him. I judged him to be Wilhelm's age, older than the three of us but younger than Alleric. Tall, fair haired and, from his build and movement, a warrior. Straight as a broad sword, he now seemed much taller than he had the night before in the tavern, slumped over the table with elbows splayed.

Alleric stepped up to each of us in turn, shook hands with genuine pleasure, then smiled, "Gentlemen, you've already met Herr Stagg. No, that is not his real name but it will do for tonight. Pardon me if I don't use your names. You understand."

Fritz and his assistant reappeared with a wheeled cart carrying several clay jugs of wine, a number of ale tankards and two pewter platters of roast meat, four different cheeses, two loaves of dark bread, chilled butter, onions, as well as a variety of foods I couldn't identify in the dim light.

When they'd finished transferring all that to the table Wilhelm thanked them, waited for them to exit, and waived us to the dinner table.

Wilhelm, Alleric and Herr Stagg listened intently as we related our experiences along the Seine and in Paris. The conversation eventually turned to our Baltic trade which had continued to expand. Alleric looked more rested that evening than he had when I last saw him, even relaxed. He'd given up French red wine for German ale and grinned enthusiastically as Wilhelm told us of a recent successful, by which he meant it was profitable to everyone, transaction with a Rostock merchant.

Our conversation shifted to Herr Stagg who explained he'd been in Emden before the arrests and remained to help other Templars reach Gotland. Nogaret's agents, like those who attacked him the night before, were turning up in England, the lowlands, even northern Germany. Nogaret paid a handsome bounty for every Templar captured or killed and didn't care which. An unknown number of Templars had been murdered, or had simply disappeared.

Eventually Alleric and Wilhelm made contact with him. I had the impression Herr Stagg's work now went beyond helping escaped Templars. Although he didn't say it I believed he was deeply involved in our efforts to find de Molay.

Alleric changed the subject once again. "You may remember that when we reached La Rochelle in late summer of 1307 Matthew was required to meet with de Molay in Paris. At that time he couldn't share with me what de Molay told him. Later, in Visby, he did. I've already told Wilhelm and Herr Stagg. Now I can tell the three of you."

I recalled Matthew's return from Paris very clearly and how I had wondered why the four fleets left La Rochelle as they did.

Alleric continued, "De Molay told Matthew that when he returned to France to meet with Clement and Philip he was taken by surprise, shock is probably more correct. He'd left Cyprus in October of 1306 with two objectives. First, organize a crusade to retake Acre as a base for our return to the Holy

Lands. Second, discourage, prevent if possible, Clement and Philip's plans to merge the three Orders.

"When he reached France in January de Molay found the Order in chaos. For years Jean du Tour had been the Templar treasurer and also Philip's treasurer. How's that for a conflict of allegiance? Without authority of the Grand Master or anyone else, du Tour lent Philip four hundred thousand gold florins from the Templar treasury. That was virtually all the movable wealth in the Templar's treasury. Philip had no intention of repaying the sum and that left the Order without the financial resources for another crusade, or much of anything.

"When de Molay returned to France he found our movable wealth gone. We had land but no coin, no gold and no silver. The greater part of the four hundred thousand florins wasn't ours, it belonged to people whose property we managed or others who had deposited their wealth with us before their pilgrimage to for the Holy Lands."

"In time the matter might have been resolved. It wouldn't be easy but if the Pope backed the Templars Philip would find it politically difficult to avoid repaying the debt. De Molay had the high moral and legal ground, on that matter."

Alleric gave a soft snort, more of a sarcastic laugh. "We've all heard rumors, probably started by Nogaret, that Templar ships left France with a great fortune in gold and silver. Nogaret wanted people, especially the wealthy land owners who placed their money with us, to think we'd stolen it. But when de Molay returned to France there was very little gold or silver in our treasury for the simple reason that du Tour had lent all of it to Philip.

"Nogaret also spread rumors the Templars had possession of the Holy Grail and a great treasure they had long ago found in the ruins of the original Jewish Temple beneath the Dome of the Rock. The lie was an attempt to turn the Jews and the Church against us. Christians would believe we were keeping the Holy Grail for ourselves and denying it to the faithful. The Jews would believe we'd had stolen their rightful treasure hidden long ago by their ancestors."

Alleric paused as though the thought of what he was about to say made him physically ill. "The loan might have been solved but it wasn't the only problem. The real problem was the stink, the rot, within the Order."

"Rot?" I stammered.

Both Alleric and Wilhelm nodded.

"Rot is the only way to describe it," Wilhelm said quietly.

Alleric pushed himself from the table, stood up and began pacing. "Maybe It began as stupid high-jinks and too much wine. Eventually, it all went horribly wrong. Not everywhere but in a few places new initiates were required to do things. Things contrary to our vows, spit on the cross, deny Christ. And other things contrary to nature.

"Somewhere, sometime a few who liked men more than women got carried away in the initiation rites. Some of the newly initiated brothers were required to kiss the backside or the stomach of the older knights. And were told to lie with brother Templars if they were overheated. Our sacred Order had been infested with perverts, animals."

It was well-known the priesthood had its share of men who were only too happy to take a vow of chastity, as to women. Men attracted to other men or boys found refuge in their Holy vows and in the Church's monastic life. But I'd never considered that men who had taken a vow to fight to the death for Christ and the Holy Lands had come to our Order with the same beliefs. I'd never seen even a hint of it in Arville.

Alleric continued, "Over the years some, not many, have been discovered within our Order. It seemed inevitable. They were defrocked and forced to leave in disgrace. A few of them reached out to the King's counselor, Nogaret. Vindictive bastards! Nogaret was only too happy to report their practices to Philip, who reported it to the Pope.

"It gave Philip power over both the Pope and our Order. Philip and Nogaret had made similar charges against Pope Boniface and wanted to try him for the same sins, even after he was dead. If Clement defended Templars accused of the same acts it would appear to be an admission that the Church and both Clement and Boniface supported such practices.

"De Molay came to France to find our Order bankrupt and subject to persecution by both Church and King for the errors of a few. It gave Philip an excuse not to repay the loan. People would not rally behind the Templars if people learned of such practices."

"That's why de Molay and the others didn't resist arrest?" I asked.

Alleric nodded. "De Molay didn't want a fight with the King or with the Pope. There was no treasury to protect. Philip already had all of it. And if de Molay and the Templars resisted arrest there would have been a civil war. It would have been seen as an admission of guilt and an attempt to protect and continue the perversions. He had no choice but to go peacefully and try to work it out, clean out those guilty and prove the Order was still loyal to King and Church, and to Christ.

"With the Pope's help and pressure from the barons, we might recover the illegal loan. At least some of the barons would support the Pope, or Philip might eventually try to take their wealth the same way he took the Jews' wealth, the

Templar's wealth, and tried to take part of the Holy Catholic Church's wealth."

As I listened to Alleric I wondered what the Templars would or could do now. De Molay had set his and therefore our course. We were trained as warriors. We were out of our element. De Molay and the Templars, all of us, had no alternative. We must pray Clement would stand up to Philip.

Alleric continued, "Within days of the arrests de Molay and the others confessed to some, if not all, of Nogaret's charges. The Pope suspected torture had been used to extort the confessions so in December he sent three Cardinals to meet with de Molay. There was a private meeting in the Notre Dame, to see if his confession was reliable or not. At that meeting de Molay retracted his confessions. Based on de Molay's retraction Clement, who was in Poitiers, did two things. First, he suspended the inquisitions. Second, he demanded the King send de Molay to Poitiers so the Pope could personally examine him. Philip refused and shortly after that de Molay disappeared."

As Alleric ceased his pacing and sat down Wilhelm spoke, "I'll keep it brief but I want to bring you current on events that may change things. We were all on the run and didn't have time to pay attention to what was happening elsewhere in Europe. We believe the Pope continues to be sympathetic to our cause but, for the reasons Alleric told you, he hasn't been willing to directly confront Philip. Maybe that will change.

"On May 1st King Albert, the King of the Romans and anticipated future Emperor of the Holy Roman Empire, was assassinated by a disgruntled relative. Philip immediately moved to have his own brother, Charles of Valois, elected Albert's successor. He's making a play to bring all of the Empire under his personal control and he's using a great deal of the Templar funds he stole to bribe the electors. The outcome is still in doubt.

"Many powerful people are not happy with Philip's ambitions. To succeed he needs Clement's blessing but Clement has not said who he'll support. Later that month, to intimidate Clement, Philip called an Estates General in Tours. His intention was to gain the nobles' support both for Charles' election and for his own action against us. Philip got both.

"Once Philip had the support of the Estates General, he sent seventy-two of the imprisoned Templars to Poitiers for Clement to interview. The seventy-two Templars were handpicked, probably by Nogaret. He already had their confessions. A number of them had been removed from the Order for their sexual practices and sought Nogaret's help. They'd tell Clement anything Nogret told them to say. Once the seventy-two men confessed to Clement he would have no choice but to join Philip's efforts to destroy the Templars.

"Philip wasn't taking chances so he personally went to Poitiers with his troops. Philip made two speeches before the trial judges and made it clear what would happen to the Pope and the judges if the seventy-two Templars, or most of them, weren't found guilty. Fifty-four were found guilty in July.

"De Molay was not one of the seventy-two. Philip controls Chinon but the lands farther south, including Poitiers, are loyal to the Pope so he won't send de Molay to Poitiers. If the Pope gets control of de Molay Philip will never get him back. We believe Philip is holding de Molay and the other leaders in Chinon.

"There isn't much we can do for the men in Poitiers but we have some ideas about de Molay and the other four leaders in Chinon.

"Henry VII, he's the Count of Luxembourg and Arlon, is Charles and Philip's chief opponent to be Albert's successor as

King of the Romans and future Emperor of the Holy Roman Empire. Clement and a number of the powerful barons, especially those in Burgundy and Normandy, may see more benefit in having Henry as the new emperor. If Henry prevails Philip could be in a difficult position.

"Right now Clement is afraid of Philip and he'll keep his Papal state in the south. Poitiers maybe but probably farther south. Southern France is not under Philip's control. Some towns, like Areles, are already within the Holy Roman Empire. Other districts have feudal allegiance to Rome. The barons in Burgundy and Normandy have been a thorn in the side of the French kings for more than a century.

"With that Philip would be surrounded. His old enemies, the Flemish lords, are to the north. Henry and the Holy Roman Empire are on his eastern flank, Clement and the barons of Burgundy are on his southern flank. The Norman barons including those in England are to the west.

"The Teutonic Knights would support the Empire on Philip's eastern flank. We believe the Hospitallers would support Clement.

"We believe Henry would support Clement but it's unlikely Henry will openly support the Templars. He might cooperate behind the curtains but will not directly confront Philip to help the Templars while there is a threat Philip would put Pope Boniface on trial.

"If Henry is elected to lead the Holy Roman Empire and actively supports Clement we believe Clement may be bold enough to confront Philip, if he has an army. If we're able to free de Molay and if he would lead the Templars as Clement's army, Philip would have few alternatives but to repay the moneys he stole, dismiss the charges against the Templars, and dispense with his threats of a trial against Boniface."

The room was silent for a long time as the possibilities of the situation sank in. It felt like a battle, or a chess match, when one of the contestants realizes the full extent of the threat and the limited moves available to him. Then, as the disastrous end seems all but inevitable, he sees the possibility of a bold but dangerous move that could dramatically change the outcome. However adverse the odds of success, they are an improvement. There is hope.

"All this depends on Henry's election," I said.

"Yes, it does," Alleric replied. "We can't tell you all the details but with our help several of our old friends are doing everything they can to secure Henry's election."

"Are you certain de Molay is in Chinon?" I asked.

"We are certain he was as of two weeks ago," Herr Stagg responded. "That's the latest information we have. Obviously I can't share with you how we know that."

Dieter chuckled. "So what do we, the three of us, do? You must have something in mind other than a lesson in European politics."

Alleric nodded. "Yes we do. We would like the three of you to go to Chinon and meet with de Molay. He needs to know he hasn't been forgotten. Do four things. Tell him of the new developments and our plan. Ask his opinion of the plan, would he lead the Templar army in support of Clement. Make it clear we're not suggesting the Templar army attack Philip. But we must be strong enough to keep Philip from moving south. Evaluate his health and ability to act if we are able to release him. And find out where he's been held after the arrests, he may be taken there again after they're done with him in Chinon.

"It is critical that he not only support the plan but he must be physically and mentally able to lead the Templars if we're able to rescue him. Clement will need an army strong enough to keep Philip at bay. No other man can rally the Templars as a fighting force and maintain the public's support.

"We also need you to get an idea how much support the people in the south have for Philip, Henry, Clement, and for us."

I looked at Dieter and Hans, then nodded. Hans and Dieter also nodded. It was settled, the three of us would go to Chinon.

I expected Alleric, Wilhelm and Herr Stagg had thought this through and had definite ideas how this should be done so I asked, "By what route?"

"The Rhone to Valence, then cross country by way of Vienne to Chinon," Alleric replied.

I recalled our, my, almost fatal effort to enter the Paris Enclos and gave Matthew and Alleric a skeptical look, then asked, "If he's in the Chateau de Chinon, one of Philip's strongest fortifications, how do you propose we meet with de Molay?"

Alleric looked at me with a slight nod. "We know the Enclos almost cost you your life. It was an excellent plan, an unpredictable interference. But your, all of you, ability to come up with the plan, then to adapt and overcome the unexpected events show you're the right men. Events are moving fast. That's good but it means we can't plan all the details. Do the best you can. No one expects miracles."

Wilhelm added, "Even if you can't meet with de Molay the mission will have great value to us if you get a sense of who the towns in southern France support and how strong Philip's forces are along the Rhone."

"I would like to tell you more but as you've already seen, Philip is looking for us," Herr Stagg added. "If you're taken prisoner he will extract all the information you have. It's not that any of you are weak, I know you're not, but we're all human.

In Bilbao be certain to stop for a tankard in the Monje Pobrea and when you reach Chinon stay at the Coeur de Lion. Consider a game of rithmomachia or chess while you're there."

CHAPTER IX:
The Rhone

Three days later the three of us signed on a Basque trading ship bound for Bilbao, Spain. A week or so later in Bilbao's sunny port we found our Templar contact in the Monje Pobrea tavern. I'd chuckled when our contact told me *monje pobrea* meant poor monk in Basque but it fit the sign over the door, an old monk with a forlorn expression holding an empty tankard. With our contact's help we crossed overland to Barcelona where we were able to sign on a Spanish cargo ship bound for Marseille. Its captain was another fugitive Templar, no doubt part of Herr Stagg's operation.

In Marseille, with the captain's help, we jumped ship. We purchased a used but seaworthy, thirty-six foot coastal craft with a draft suitable for the Rhone and had it modified similar to those made in the boat we used on the Seine. While the carpenters worked on our boat we purchased an assortment of clothes suitable for various roles, wealthy merchants, dock workers, and Black Friars.

From Marseille we made our way west with smooth seas and a fair wind to the Camargue at the mouth of the Rhone, then a few miles upriver where we sheltered for the night. We were fortunate, this was not the season for either the fearfully strong mistral winds or the snow melt from the Alps that fed the Rhone's roiling spring floods. After the grandeur of Paris and the busy Seine commerce both the Rhone and the countryside of southern France seemed beautiful, peaceful and above all clean.

There were no quaint St. Adela inns along the lower Rhone so we continued on to the old Roman city of Arles. It was still warm and the beautiful trees and meadows filled with color made it easy to forget our purpose. Philip, Paris and Chinon were far away. Arles was a journey a thousand years back in time to the true Roman Empire, not the clumsy affair we called the Holy Roman Empire. The old theatre, arena, necropolis, baths, obelisk and the aqueduct and mills were now just monuments to a time that must have been greater than our own.

We spent a day looking for evidence of Philip's power but found nothing, neither physical power nor in the hearts of the people. The Templars and the coming election of a new emperor seemed distant matters but there was genuine enthusiasm for Clement, and little response one way or the other to our neutral comments regarding Philip.

Two days later we spent a sunny afternoon in Avignon's open market using our time to size up the town and people. Apart from the old fortress at Beaucaire, it was not in good repair and wouldn't support a guard of any size, there were no fortifications and no sign of Philip's troops.

Undoubtedly Philip had supporters in both Arles and Avignon, whether spies, sympathizers, or acknowledged representatives. Philip would receive information regularly but not timely about everything that happened along the Rhone. Even rumors and speculation would reach him. Perhaps even news of three strangers posing as merchants coming north. But it would reach him too late to be of value.

That evening we visited several of Avignon's riverside taverns, listening to the locals, the boat crews and the other river merchants. A few tankards with games of draughts and teetotum bought more talk. Locals like to impress strangers, especially those who loose gracefully and are willing to buy the next round. Beyond a few open ended questions we said little and listened. Nothing was said of the Templars and little was said of the King but Clement had a great many supporters. There were rumors Clement intended to establish his Papal Court in Avignon. If true it would bring great fortune to the town and the people already loved him for it.

Early the next morning we set out for Roquemaure on the Rhone's west bank and a look at its two castles, one on the east bank and the other on the west bank. Either might be a formidable obstacle on any run up or down the Rhone. We left Avignon in sunshine. Mid-morning the weather changed to a cold rain blown by a sharp wind straight down the Rhone valley. In the dismal weather the two castles, both built of grey stone that blended with the low drifting clouds, looked almost ghostly and far more threatening than I'd anticipated. From what I could see the castle's two towers, one round, the other square, on an island near the river's the west bank were in excellent condition. I feared they might be well-manned.

The thought of an inn with a warm fire and hot food urged us on until we pulled to the Rhone's bank just down river from the two towers. The dock master, unhappy to leave the comfort of his shelter, curtly directed us to a slip for our craft and collected his fee. When we asked where we might find lodging he simply replied "*Le Centurion*," pointed towards the far end of the market square, and disappeared into his shelter. Fortunately it wasn't hard to find. Hanging above the inn's entrance was a wooden relief carving of a Roman shield with the helmet of a Roman Centurion. It had rooms for the night, a large fire in the great stone hearth, hot food, good wine, and few other guests.

The weather cleared over night but even with clear skies and a warm autumn sun Roquemaure's market didn't open until mid-morning. From *Le Centurion*'s open windows we had a view of the market operations and a view of the dock-master. He was slightly taller than the average man and had at one time been very fit. Now he carried a belly that told us he enjoyed his food and drink, and had given up strenuous exercise. He wore a dagger but it looked like it hadn't left its old, dried to the point of cracking, leather sheath in a very long time. In many ways he was the opposite of Milun. He needed new clothes or at least his current uniform should be mended. Both his hair and beard, most recently washed by last night's storm, needed a barber's attention. Regardless of his personal appearance it was clear he knew everyone in the market by name and everyone knew him.

We brought the dock-master, Claude-Jean, a tankard of excellent local wine for his mid-day meal to let him know how much we appreciated his help the evening before and invited him to join us after the market closed for a tankard and a bite to eat. He quickly accepted and predictably asked what brought the three of us to Avignon. We swore him to secrecy before telling him we were on our way north to buy wine for export to Spain and Italy.

When the market closed the three of us found him waiting for us just outside *Le Centurion*. No sooner had we stepped through the tavern door when the waiter, with a grin and cheerful greeting, waved to him. Claude-Jean called back he needed a table for himself and three wealthy wine merchants. Several in the room called out a cheerful greeting to him as we crossed the room to our table and Claude-Jean stopped to pat each of them on the back and ask how they and their wives and children were. Claude-Jean not only knew each of the men by name but also knew the names of each man's wife and child or children. He made a point of saying a little something flattering about each man and his occupation. As we had counted on, each time he stopped at a table he introduced us as wine merchants on our way north.

As we sat down I put my coin purse on the table and with a sweeping motion ordered a tankard of their best wine for each of us. Claude-Jean's reaction was one of joy and he immediately told us the inn's pork stew was not to be missed. I nodded to the waiter, ordered a serving of stew for each of the four of us and asked the cost. Upon hearing the number I handed the sum to the waiter.

Half way through his tankard Claude-Jean informed us the Rhone was a border of sorts. Philip controlled the Rhone's west banks and the Pope controlled the east, which was part of the Comtat Venaissin. The family that owned the Chateau de l'Hers, on the island near the river's east banks across the river from Roquemaure's castle was loyal to the Pope and Chruch more than to whoever happened to be the French king.

I leaned in a little and assumed a conspiratorial grin. "But who collects the tolls on the river traffic?"

Claude-Jean shrugged. "Both. It's always been a peaceful and mutual sharing of the river tolls."

Then he leaned in. "But now we have a French Pope, God be praised, and the word is Clement will establish his Papal Court in Poitiers or …"

He paused, looked around to see if anyone was close enough to hear, then whispered, "even further south."

"You mean here?" I whispered.

"Well, I have it on good authority, men very close to Clement, all close friends of mine, that both Avignon and Roquemaure are being considered. It will most certainly be a Rhone town. Clement prefers Roquemaure, he's stayed at our castle many times, but Avignon is safer, it's farther from Philip."

From Claude-Jean's smile it was clear he foresaw his own position, both as to authority and compensation, was on the rise. If the Pope moved the Papal Court to Avignon or Roquemaure or anywhere on the Rhone, river traffic would increase both in volume and value. The fee income would increase, substantially. The local bishops and the Church would want the lion's share of those fees but the Holy Roman Empire would object to that, so would Philip. The great powers could fight over fees but Claude-Jean and his friends would still profit greatly.

I asked, "What's the Rhone like between here and Lyon? I hear even that cursed plague of Vikings couldn't make it past Valence."

Claude-Jean looked surprised. "You know about Vikings? It's true they could manage the Rhone this far north, even up to Valence. And they caused terrible mischief wherever they went. So did the Muslims before them, until Charles the Hammer put an end to that scourge. But the Muslims didn't use the Rhone. Our poor lands were ravished first by Muslims and again by Vikings."

It was apparent he didn't consider Caesar's invasion of Gaul a scourge.

"North bound river traffic such as yours can't make it on its own beyond Valence. It's the current and the winds. Not as bad now but you should see it in the spring after a heavy winter in the Alps. My God it's wild. And the mistral winds from the north, such winds. Every winter and spring when it blows down into the Gulf of Lyon no boat on the Rhone is safe. It's dangerous enough if you're headed down river that time of year but making headway north is simply impossible during the spring floods or the mistral winds. The Rhone is our life but it's also brought death."

He took a drink of wine and wiped his mouth, then added, "The river can be dangerous. Maybe you're better buying wine here. We have excellent wine this far south. I can introduce you to several of the vintners, they're all good friends of mine. How far north were you planning to go?"

Dieter said, "We haven't decided. It depends. We thought we might buy some of the Rhone valley's excellent wines. Maybe take it round to Italy or perhaps to Spain. We haven't yet decided. Should fetch a handsome price wherever we take it.

"If we can't make it all the way to Vienne on our own is there another way?"

Claude-Jean shrugged as he ate. "I suppose. If you had the money you might find a horse tow as far as Vienne. But by God it's expensive. Still it's faster and safer than over land. Of course, from Vienne north you'll have to go overland. But that's dangerous, the land's full of thieves. Maybe you should buy your wine here. I can take you to the best vineyards."

I asked the question that had worried us. "How safe is it for us north of here? I mean are there robbers, thieves, on the river too? Who protects the merchants and the river traffic?"

Claude-Jean frowned and pursed his lips in thought. "Well, there's the chateau in Montfaucon, on the Saint Maur rock farther up the Rhone. It will also require a toll. As imposing as the castle is there aren't more than a dozen or so guards. And it's inferior to our own castle in every way. Completely unsuitable for important guests or merchants like the three of you."

"And north of Montfaucon?" I asked.

"Beyond that there is little until you reach Valence," Claude-Jean responded with a shrug of indifference.

"What of thieves. Is the river safe?" I asked.

126

"There are a few thieves on the river. But the three of you look able to handle them. We haven't had much of a problem since a dozen or so were hung several months ago."

"Does Philip try to protect the river?" I asked.

Claude-Jean chuckled and took a long drink. "No, no. South of Lyon he doesn't have troops and he doesn't have officials to collect the fees and tolls. Several Houses, Dukes and Counts, Bishops and Archbishops, even the Pope, and a whole lot of lesser lords all want a share of the river fees and they all have toll collectors. But they're not as enthusiastic about providing safe passage for merchants or pilgrims once the fees are paid."

Dieter laughed. "You mean we're on our own?"

Claude-Jean grinned and nodded, "That's about it. But God forbid you don't pay your fees. Then they take a great interest in you and your cargo."

Five long, hard days later we reached Valance and arranged for a horse tow to Vienne. It was outrageously expensive but three equally difficult days later we arrived in Vienne. We stored our boat but doubted we would ever see it again. Our story that we were merchants in search of goods to buy and transport to Spain or Italy would be questioned if we sold the boat. And there was always the chance that we might find it useful again.

It took another two days but with diligence we found six horses for our overland journey to Chinon. Four were the extraordinarily comfortable gaited Icelandic horses. A wealthy aristocrat had brought them south from Normandy, then died. His widow and daughters had no use for the animals. The other two horses were common palfreys. Each of us had two horses. Ride one in the morning, halter the other, then switch for the afternoon. We could move very fast. Six young, healthy horses cost a great deal but Alleric had insisted it was critical we have excellent mounts, a weak or lame horse might jeopardize our efforts.

To say distances are inexact is an understatement. Distances are measured in days of travel and that depended on too many factors to name. Opinions ranged from nine to seventeen days to reach Chinon. Even if the old Roman roads were in good condition, which was always a question, with luck and fair weather it would take two weeks on horseback, maybe more, maybe less.

Vienne was significant for another reason. It was here, in October, that we first heard rumors Clement had issued a Bull calling for a general church council in 1310 to be held in Vienne. Apparently, the council was to try Templars.

The city was alive with the rumors, many contradictory. It wasn't clear to us what Clement had actually done. Apparently, Clement had also called for trials with three distinct jurisdictions. Diocesan committees were to investigate individual Templars found within its borders but the final decision on the accused would be left to a council of the province. District Papal commissions would try the activities of the Order within its district. Pope Clement reserved personal jurisdiction to try de Molay and the other leaders.

Rumors were just that, rumors. How the trials would work and when they would actually begin was impossible to predict.

Adding to the confusion, we also heard the king's representatives in Chinon had obtained another confession from de Molay but the Pope had for the second time granted de Molay absolution. What was encouraging was that Philip had not been successful, so far, in his efforts to have his brother, Charles, elected King of the Romans.

Our overland journey to Chinon took another eighteen days. We used a series of six guides and traveled without a guide for four of those days making it difficult for anyone to discover where we were bound and where we'd come from.

There had been only one incident. We'd been traveling for two days without a guide west of Lyon and camped on the edge of a meadow outside Riom. Our location was fine, level ground, plenty of fire wood, and the meadow that provided excellent grazing for our horses. A quarter moon on the western horizon and stars provided a little light but scattered clouds blocked most of it.

We belled the horses, hung a feed bag of grain around the neck of each, then tethered the animals to our picket line. As we laid out our bedrolls between the campfire and the picket line Hans suggested we sleep lightly that night as a few of the travelers we'd met earlier that morning had more than a passing interest in our horses.

Dieter and I agreed it was a perfect night for a little horse theft so we left the top blankets where they were and stuffed branches beneath them, then moved our bedrolls into the shadows on the other side of the fire. As I drifted off to sleep I felt a little foolish about our precautions but shrugged it off, there didn't seem to be any harm and neither Hans nor Dieter had objected.

Sometime later I woke with a start, Dieter had his hand over my mouth and was whispering, "Someone's on the picket line."

It took a moment to clear my head but I could hear horse bells jangling. Hans was already awake, sitting up. Whoever was on the picket line wasn't making an effort to be quiet about it. Without making a sound I fitted a bolt in my crossbow, Dieter and Hans were doing the same. Dieter motioned for me to go right and for Hans to go left around the fire, then he followed Hans. In the darkness I could make out two men, each holding the leads for two horses in one hand and trying to untie the lead for a third.

Without making a sound Dieter suddenly appeared out of the shadows beside one of the men and I heard him say in his booming voice, "Can I help you with that?"

The startled man threw up his arms, let a thunderously loud fart, screamed, "Jeeeeeeesus Chriiiiiiiist," dropped the leads to both horses, grabbed his rear with both hands, and ran stumbling into the woods.

Hans and I were both laughing as the second man, wide-eyed and open-mouthed in the fire light, looked at his retreating friend, then at Dieter, dropped the leads, and followed his companion. As we rounded up the horses we joked about the one man's reaction to Dieter's question, he'd be cleaning his underwear when he finally stopped running.

It all looked like a bungled, incompetent attempt at horse theft until we looked at our blankets. Each had two crossbow bolts in it. No wonder they didn't worry about the noise, they thought they'd killed us. There must have been a third man but I didn't see him. Neither had Dieter or Hans. Suddenly it wasn't so funny. They'd tried to murder us, and a third man we hadn't seen had most likely been standing in the shadows, undoubtedly with a bolt in his crossbow. But he hadn't shot. Perhaps the thought of his one bolt against our three stopped him.

In Tours we sold our horses and purchased clothing for our new roles. All that required four additional days as we evolved from cross country riders to modestly wealthy merchants looking to buy and export fine wines of the Loire valley. Each day we moved and each day, as we changed our appearances, we crossed one or more strata of Tours' economic life. We left no traces of the three men who had arrived one afternoon with six fine horses. Tours was a large city, nothing like Paris but large enough to get lost in. No single person could directly connect the three modestly prosperous merchants with the three roughly dressed riders carrying crossbows.

Philip was a popular king in the region. Most people we talked with were quite aware of the October arrests and the charges against the Templars but none were willing to publically express sympathy, much less support, for de Molay. Few were interested in any but the most salacious charges and many believed every Templar not only had sex with men and boys but also with their horses. Chatter and laughter in the public houses and inns were coarse and loud when it concerned Templars. Story after story, each baser than the other, filled the rooms with laughter and each was accompanied with crude, barnyard gyrations depicting sexual acts.

Comments regarding Clement were few and guarded. No one wanted to damn him but none praised him. Usually the reply was a shrug and a nod. I recall one man who expressed his view and most likely that of a great many others when he said, "Well, at least he's not Italian. We'll see."

Our attempts at conversations about the Holy Roman Empire elections ended quickly. Few seemed to have any awareness or interest in the matter. A shrug or a blank stare was the most frequent response.

CHAPTER X:
Chinon

The following morning we rented a small barge to take us down the Loire to its confluence with the Vienne then up river to Chinon. We'd heard of the Chateau du Chinon and from the river it was just as imposing as its reputation. Built high on a rocky bluff along the river's north bank the Chateau had a commanding view of the surrounding lands and its Tour du Coudray stood well above the chateau's curtain wall. If properly garrisoned, each of the chateau's three fortifications would, for all practical purposes, be impregnable. Philip wasn't taking any chances with his Templar prisoners.

We settled into the Coeur de Lion, an inn befitting our new roles as wealthy wine merchants. After our quiet dinner the inn's proprietor, Robert Dijon, invited us to adjourn to what he proudly referred to as his gaming room. Robert led us down a short hall to where a rather fit looking man, I thought him to be in his mid-thirties, sat next to a wide, heavy oak door. Robert introduced the young man as, Alexi, who, with a polite nod and a smile, opened the door for us.

We entered a spacious rectangular, wood paneled room. A half dozen candelabras, each with a dozen candles, hung from the heavy beams. Two grand, stone fireplaces, one on each of the room's two long walls, provided warmth. Several Turkish wool rugs covered most of the room's limestone floor. Three walls were decorated with colorful tapestries depicting a variety of hunting scenes and battles.

The combination of rugs, tapestries, paneling and the vaulted ceiling gave the room and its seven gaming tables a quiet warmth, and dignity. Two tables each seated two people. Four tables seated four each. The waist high, round, center table was built for dice games and could accommodate eight men, all standing. In the corners to our left and right were two chairs, conversation settings where two men could quietly discuss a private matter.

A variety of common games and several I didn't recognize were displayed on shelves next to the fireplaces. Robert proudly showed us his collection of beautifully inlaid jeux de tables and chess boards with elaborately carved pieces for each.

Two gaming tables were occupied at the time by gentlemen deeply involved in chess. At a third table four men huddled as they quietly discussed something, a business transaction of some nature by the look of them. A musician played his psaltery quietly in the far corner to our left. The four chess players paid no attention to us. The musician granted us a brief, faint smile and a nod. The four business men stopped to look at us. At first all four appeared annoyed with the interruption but finally annoyance changed to indifference.

In the far corner to our right another man, by his dress and demeanor I judged him another of Robert's employees, sat behind a small, artfully carved desk. The man nodded to Robert who smiled and nodded in return.

Centered on the room's far wall was a long table with several clay pitchers, the types used for cooling wine and ale, and an assortment of clay cups, wooden tankards and metal goblets. To the left and right of the table were doors. A man dressed in a uniform identical to that worn by Alexi stood behind the table. Above the table hung a beautiful tapestry almost as long as the table and half that as wide. There was no mistaking the message. The tapestry depicted a reclining woman, nude.

In a voice meant only for the three of us, Robert explained, "Our guests may find a variety of relaxation at the Coeur de Lion, whatever your selection may be. Simply a quiet place to discuss business, a peaceful escape from the pressing events of the day, a pleasant evening of gaming for agreeable stakes, or an evening with gentler, very attractive company."

Robert nodded towards the tapestry above the long table at the far end of the room. "I assure you of the finest quality here. All healthy, young, beautiful, and very charming."

With that he waived to the refreshments on the table. "Please enjoy our selections of wine, ale and cheeses. Tonight the refreshments are included in your lodging fees."

He nodded towards the man in the corner, and as we made our way across the room he added, "Let me introduce Geoffroi, our gaming room concierge. He will answer all your questions and arrange for your requests.

"Usually there is no charge for the gaming room. Only for the wine, ale, food, arrangement of games, and other services you select. If you enjoy an evening of gaming let Geoffroi know what game you prefer and the stakes you are willing to risk. He will find suitable participants. The fee for games depends on the stakes. For all dice games, backgammon, passé-dix, hazard, and highest points, we permit only the use of our own dice and the game will be called by one of our employees. Let Geoffroi know if you prefer an evening with more charming company in more private accommodations."

Geoffori rose when we approached but did not extend his hand, rather he gave a slight bow and quietly said, "Good evening gentlemen, welcome to Coeur de Lion."

The plain oak working surface of his desk was not much different than one would see in a successful counting house. The pen, ink and a ledger were neatly arranged. He'd discretely closed the ledger as we approached. To one side were two stacks of linen strips, one of blue, the other of red.

With a slight bow and smile that communicated how much he enjoyed his inn and providing for his guests, Robert said, "Please excuse me now. Enjoy your stay. You will find we are all very discreet at Coeur de Lion. Simply make it known what you wish and Geoffroi will make the necessary arrangements."

We stayed at a table close to one of the fireplaces to enjoy a glass of wine, watch life in the gaming room, and silently consider the Chateau du Chinon. Herr Stagg hadn't said what would happen or who would make himself known to us. He'd only suggested we enjoy a game of rithmomchia or chess at the Coeur de Lion, so we waited.

Before retiring for the evening we asked Geoffroi what wineries we might inspect the following day, we wanted only the best wines. Geoffori nodded and said he would make arrangements for us. We should be ready following breakfast the next day.

When Dieter asked what the charges would be for such services Geoffroi smiled and said it would be on our bill. He assured us we would find it most reasonable. It didn't seem polite to argue the matter so we let it go with an uneasy feeling that we might regret not pressing for more information. We had to trust Herr Stagg.

After breakfast we found a guide and three strong, gaited horses waiting for us. Our guide, Gilbert, not yet eighteen he said, proved both knowledgeable and courteous. We toured four wineries that day and sampled their wines. Their reds were excellent and reasonably priced.

Gilbert was well-known in the region and at each winery we were greeted with enthusiasm. He introduced us as wine merchants but was vague about where we were from or where we were taking the wine we purchased. Without being instructed he understood it was not good to disclose too much information before beginning negotiations.

At each winery we were met with a small tankard for tasting samples of their wares. As we toured the winery a lad, ten or eleven by the look of him, followed us carrying a platter of roast meats, a loaf of a light bread, and a variety of local cheeses for our enjoyment. When we finished the tour we found a groom had watered and brushed our horses.

It was a beautiful fall day, cool but not cold and the leaves were changing. But I worried that we'd accomplished nothing. As we returned to our lodging that evening Gilbert grinned and said, "There are four more wineries I suggest you gentlemen see tomorrow. As you've seen, the presence of three mysterious wine merchants has people excited. Tonight there'll be a talk in the wine community. The others wineries will hope to see you and disappointed if they don't."

Gilbert pointedly suggested we visit the gaming room that evening. Robert had two visiting jongleurs, itinerant musicians and poets he explained as if we wouldn't know. Both had been to the Coeur de Lion several months ago and had been a popular entertainment for his clientele so Robert brought them back. Because this was special entertainment, Gilbert explained, there would be a modest charge on our bill.

We spent the evening in Robert's gaming room listening to the entertainment, enjoying an excellent wine from one of the vineyards we'd visited that day, and watching the other patrons. We'd done what Herr Stagg suggested and there was nothing more to do but wait.

Robert was a good businessman. The entertainment filled his gaming room and the patrons drank a great deal. The dice table was busy and at times rowdy. Several of the poems were suggestive, even explicit. A number of the patrons used one or the other of the two doors at the far end of the hall.

I watched as Geoffroi managed the evenings events with quiet efficiency and discretion. When a gentleman approached his desk and quietly made his desires known, Geoffroi nodded, made a note on his ledger and handed the gentleman a strip of colored linen cloth. The gentleman resumed his seat and sometime later Geoffroi nodded to the man and then towards one of the two doors.

As I watched I saw something I hadn't noticed before. Two cords extended upward to the rafters from two levers on the wall next to his table. Whenever the lever was pulled up Geoffroi would nod to the next man. As the man entered one of the doors Geoffroi lowered the lever to await for someone behind the doors to pull the cord and raise the lever once again. Since none of the men who entered either of the two doors returned to the gaming room it was clear there was another exit.

Later that evening I asked Geoffroi the meaning of the colored cloths. He explained the red cloth was for a half hour, the blue cloth for an hour. Then he added with the hint of a smile, "As with the wine and ale, a gentleman can enjoy one or two glasses, or as many as he wishes."

Our tour the next day was as informative as the prior day's. Our presence and our business seemed to be common knowledge in the wine community and at each winery we were greeted by name and the same courtesies we'd received the previous day.

That evening as Gilbert gathered the horses to return them to their stable he thanked us for two days in the open air and away from his usual tasks. His parting comment as he swung into the saddle was, "Geoffroi said you don't want to miss the entertainment this evening, in the gaming room immediately following dinner. He said you should not be late. And if you want anything for tomorrow let him know. He'll arrange it for you."

Robert had prepared an excellent dinner for his guests, roast venison, excellent honey bread, fresh butter, sauté vegetables, and a variety of local wines. After dinner the three of us retired to the gaming room to watch the promised evening's entertainment and enjoy a final cup of wine for the evening. Alexi greeted us as usual, opened the door to the gaming room and quietly closed it behind us.

CHAPTER XI:
Monsieur Noir

The room was empty except for one man seated at a table for four near the left fireplace. We were early I guessed, but the candelabras were lit and fires in both fireplaces were burning. We poured ourselves a cup of wine, took our seats at another table and waited for something to happen.

We'd just sat down when the man turned to look at us, smiled, went to the refreshment table and poured himself a cup of wine. He brought a platter of cheeses and placed it before us.

As he approached he said, "Good evening gentlemen. I'm Monsieur Noir. Please call me Albert. I understand you gentlemen enjoy both rithmomachia and chess."

To remove any doubt Albert assumed a Templar stance of identification.

Wondering if we might be interrupted I turned to see if the door was barred.

Monsieur Noir smiled. "Don't worry, Alexi has tyled the door."

Albert sat down. "Herr Stagg sent a message that I should expect you."

"Do you have any ideas how we might reach de Molay?" I asked.

"Yes. He's being held in Chinon, the Tour du Coudray. Other Templar leaders, Caron, Gonneville, Charney and Pairaud, are also held there. All in separate cells. We have extensive knowledge of the chateau and the tour. You'll be told later. Four days from now one of you will meet with de Molay and, if all goes well, the others."

I sat back, amazed at what I was hearing. One of us would be face to face with de Molay.

Albert continued, "We've been working on this since we learned de Molay was in Chinon. But do not ask who the others are. As I'm sure Herr Stagg told you, if you are caught by Philip's men or those of certain bishops you will be forced to tell all you know. It's best you know only what is absolutely necessary."

"You were here, in the gaming room, last night. I remember seeing you at the dice table. Later you left through one of the doors beside the refreshment table," Dieter said.

"Yes, I was here last night. If asked, a great many people would swear to that. But no one knows we met and no one will see me here tonight. Before you return later this evening, the three of you must decide who will be the one to meet with de Molay. When you return enter the room single file, the man you select will be the last in line.

"Tomorrow the three of you will revisit two of the wineries. You decide which two. At each you will enter into agreements to purchase wine for export to Portugal by way of the Vienne and the Loire.

"The following day two of you will conclude the transaction and arrange for payment and transportation of the wine. On the morning of the third day, those two will make a show of leaving for Portugal with the wine. If anyone asks where the third man is you will say he's gone ahead to arrange for export licenses and fees."

He paused to see if we were following his plan and when satisfied we were he continued. "The other two will leave the Coeur de Lion. They'll travel with the wine and wait at a safe location before you all continue on to Nantes. For obvious reasons of security the contact person will not know where or when that will be."

"How are we to arrange for payment. Normally the Templars have done that," Hans said.

"A merchant banker in Tours, and from time to time a patron of the gaming room, has agreed to bank your transactions. His name is de Veron, Charles de Veron. He was also here last night and one of you will meet him later this evening. He and his brother, Johann de Veron, manage their family's banking house. Johann manages the Nantes office, Charles the office in Tours. They are well-known and respected all along the Loire.

"Tonight there will be a game of rithmomachia or chess. You will decide which it will be. Charles will lose but the four of you will become great friends.

"Tomorrow after you have selected the wines to be purchased you will visit his offices. A very large deposit will be made to his firm and he will agree to bank your transaction. He will issue a letter of credit that will be good all the way to Saint-Nazaire.

"The four of you will have dinner here tomorrow evening and attend the gaming room activities. You will not gamble as there will be entertainment. The four of you will make it clear to everyone that you have all become great friends."

"How much is this deposit? Perhaps we didn't bring the required sum with us," I asked.

"It will be taken care of. You don't need to know by whom or how it will be done. As far as the world knows you brought a great deal of money with you and decided to use de Veron only after you met him in the gaming room.

"It's well-known by patrons of Coeur de Lion that de Veron is an expert at both games. So when he loses it will be the subject of talk. Be a gracious winner. He will be a gracious loser. It will reinforce your reputations both as gentlemen and as very clever business men. The one selected to enter the chateau must not be the one who plays with de Veron."

Albert smiled, the first real smile I'd seen from him, then stood up. "Gentlemen the other patrons will soon be waiting to come in. They've been told the room is being prepared so you must leave by the left door at the end of the room. You'll be shown the way out. Wait a while then return by the main door."

We did as instructed and it was an education for three men who'd in their youth taken vows of chastity. The lady in charge, polite and very attractive, smiled but said nothing as she led us down a long hall, past a half dozen closed doors, to the exit. She was the only person we saw as we made our way out. I must admit I was disappointed.

After listening to Albert we quickly made our decision, I was to be the one to meet with de Molay. It followed that Hans, our estate manager and very quick with numbers, would be our rithmomachia champion.

When we returned to the gaming room I recognized de Veron from the night before. He was sanding by the center table talking with three men. Whatever de Veron said must have been funny, the others were laughing. Average height, graying hair, about Alleric's age with the beginnings of a stomach but very fit I thought. As I came closer I saw his very genuine smile and clear, blue eyes. He was in friendly territory. He knows these men and likes them. They know him and like him. More than that they trust and respect him.

As we made our way to the table Geoffroi appeared next to de Veron. I was always amazed at the way Geoffroi made his way through the gaming room without being noticed and seemed to suddenly appear out of thin air. Hans nodded as a signal that he was the man for the game and stepped forward.

Dieter and I held back to watch Geoffroi introduce the two men.

Geoffroi stepped around to Hans' left side, so as not to interfere with the two men shaking hands, and smiled. In a voice just loud enough for others to hear he clearly announced, "Monsieur de Veron please let me introduce Herr Schmidt. Herr Schmidt, Monsieur de Veron. As the two of you requested I have arranged a friendly game, the stakes as you both requested are being held for the prevailing party. Herr Schmidt as the visitor to our gaming room may choose the game. "

"Rithmomachia please," Hans responded.

De Veron smiled and nodded. "Excellent."

As the two men shook hands and took their seats across from each other the nearby patrons politely moved out of the way while others resumed their own games or conversations. Geoffroi reappeared with wine for the two contestants then left the men to their game.

Dieter and I found two chairs across the room to wait. I could not read either contestant's emotions. Each appeared to be deeply involved in the game as if reading a financial ledger alone in the private of his office. Each contestant had blocked out everything but the game and may have forgotten the rest of us were in the room. From our vantage point, neither Dieter nor I could actually see the board or the pieces or the moves. I looked around the room and realized the board and game's progress could be seen only by the two players.

No one but the two contestants knew whether the game was played well or not. Even if Hans were a rank fool, which he was not, no one but de Veron would have known. The deception was taking place in plain sight of everyone. My admiration for Albert and Geoffroi grew.

I don't recall how long the game lasted but everyone in the room had long ago lost interest. Finally de Veron stood and with a broad smile reached out for Hans' hand. "Excellent game. Thank you, Herr Schmidt."

With that he turned to address the room and with his left hand deftly moved the pieces so no one could tell where the pieces were when the game ended. With his right hand raised de Veron announced, "Gentlemen, we have a brilliant player and I propose a toast to the gentleman and winner, Herr Schmidt."

There was brief, polite applause and lifting of tankards, then everyone went back to whatever he'd been doing before de Veron's announcement. Hans and de Veron made their way to Geoffroi's table where, to all appearances, an arrangement for payment to the winner was quietly made. After that the two men moved to the wine table to refill their cups.

Dieter and I waited to see if Hans would rejoin us but he didn't. He and de Veron found two chairs across the room, where they chatted and laughed a great deal. Hans had been an estate manager for many years before the October arrests and afterwards a businessman in the Baltic. He and de Veron had a great deal in common.

Whenever the opportunity presented itself de Veron introduced Hans to men on their way to the wine table or to Geoffroi's desk. As far as everyone in the room could tell, the two had become great friends, just as Albert had predicted.

After a time Hans waved to Dieter and me to join himself and de Veron for a final cup of wine. As we parted for the evening de Veron smiled broadly. "I'll see you gentlemen tomorrow to complete our arrangements. I know you are very busy so I'll thank you now for permitting Johann and me to be of assistance in your banking needs. Please do stop in Nantes to see him. He may be of help should you encounter problems."

A room full of Chinon's most respected men representing the Loire Valley's commercial and financial interests, and half a dozen of the Loire valley's aristocracy were now witnesses to Hans' skill. Our new friendship with de Veron established our position as trusted and respected merchants in town on the business of making themselves and a few of the local families very wealthy.

All of it had been arranged by Geoffroi and Monsieur Noir without anyone, except the participants, being aware of it. I had a new sense of hope. Not just hope but an expectation that we would be successful.

With Hans fully occupied in his game Dieter and I had decided to purchase our wines from the Loire Winery and the Chinon Vineyard. Later, as the three of us bid Geoffroi a good evening, he simply nodded and replied, "Both excellent choices."

I found his personal approval rewarding.

The next morning the three of us set out for the first of the two wineries. About half way Gilbert pulled up his horse and motioned to a wooded area along the Loire to our left. With a smile he announced, "Nature calls me, sirs. I'm going into the woods up ahead. I'll be a while. I suggest you rest along the river, that spot over there by that old oak is nice. You'll find a little clearing with a beautiful view of the Loire and plenty of grass for your horses. Take your time. When you're ready I'll be up the road waiting."

It was a pleasant place to stop and at the base of the tree, very clearly drawn in the dirt, was a large, five paces by three, diagram of the Chateau du Chinon. Next to it was another of the Tour du Coudray. The drawing of the tour showed each level and the locations of the five cells. There were no indications how I should gain entry and nothing about what or where I should go within the chateau. Neither the chateau nor the tour were unique. Both were utilitarian, meant to keep enemies out, prisoners in, and control the river.

When we were confident I understood the chateau and tour we scuffed out both diagrams, then scattered leaves, trigs and stones over the dirt. It was clear several people had been there and something, no longer discernible, had been erased from the dirt but with the fall winds or a little rain even that would disappear.

Gilbert said nothing about the diagrams. I doubted he had any idea what was in the dirt below the oak.

We took our time negotiating for one hundred oak barrels of the Loire Winery's best red wine, a wine the Romans called claret, to be delivered dockside to our barge by noon the following day. Later we settled a similar agreement for one hundred fifty barrels at the Chinon Vineyard with the same terms of delivery.

That afternoon we met briefly with de Veron. He confirmed our deposit and issued his letter of credit. It took him less than an hour to complete our business.

Robert met us as we returned from our day's work and cheerfully announced, "We have a special dinner tonight, roast boar and a variety of fresh vegetables. And the Loire Winery sent over a quarter cask of their best wine, the same one you purchased this morning. Gilbert will care for your horses. Come in and let's open the cask now."

Robert turned to me. "Oh, Erik. I almost forgot. Geoffroi says you left something, I don't recall what he said it was, in the gaming room last night. You should see him before we start dinner. Don't be late or we'll start without you."

I didn't recall having left anything in the gaming room.

CHAPTER XII
Tour du Coudray

When I entered the gaming room I found Monsieur Noir, not Geoffroi. Monsieur Noir barred the door from inside and asked me to take a chair next to him by the fireplace.

"Tomorrow morning Hans and Dieter will complete the shipping arrangements for the wine. At breakfast they'll make a point of telling the other patrons that you've left to make arrangements between here and Saint-Nazaire and will meet them there. I'll tell your two friends where to stay each night. We've already made arrangements."

He paused to be certain I was following him. When I didn't have a question he continued.

"Tomorrow morning, before dawn, come directly to the gaming room. Don't bring anything with you and don't wash or trim your hair. We'll have clothes appropriate for your new job, helper to the night jailer at the chateau. The night jailer, Marcus Blanc, goes by the self-proclaimed title 'Marquis du Blanc.' He thinks it's quite clever. So always address him as 'your lordship' or 'Marquis du Blanc' or simply 'Marquis.' Marcus is not very bright but he's a first cousin of the head jailer.

"Marcus has the night shift at the Tour du Coudray. Vespers bells to morning prayers. It's a long shift. Marcus is responsible for feeding the prisoners in the tour, once after Vesper bells and again before morning prayers. And cleaning out the filth from their cells. Understandably he doesn't enjoy it.

"His bad hip makes it difficult to carry the food and water up all those stairs and carry out the filthy waste buckets. No one else wants the job so they let him have a helper but Marcus must pay the man out of his own wages. He's not a generous man so he goes through several helpers a year.

"His current helper, Piers, will introduce you to Marcus tomorrow evening and will explain he's not been feeling well, the runs, and wants you to stand in for him until he's feeling better. He'll show you the job that night so you'll know what to do while he's out. Marcus will do anything to avoid the work so he'll let you be his helper for the next few days."

I nodded. "Can anyone trace me back to the Coeur de Lion?"

Albert shook his head. "No. Piers is being paid a handsome sum to help a group he believes are thieves take a load of stolen goods to Saumur. He was told they'd provide someone to take his place while he's gone. I doubt he'll ask any questions. Our people are not from around here and used false names. After the goods are delivered Piers will go back to work and our people will simply disappear. Piers won't have any information that would help Philip. If Piers is interrogated he would have to implicate himself in the theft."

"What name should I use, if Piers or Marcus ask?"

"Philip," Albert responded with a grin.

"While you're performing your rather distasteful duties you'll be able to talk with de Molay and the others. But remember, when you're around the Marquis or any other of the chateau crew don't hurry. Be slow and a little clumsy, say as little as possible, grunt a lot, and act stupid. If you're quick or clever Marcus will think you're out to get his job."

I was late for Robert's special dinner and everyone had started on the wine. But the roast boar was tender, excellent in every respect. And the wine, too. It would be some time until I enjoyed such a feast again.

I didn't sleep well that night, neither did Hans or Dieter. We stayed up well into the night talking of old times in Cyprus and in the Baltic, the attempted horse theft on our way to Chinon, anything but what we were doing now. I told them nothing about my assignment and they told me nothing of theirs. We all believed it would be a long time until we would see each other again, maybe an eternity. There was no noble sense that we were Christ's warriors protecting pilgrims in the Holy Lands from the scourge of Islam. Our foe was our king. And our pope, Christ's vicar, didn't seem to care what happened to our Order or to us.

In the morning, as usual we were up before the sun, As I left I looked at my two friends and nodded. "*Deus Vult.*"

"*Deus Vult,*" each responded.

I wondered how the next week would go and when I would see my companions again.

In the gaming room Monsieur Noir had set out the clothes I was to wear for the next few days. Albert laughed as he watched my reaction to the disgustingly filthy remnants fit for the trash fire.

He nodded to the back doors. "Use the one on the left. We've set aside a room for you. There's a bed so you can sleep but stay in the room. And take these clothes with you.

"I'll come for you when it's time. You'll leave by the back door. In the meantime you don't have anything to do until mid-afternoon. Rest if you can. You work the night shift and will be up all night."

To my surprise the little room was neat and clean, and the bed quite comfortable. There were no windows so I had little idea of the passing of time. I hadn't slept well the night before so I lay down to rest.

I woke as Albert was shaking my arm. "It's time."

When I finished changing into the clothes for my new role I felt as though I'd rolled in a pig pen.

Albert looked at me rather critically. "Still too clean, but by the time you get to the chateau you'll be covered in dust and that will help. Run a little on the way, enough to sweat. Then rub dirt on your face and neck. That will help. You'll look the part. It's a long walk so you'll need to leave for the chateau well before Vespers. It wouldn't be right to arrive clean and riding a good horse. Wouldn't fit your new status in life."

Albert laughed as he handed me a small tankard of wine, very cheap wine by the taste of it.

"Take this with you. Drink it on the way. Your breath should smell of cheap wine. If you show up for work sober they won't trust you. And you don't want to be the only sober jailer in the tour.

Albert looked me over from head to toe once more then nodded his approval. "Play your part. Don't contact de Molay tonight. Don't even look at him. Wait till tomorrow night when Piers isn't there. Each morning when your shift is done come back the same way. Remember the oak along the river road?"

I nodded.

"Stop there on your way back in the morning. Take a piss, rest, look at the Loire. But don't fall asleep. If Gilbert rides by with another man then it's safe to come here. Hide in the bushes and wait until the lady you met the other day comes out and shakes a rug. Don't say anything, just follow her in and go to this room. Stay here until it's time for your shift. Get some sleep, I'll come for you again. We'll have food waiting for you when you return so if possible don't eat whatever Marcus is serving. You must stay healthy."

Albert looked at me to be certain I understood then continued, "If you don't see Gilbert by noon then something's gone terribly wrong and it's not safe to come here. You'll find a leather pouch concealed beneath the oak. There'll be money in it, enough for your escape. And there'll be a change of clothes. Not far down the river there'll be a small boat hidden in the bushes where a small creek runs into the river. Head for Saint-Nazaire as best you can."

I looked at him and frowned. "What do I do in Saint-Nazaire, where do I go?"

"One of us will find you before you get there."

Albert escorted me to the back exit, opened the door, looked around to be certain no one was there, then waved me out the door. As I left he quietly added, *"Deus Vult."*

Macus Blanc was everything Monsieur Noir had said, slovenly and drunk. Piers was no better. I tried to fit in with a generous portion of submissive fear and no direct eye contact. I could tell the Marquis liked that.

As Marcus looked me over I kept my head down, tried to appear as though I expected to be hit, and looked only at his old, dirty boots.

"You're new here aren't you?"

I nodded.

"I don't pay for the first day. You're here to learn and I don't pay you to learn."

"Yes, your lordship," I replied trying to sound like a whipped dog.

"Tomorrow, if you do a good job, I'll pay you the next day."

He paused as he looked me over evaluating how much he could get away with.

Finally he said, "Four deniers a day."

Geoffroi had told me the usual pay was six per day, hardly enough to shelter and feed oneself and enjoy a tankard of cheap wine at the end of the day.

"Yes, your lordship, thank you your lordship," I responded with a few head bows, eyes lowered.

Marcus sat back in his chair watching me, obviously pleased I'd accepted his bargain. He took a long drink from his tankard. "Get about your work then."

I followed Piers to the back of the chateau's kitchen, where he directed me to a single bucket of what looked and smelled like leftovers from the troops' mess made into a chunky stew by adding what was left of the wine and ale, then reheating the whole thing in the bucket. From the look of it neither the bucket nor the ladle had been washed, ever.

Piers looked at the stew, grinned, scooped a ladleful from the bucket into an old, unwashed, wooden bowl, pulled a wooden spoon from his pocket and dug in.

He looked at me. "Eat."

I recalled Albert's instruction not to eat but there didn't seem to be an alternative so I stifled a gag, found another old bowl on a nearby table, wiped it with the sleeve of my shirt and scooped a half ladle of the stew into it. I didn't have a spoon so I drank the liquid then used my fingers for the smallest of the fatty chunks. Piers grinned his approval. I tried to think of the roast boar I'd had the night before but couldn't quite manage it.

Using the ladle as his baton Piers led the way up the tour's narrow, hardly wider than my shoulders, stone steps to the tour's second level. I followed with the stew bucket and the empty waste bucket Piers handed me as we left the kitchen. Each small, stone cell had a solid oak door with a small interior door just big enough to pass the waste bucket through.

Piers unlocked the first cell's interior door, looked in and yelled, "Hungry?"

In response a food bowl appeared and Piers poured two ladlefuls of stew. When the bowl was removed Piers motioned for me to pass the waste bucket through. I tried to look through the interior door as I handed the bucket to the prisoner but could see nothing other than a dirty canvas mat before I recoiled from the stench. A moment later the bucket reappeared.

Piers recoiled from the bucket and yelled, "For God's sake don't spill it."

We continued through the other cells, five in total. By the end of it the stew was gone and the waste bucket was full. As Piers followed me down the stairs he made a point of explaining several times that if I spilled the waste bucket he didn't want to be below me and I'd have to clean it up myself.

At the bottom he once again led the way but this time it was to the garderobe on the south curtain wall. Far below us and a dozen paces or more from the curtain wall two men waited with shovels and an old wooden litter.

Piers broke out in a wicked laugh. "We throw the kitchen scraps, the old hay, and the crap from the stables and waste buckets down here. Them damn fool farmers, like those two, come by every couple days to pick it up."

He grabbed the waste bucket from my hand and tossed its contents at the men below. The men apparently knew what Piers was doing as they were waiting well out of range of the flying waste. They replied with obscene gestures and equally obscene comments about Piers' mother.

Piers laughed. "Damn. I like to get them farmers if I can. The damn fools say their crops grow better if they add this to the soil. I think they say that just to piss me off."

I nodded and grunted as I watched the two farmers shovel the accumulated waste onto their litter and haul it away.

Piers laughed. "Ja, I'm sure glad I'm not one of those stupid farmers."

I grunted and nodded in response. Right now it seemed a better occupation than assistant night jailer.

"What do we do now?" I asked.

"Wait for morning bells. Then do the same thing."

"Wait. Right, I'll wait," I mumbled as I nodded.

I looked around trying to look very confused. "Where do I wait?"

"Wait by the kitchen if you want. Sometimes the cooks will give you food or a drink of ale if you help them, carry things for them, sweep a little. You can sleep if you find a dark place with no one around. When you hear the morning bells we feed the prisoners again. And dump their waste. Then you go home."

When I asked the cooks if I could help they seemed pleased and gave me a broom to sweep the kitchen. After I finished sweeping, I didn't do a good job of it, they gave me a small platter of real food, not the prisoners' stew. After that I found a dark corner and stayed out of sight. At morning bells we fed the prisoners and disposed of their waste.

As we left the garderobe I asked, "Do I get my four deniers now?"

"No, his lordship said you won't get paid tomorrow cause you was just learning today. But you'll get paid for tomorrow's work, the next day. The marquis always pays the next day cause he thinks you may die and he won't have to pay you."

I squinted at the ground and shook my head. "Oh, ja I don't get paid tomorrow cause I'm just learnin' today. I work tomorrow but don't get paid till next day cause I may die. Why does he think I'm ga'na die?"

Piers looked at me for a moment, then said, "Ja, well, don't worry about it. I'll get well soon and then you won't have to work at all. I'm going home but don't you be telling the Marquis du Blanc anything bad about me. If you do I'll never let you take my place again when I'm not well. And you'd miss out on a fair day's wages."

"Oh, ja. See ya," I replied.

I stopped to see Marcus on my way out but he wasn't around so I waited. When he finally showed up he was drunk. I shuffled a bit to get his attention, "I fed the prisoners and threw out their waste. Can I go, your lordship?"

Marcus nodded and waved me away, then said, "Be here on time tonight. I won't tolerate a late helper. If you're late you won't get paid."

I nodded and grunted. That seemed to satisfy him.

As I waited beneath the oak for Gilbert and another man to ride by I felt certain I'd convinced both Marcus and Piers I was too stupid to be dangerous. Thankfully, it wasn't long until Gilbert and a second man rode by at an unhurried trot.

Back in the quiet safety of my little room I washed but did not shave or trim either hair or beard. At a knock on my door I opened it to find Albert.

"How did it go last night?" he asked.

"Well enough, I think. But what they feed them. My God I don't know how they make it."

"I'll have the cook provide you some extra meat. You can add it to their food. Do you think you'll be able to talk with de Molay?"

"Piers only had the key to the interior doors, one key fit all five. It was obvious that key would not fit the cell door lock. I may still be able to talk to de Molay. No one will be around while I'm feeding the prisoners and collecting their waste. The smell, if nothing else, will keep them away. But it won't be the same as a real face to face talk. It's also possible he won't recognize me as a Templar. He may believe I'm there to trick him."

"Where are the keys to the cell doors, not the interior doors?"

"I can't say for sure. When I met Piers he already had the key to the interior doors. He didn't show me where he got it and I couldn't ask or he would get suspicious. Neither Piers or Marcus carry keys with them and I didn't see them in the room Marcus calls his office. Tomorrow I'll ask Marcus for the key. I think he'll show me where all the keys are."

Albert thought a moment. "It may be worth the risk to make a copy of the key rather than use the actual key. And it might prove useful later. Tonight I'll have a block of wax for you. If you find something that looks like it may be a key to the cells make an impression. But if you're caught try to squeeze it, destroy the impression. Tell them you found the wax on the way to the chateau, didn't know what it was but it was nice so you kept it."

I showed up before Vespers bells which seemed to please Marcus. It showed I was afraid of him. But it also irritated him. If I'd been late he would have an excuse not to pay me for that day's work. I sat quietly on the floor outside the room he called his office. It had a small table, a single chair, and a half door. There was no place to put or hang, much less hide, anything. The keys were not in his room and they weren't on his belt.

Vesper bells hadn't rung yet and I was tempted to ask if I could start anyway but I recalled Albert's advice, don't be quick and don't be clever. So I decided to wait until after the bells stopped.

I hadn't moved when Marcus came out of his little room. "Did you hear the bells, dumbass?"

I nodded.

"Well get your sorry ass to work if you want to be paid."

I slowly got up, knuckled my forehead and said, "I need the key your lordship. Piers didn't show me where it is."

Marcus shook his head in disgust. "Stupid fools. Follow me."

Candle in hand he led the way down a short hall to another door, opened it and took a key off a wall hook. In the flickering light I saw there were three or four hooks on the wall, but only two had keys on them. Marcus took the key closest to the door.

"Here, dumbass. It's the one closest to the door. Be sure you put it back on that same hook after you're done. If you don't then you don't get paid. Understand?"

Marcus stopped and sniffed the air. "You smell like roast meat. You been to the kitchen already?"

I nodded and slunk down the hallway to the sound of his laughter.

Buckets in hand, ladle in the stew bucket, and more than two pounds of the best cold, roast venison and another pound of fresh vegetables wrapped around my waist in a cloth beneath my loose shirt, I climbed the stairs to the prisoners' level.

I stopped at the first door and unlocked the interior door. A food bowl appeared and I ladled stew into the bowl then added two strips of roast venison and several vegetables. I could see only a shadow in the darkness so I leaned close to the opening and whispered, "I bring greetings from the East brother. *Deus Vult*."

There was a long pause, then a shaky, weak voice responded, "*Deus Vult.* I am in search of further light. Do you bring it?"

"Together, with God's grace, we may find it," I answered.

"Who are you?" the voice said.

"A brother of the Temple. Who are you?"

"Master of the Temple."

"I don't have much time," I said as I handed him the waste bucket. "I must feed the others. We will talk tomorrow after Vespers."

All went well that night and I made no further effort to talk with de Molay in the morning feeding. There was no reason to take the risk. Marcus was fast asleep in his chair after I finished feeding the prisoners so I returned to the key room. As I placed the interior door key on its hook I lifted the other key from its hook and pressed it into both sides of the wax block then returned it to its hook. Marcus was snoring loudly as I left.

Monsieur Noir examined the wax block and nodded his approval, "We can make a key from this. We'll have it ready when you leave for the chateau this afternoon. It'll be sewn into your jacket hem. You'll need to remove it and then find a place to hide it. Can you do that?"

I nodded. I could hide it in de Molay's cell, beneath his waste pot. It would be the last place they'd willingly look for anything.

That evening as I shuffled down the hall to the key room I heard Marcus shout my name so I made my way to the half-door of his office.

"Yes, your lordship," I said trying to sound as frighten as I could.

I looked at Marcus out of the corner of my eye, careful not to make eye contact. It was clear he was already drunker than usual. He started to rise but belched and fell back into his chair. His belch filled the small room with the odor of spiced sausage.

"Too good for your wages, are you?"

I had no idea what he was trying to say so I hunched over a little more, shook my head and grunted. As I did it occurred to me that I should be paid four deniers for yesterday's work. I wondered if he'd concocted an excuse not to pay me.

"Too good to come for your wages? You expect me to chase you down and pay you?"

"No, your lordship, no. Piers didn't say nothing about that and I didn't want to bother you."

"I'll pay you this time. Piers, that worthless bastard. If you want your wages you need to come to my office first thing after Vesper bells. Got it?"

Marcus slumped back in his chair, "If you forget I'll just understand you don't want to be paid. I'll keep the money for myself."

"Yes, your lordship. Thank you, your lordship."

With that he tossed four deniers at me, one at a time, counting them out as he did. When he finished he laughed and waved me away as he would a fly.

I knocked on the interior door of de Molay's cell. Instead of a food bowl I saw an apparition framed by a black hood. Its dark eyes glared at me through a tangled mass of uncut, grayish white hair. It moved closer until its beard, bushy eyebrows, and those dark, unblinking eyes filled the opening. The eyes studied me, then, apparently satisfied with the examination, pulled back.

"God be with you brother," he whispered.

"I'm going to feed you and empty your waste, as I usually do. After I do the same for the others I'll return. I have news."

He nodded, stepped back and handed me his food bowl.

When I returned to de Molay's cell and inserted the new key into the door's main lock, it seemed to stick. Either the key wasn't worn smooth or the lock had rusted from lack of use. With effort and more noise than I wanted, the key finally turned. I pulled the bolt back, more noise. I waited to see if I'd alarmed anyone. Satisfied no one had heard I began to pull the door open. Its rusty hinges made a frightful sound that echoed through the tower. I waited a moment then opened the door just enough for me to squeeze into the cell.

The noise hadn't bothered de Molay. With the hood of his robe pulled over his head, he was sitting on his mat, back against the wall, chewing on one of the strips of cold, spiced venison I'd included in his stew.

I looked around the cell, about five paces by three in size, I estimated. Its only furnishings an old canvas mat stuffed with straw, a thin woolen blanket, a spoon and bowl, and a pot for waste.

I sat down in front of him on the cold stones of his cell.

"Have you come to rescue me?"

"No, to talk with you. To find out what you want us to do. We need your guidance."

He nodded but didn't stop chewing.

"First, where were you held after your arrest last October? We searched for you but couldn't find you."

He seemed to ignore my question as he continued to chew the venison. Finally he spoke, "You wonder why we, I, didn't resist Nogaret when he arrested us. Why we opened the gates of our strongest fortification to our worst enemy without a fight?"

I nodded.

"Because we're innocent of the charges. When I returned from Cyprus and met Clement in Poitiers I told him of Philip's allegations there had been irregularities in some of our initiation rites. It was March or April before the arrests. I asked him to help investigate and remove those involved. He told me he would and that he had confidence in our Order. I trusted him.

"Clement knows the problems caused by such men. Philip threatened to try Boniface for the same perverted acts even though Boniface was dead. Philip is despicable and Nogaret, too. Let the dead rest in peace.

"If there'd been a battle, even if we'd won, the Order would be lost. The people, our support, would turn against us. They would see us as a threat to their own peace. Even if we won every battle we are not an order that governs. There must be a king as well as the Church.

"The people would believe Philip's allegations were true and we were protecting those who had sinned. If Clement openly supported us the people would believe the charges Nogaret made against Boniface were true. The Church cannot condone or even tolerate an order that permits such actions or brings harm to the Church's people."

He paused to take another bite of venison. "This is excellent, after our usual fare. If we'd resisted arrest Clement could not, would not, help us. He will not directly confront Philip. He's afraid of Philip and Nogaret for good reason. They've already murdered two popes.

"Clement needs Philip. Clement's the first pope not in Rome and there are a great many cardinals and bishops who want him out and the papacy back in Rome. Bishop Marigny, a sadist, feels free to ignore his Pope, even undermine him. His brother, half-brother really, is Philip's Chamberlain.

"And there are plenty of other bishops and cardinals who agree with Marigny."

He paused then added, "I was held in the Corbeil, Bishop Marigny."

As I told him what Clement and Philip had done since the arrests De Molay chewed on the venison, his head down, staring at the floor. I wondered if he was really listening. After finishing the last strip of venison he looked up. "Do you have more venison?"

I handed him another slice and said nothing more as he resumed eating, eyes focused on the floor stones.

Two venison slices later he spoke, "If Clement's wise, and I think he is, he'll establish his Papal Court in the south of France, as far from Philip as he can. The farther south he goes the stronger he is and the weaker Philip is.

"Clement will help us. From what you've told me he is, as much as he can. Three separate investigations, a brilliant move, it will work in our favor. His recent absolution of me and the others shows he's still with us. If he controls the investigations and the trials then all will be well. We must trust Clement, have faith in him, and in God."

I was encouraged. He had been listening so I explained the recent developments in the Holy Roman Empire and the possibility of an alliance that would isolate Philip. At times he nodded. Other times he uttered an "ah" or an "ummm" as if I'd just said something he thought particularly significant.

When I finished I asked, "What do you think of the plan? Could you lead the Templars if Clement and Henry were to stand together against Philip?"

"That's a big if, Erik. Even if there were such an alliance and even if the barons you mentioned were to join it, I am old. I don't have the strength I used to have. Maybe before the torture, before the isolation and privations, before the Templars were scattered. If we still had our wealth."

His voice trailed off as he shook his head.

"No, not now. I doubt I'd survive a rescue and I'm not strong enough to lead an army against the King. Even if this matter of the Holy Roman Empire is resolved in Clement's favor, our favor, and Henry is elected King of the Romans, it's too late. Philip asked for and got the support of the nobles at the Estates General in Tours.

"It might be possible if we had more time, if we hadn't lost Acre in '91, if du Tour hadn't given Philip all our moneys, if I were stronger, if Henry had been elected a year ago."

There seemed no reason to press the matter so as de Molay slowly chewed on the last strip of venison I asked a question I'd thought about for years. "What of the Holy Grail? Did the Templars find it?"

His eyebrows furrowed as if he hadn't understood the question. "You mean the relic? Christ's cup from the Last Supper?"

I nodded. "The same one Joseph of Arimathea used to capture Christ's blood when He was on the Cross."

He put his hand on mine. "Erik, there are actual relics from events and saints. Perhaps Christ's cup, chalice or grail exists somewhere but the Templars do not possess it or know who does. We've never possessed such a relic."

He paused, then added with a gentle smile, "But we do possess the true Holy Grail. The true Grail is here, in this cell."

He let a moment pass as I tried to understand the apparent contradiction. When I shook my head he continued. "Erik the true Holy Grail is not a thing, a thing to be possessed by a single man.

"Christ did not say that anyone who possesses or believes in this cup shall have eternal life. He said that anyone who believes in Him shall have eternal life. It is the belief in Him that is the Grail. The Grail is the vessel for that faith, the belief in Christ and His teachings, and trust in God. The true Grail is all who believe in Him and seek to preserve that belief. That faith and belief are open to everyone. Open your mind and heart to Christ and to God and you become the Holy Grail.

"There are many people who would destroy that belief, wipe it from the face of the earth. Some would kill all believers. Islam would destroy that belief by killing all of Christ's believers or replacing Christ's teachings with a belief in the teachings of Mohammad. Others would destroy it by causing people to lose hope and with that lose their faith. Philip and Nogaret, and Marigny, would destroy the Grail by physical and mental privation and pain."

He was silent for a moment. "If a few men hadn't perverted our rites and undermined the people's support for our sacred Order. If it were only a matter of the return of our wealth."

De Molay was silent for a long time as he chewed the last of the venison. When he finished he said, "Tell me more of your work in the Baltic."

I did and was surprised. It seemed to cheer him.

He smiled. It was a sad smile, but a smile. "The Crusades are over, Erik. The world has changed. Matthew and the rest of you have found our future, not as Templars but as men of commerce and finance."

He cocked his head and looked at the cell door as if listening for something. "You must go now. There's too much at risk. Carry my message to the others and trust in Clement. He will save the Order, if it's possible, if it's God's will."

"And if Clement does not?"

"Then *Deus Vult*. It is God's will. Look to your future in the Baltic, not the Mediterranean. And to commerce and trade, not armor and arms."

I had two more nights at the Chateau du Chinon and put them to good use. I met with Pairaud and Charney the next evening and with Gonneville and Caron the last. All were in terrible physical condition, thin, emaciated. All bore marks of torture and abuse, physical, mental and emotional. When I explained the events since their arrest and asked their views on the future, the answers were essentially the same. Our fate was in Clement's hands and we must trust in him and in God.

Marcus remained oblivious to my nightly visits with the prisoners and Piers returned to work as scheduled. When I came that next evening to collect my four deniers Marcus was drunk but paid me. Piers, thankfully, ignored me. As I left for the last time it struck me that neither Marcus or Piers had ever asked my name. In their opinion I wasn't worth the effort to ask.

Monsieur Noir agreed there was nothing more I could accomplish in Chinon. I spent the rest of that night hidden away out of sight of the other guests, thankful to be done with collecting waste buckets. But I didn't sleep well. I could not stop thinking of the men held prisoner in Tour de Coudray and Philip's other prisons.

CHAPTER XIII
Nantes

With the dawn Gilbert and I set out on horseback for Montsoreau. I was to all appearances a game keeper, a professional hunter employed by some landed lord. As such my attire was suitable for whatever weather I might encounter, sun, cold, wind, rain, even a night in the wild. In the small of my back, a misericordes; slung across my back, a crossbow and a half-dozen bolts. Tucked into my jerkin's inside pocket was a leather pouch containing a variety of common coins. Monsieur Noir explained two gold florins had been sewn into the calf of each boot; it was enough to bribe my way out of difficulties.

As I left Geoffroi handed me two saddle bags. Food for my travels, he said. Later, on the barge, I made a quick inspection and found a large, round loaf of coarse, dark rye bread, two onions, a dozen boiled eggs, two dozen strips of jerked venison, an equal number of dried roast boar, and a large leather wine skin of excellent Loire Valley red wine. It was more than enough food and wine to last me several days.

Gilbert wished me well as he saw me off on a Loire river barge and good naturedly reminded me not to lose my boots. His final instruction was that I stop in Chenehutte and stay the night in the small inn on the Lorie's southern bank where a small stream flows into the river. It wouldn't be hard to find; it was the only inn. If nothing developed by noon the next day I was to take the river trail east to the small town of Treves where I should take the first available barge to Nantes and then a different barge to Saint-Nazaire. There I was to stop for a drink in the Fille Par La Mer tavern and look for a man with a patch over his left eye and an oak tankard carved with two fleurs de lis.

When I told the barge master my intended destination was Chenehutte he gave me a quizzical look, shrugged, but accepted my fare.

It was late afternoon when the barge pulled into a small cove that cut into the thick, hardwood forest lining the river. All I could see were a marshy meadow and a short, half submerged dock. Fall winds had cleared the leaves from the trees leaving so many scraggly skeletons. The meadow's grasses and bushes had turned to shades of umber, ocher and sienna. With the sun setting it made for a depressing scene.

I looked at the barge master for an explanation. He said this was Chenehutte and he had to reach Gennes that evening with his cargo and he was late. It was clear he wasn't going to stop, so as the barge slid alongside the dock I stepped off. The barge continued down river.

As I made my way into the meadow I saw the remains of a small inn tucked into the forest at the far end of the meadow, a long bow shot from the dock. No smoke rose from its rock chimney. Not so much as a candle indicated it was occupied. The inn's west end had collapsed, taking half the porch overhang with it. Judging from the thick weeds and brush growing up through what remained of the porch floor, the inn had been abandoned years before.

There must have been some reason I was to stop here but the best I could guess was that it was a safe location. No one would look for me here. As I thought of de Molay and the others back in Chinon and surveyed the decaying remains of Chenehutte I had every reason to believe our mission had failed and I'd failed.

My next thought was that I still had plenty of food in my saddle bags, excellent food really. Enough to last me several days. And I had shelter for the night and flint to start a fire to keep me warm and cheer me. Perhaps with the morning light my spirits would lift and I could continue on to Saint-Nazaire.

I made my way through the meadow to the inn. The overhang groaned with my first step onto the few remaining boards of the inn's porch. As I considered whether the structure would collapse on me the old door swung open and Dieter, grinning broadly, stepped out to greet me.

"By God we were beginning to worry something had happened to you."

He gave me a bear hug, then shouted into the inn, "Hans! It's Erik. Light the fire and let's eat. He's probably starved."

I looked around the meadow. "Where's our wine, the barge? How'd you get here?"

Dieter laughed. "The barge is safe in Treves, just down river, a short ride from here. Our crew is watching it. Hans and I rented three horses and rode back here to meet you. They're tied in back, out of sight. We told people we we're looking at the country side for our baron and would be back in the morning.

"The country's full of Philip's men and if they aren't Philip's men then they work for one of the bishops, or their bounty hunters. All of 'em the devil's own if you ask me.

"Monsieur Noir suggested we visit this old inn. He said it had been abandoned when it couldn't compete with the better river ports down river. It was a safe place for the two of us to wait for you and hide if things went wrong in Chinon. There's no one here to ask questions."

Hans lit the small stack of kindling in the inn's massive, stone fireplace and asked, "What's for dinner? Monsieur Noir said you'd bring dinner and breakfast, too."

"My God that man thinks of everything. I wondered why I had so much food and wine. It never occurred to me it was for all of us."

We ate on the inn's cold, stone floor, close to our small fire, our only light and warmth in the moonless night, with a cold draft slipping through the remains of the inn's wooden walls. As I related the events of the past few days the mood of our reunion changed from joy to deep concern for our imprisoned brethren and our Order. We were safe but they faced a long winter of hardship and torture.

Late in the afternoon a few days later we and our cargo reached Nantes. We hadn't encountered any difficulties along the way but as our barge tied up at the assigned inspection slip a runner stepped aboard and announced he had a message for Hans, Dieter or Erik.

Dieter stepped forward. "I'm Dieter."

When satisfied he had the right man the messenger handed Dieter a sealed envelope and disappeared into the busy crowd. The three of us found a private place to open the envelope. In it was another sealed envelope and a note signed "J." The note read, "This arrived early this morning from A. G rode straight through. It must be urgent."

I tore open the second envelope. Its note read, "De Caron died last night while being interrogated. Before he died he divulged a meeting with a night jailor, a Templar. Piers and Marcus are being interrogated. Philip's agents are looking for Marcus' temporary helper. Everyone is suspected, including all recent strangers in Chinon. De Molay has been removed from Chateau Chinon. His whereabouts are unknown. Burn this message and the envelope. Leave France immediately!"

Hans was quick. "I think we know who A is, Albert. My guess is G is our young guide, Gilbert, and J is Johann de Veron."

We must escape with our information but we doubted the authorities had connected the three of us to the missing night jailer. No one at the chateau, including Piers, Marcus, and the five Templar leaders, had an accurate description of any of the three of us. That night we decided we could not abandon our goods.We must escape, but to abandon our goods would raise suspicion. Any number of people could give accurate descriptions of the three wine merchants who had suddenly and inexplicably abandoned their valuable cargo, and connect us to the Coeur de Lion and everyone we'd met there.

Once Philip's men and the bounty hunters had our descriptions they would search the Loire towns and Saint-Nazaire port. Anyone who fit our description, especially those trying to sign on ships bound for foreign ports, would be arrested.

The best course was for us and our goods to clear the port authorities as rapidly as possible and find a ship bound for somewhere far from Philip's control.

Unfortunately, before we would be permitted entrance to the port with our cargo of wine we had to pass inspection and pay our tolls and taxes at Nantes' massive chateau, the old castle of the Dukes of Brittany. Nantes was firmly in Philip's control and Philip needed funds. Exporting of Loire Valley wine was apparently an excellent source of taxes, exorbitant taxes. All that was required of Philip's port agent was to over-estimate the cargo's value or its volume, preferably both.

We met with Monsieur LeFeete, the 'Representative of the Crown for Exports from Nantes,' as he referred to his official position. It became clear that he believed we were illiterate, innumerate and fundamentally stupid. It occurred to me that in his view, all merchants ranked somewhat lower than street sweepers, both in intelligence and inherent worth. At a hand taller than I was and thin, he had a gawky but aristocratic, appearance. He'd neatly trimmed his mustache and beard to emphasize his long, narrow nose, high cheek bones, and prominent jaw. His eyes were the color of his dark brown hair, his clothes fashionable, his complexion pasty.

In the process of inspecting our goods to determine the appropriate export tax, he miscounted the number of wine barrels. He said his assistant had counted 275 whereas I knew we had 250. And he inflated the value of our cargo far beyond what showed on the bills of sale provided by the two wineries.

Wine, he lectured, was taxed at its value at the port, not by what we paid for it in the Chinon wineries. In simple terms he believed it was taxable at the cost of the wine, plus the cost of transportation from Chinon to Nantes, plus his estimation of our expected profit, plus a factor he couldn't explain, other than his estimate of the value of our personal efforts and expenses to get it all to market.

LeFeete was arrogant enough to believe that the higher he set the value of our personal efforts and the greater his estimation of our profit the more we should be flattered. And we should gladly pay for such flattery. LeFeete also knew our product was going to stay in Nantes until we paid his demands and if we didn't pay it soon the Atlantic winter storms could keep us in Nantes until spring. LeFeete seemed to take pleasure that both time and weather, his powerful allies and our equally powerful enemies, were clearly in his favor.

The thought of either paying an excessive tax or staying in Nantes beyond what was absolutely necessary was unacceptable. If we simply paid the demanded tax without negotiation it would raise suspicions, both as to who we really were and whether we had goods we had not declared. Most likely LeFeete would feel he'd foolishly underestimated the value of our goods or we'd pulled a fast one on him. Either way, LeFeete would give us additional and unwanted scrutiny that would delay our departure and increase our risk the authorities might link us to Chinon's missing night jailor. We had no choice but to go through the usual negotiations involved in the export of wine.

Hans, Dieter and I had the same thought, the mysterious "J" had to be Johann de Veron and it was time to pay him a visit. So we thanked LeFeete, apologized for taking so much of his valuable time in the inspection, and explained we had urgent business and would see him again the next morning.

LeFeete seemed to accept that as our acknowledgement that he had us but we weren't quite ready to admit it. He just nodded and smiled politely as he said, "I look forward to seeing you then."

Monsieur Johann de Veron was kind enough to see us immediately. As I started to show him our letter of credit issued by his brother he smiled and stopped me. "It's not necessary. I've been expecting you. I'm already aware of the business arrangements between our firm and yours. How may I be of help?"

I learned sometime later, in Lubeck, that Herr Stagg, Alleric and Monsieur Noir had established the relationship with the de Veron brothers shortly after our meeting with Alleric and Herr Stagg in Emden. All had been arranged well before the three of us reached the Coeur de Lion.

Johann had his brother's same easy manner, happy and confident. It was impossible to say who was the older, both seemed to be Alleric's age. Both struck me as intelligent, physically vigorous men who enjoyed a day on horseback or a day reading ledgers and could do each exceedingly well.

He listened sympathetically as I summarized our difficulties with Monsieur LeFeete, then smiled. "Yes, yes, I understand. I suggest, with your permission, that I meet with LeFeete this afternoon. Please come by my office when we open tomorrow morning. Perhaps the matter can be resolved."

I don't know what transpired between Johann and LeFeete that afternoon but when we met with Johann in the morning he informed us that the four of us had a meeting with LeFeete shortly before noon at the Nantes Society. He added that he and LeFeete were members of the Society and he anticipated no more problems. But it required a payment, undisclosed to the crown, of a barrel of our wine and two gold florins. The wine had already been transferred to LeFeete. Payment of the florins would be made at the meeting. At the appropriate time I was to place the two coins beneath my wine cup.

The Nantes Society's Hall was similar to the Emdenhaus where we had met with Herr Stagg. Over a very excellent Loire valley red wine, a fine roast beef with a variety of sauté vegetables, a delicious loaf of bread with fresh butter and plum jam, and a variety of local cheeses we quietly resolved our issues.

Monsieur LeFeete announced his regret that his assistant had miscounted the number of wine barrels and after his personal review of the cargo he determined we had exactly two hundred forty-nine barrels. LeFeete then continued "I have personally sampled your cargo and determined its value for purposes of the king's export tax, is exactly what you paid for it in Chinon.

Johann smiled. "Monsieur LeFeete has been kind enough to have a quarter barrel of his finest wine delivered to our Society. We're enjoying some of it with our meal."

I thought, but did not say, it was hard to argue the barrels had somehow multiplied en route to Nanates and it was most generous of him to take just one barrel of our wine, keep three-fourths of it for himself, and give a quarter of it for our meeting and the enjoyment of the other members of his Society. His fellows would think him a very generous man.

LaFeete continued with a smile. "Monsieur de Veron informs me we may expect to see more of you in Nantes, if your venture results in a handsome profit. And I have not a doubt that it will."

Johann lifted his wine cup in a toast. "Here's to profits and the future."

After the toast I slipped two gold Florins beneath my cup. I think LeFeete was the only one who noticed. LeFeete nodded his appreciation as he pulled my empty wine cup to his side of the table being careful not to let the two coins slip from beneath. After refilling my cup he moved it back across the table. As he did it, he tipped the cup slightly with his right hand and raked in the coins with his left. He was very good at it.

With the transfer complete he announced, "Your export license will be available tomorrow morning. Everything will be in order."

Lubeck law had all but eliminated such corruption in the Baltic trade. This and later transactions reinforced my growing belief that Templar morality fit far better with Lubeck law than with French corruption. Under Philip's administration corruption had become rampant and it rubbed me the wrong way to participate in such activity. But we had no choice but to quickly complete our transactions. This was not the time or place for moral outrage.

With our taxes paid and permission granted our barge was allowed into Saint-Nazaire harbor and access to the Atlantic. The 'Certificate of Payment and Permission' was a piece of work. It had all the flair of England's Great Charter signed some hundred years before. One would think LeFeete had signed over Nantes and Saint-Nazaire to us, all with multicolored ribbons, scrolling signatures, and red wax seals impressed with unrecognizable symbols.

CHAPTER XIV
King verses Bishop

The long voyage around the headlands of Brest, then up the French coast to Amsterdam and Emden was always risky this late in the season but we had no choice. We had information Matthew and Alleric needed. If we waited in France we would run the risk of encountering Philip's bounty seekers. And this might be the last of the French wine to reach the Baltic until Spring.

On our return to Lubeck we made a handsome profit on the Loire Valley wine, enough to finance the purchase another ship and refit two older ships. Our fleet, a Templar fleet, would be large enough and strong enough to both transport cargo and protect itself from the svear pirates.

Years later it would be easy to look back and understand Philip's strategy and Clement's counter-moves but in early 1309 nothing was clear except that Philip was still on the offense and had the upper hand. Templars were reeling from the arrests, our leaders were imprisoned and those still free were scattered over Europe with few resources. Clement was weak, confused, besieged by the bishops in northern France and all of those in Italy, fearful of Philip, terrified of Nogaret, and uncertain how to preserve his Papacy. Templars were not his first concern each morning or his heaviest burden at night.

The winter of 1308 and 1309 is remembered by most people for the terrible cold and the great dying of cattle, a plague some say. But I remember other events, events that gave us hope. In late November, 1308 Henry VII was elected King of the Romans and crowned in early January. With his coronation our hopes rose that Clement would be emboldened to stand up to Philip. A league between the two great offices, Pope and Emperor, would strengthen both Clement's papacy and Henry's rule over the Empire, and weaken Philip. Perhaps it would save the Templar Order.

Philip wasted no time in grieving his brother's election loss. Less than a month had passed since the coronation when Philip renewed his threat to try Boniface for sodomy and heresy. It would be a show trial, Boniface was already dead, murdered by de Nogaret. But the prospect of dragging the name of a dead Pope through the dirt terrified Clement. Just the allegations undermined public support for Clement and the Catholic Church.

Dieter, Hans and I often talked of the affairs in France. Philip had entangled Clement in a long, slow, deadly serious chess match. The Templars were just one of many pieces on the board and certainly not the most important. There were moves and counter moves, feints, attacks and retreats. More than a few pieces were being sacrificed to a player's larger ends.

Some players, like Henry and the Italian bishops, even the French nobles, had games of their own and interests of their own. Pieces were not owned by any player. A piece could suddenly change sides, black to white, white to black. Allegiances changed in outwardly unpredictable ways. But always in accordance with the piece's single loyalty, its own survival and advancement. Though the game the power of each individual piece changed, enlarged at times, diminished at times, with the unpredictable ebb and flow of wealth and public opinion. Each player and each piece sought to gain the peoples' fickle favor but some were more capable than others in the manipulation of that opinion.

Over the long winter Philip refined his response to Clement's gambit of separating Templar trials by jurisdictional and geographical distinctions. Philip's strategy would take time but he was a patient man.

About the same time, March of 1309, Clement finally settled on Avignon for his papal court. He went as far south as he could. Avignon was well outside of Philip's direct control and just a hard day's ride from the safety of the Mediterranean and about the same by the Rhone. It was a wise move I likened it to a castling move on a chess board.

I believed, or at least hoped, the combination of events set the stage for Clement and Henry to openly ally and by doing so curb Philip's power.

We were not idle. Alleric sent word that the three of us were to supervise the repair and refitting of our ships in preparation for the Baltic's spring trade. All three of us were ready for a change. There was little we could accomplish either by a return to France or by remaining in Emden.

Our return to the Baltic was a welcome change. Philip wasn't popular in Lubeck and his feud with Clement didn't help his image. His attack on the Templars was seen for what it was, a bold theft of their property.

Public sentiment in Lubeck favored the past two centuries of Crusades as a noble, even romantic, effort. But with the fall of Acre a generation before, enthusiasm for another Crusade had faded. There was an uneasy sense the time of Crusades had passed and with it the usefulness of the three Orders. In the years since the fall of Acre people of western Europe, particularly in the north, had come to see the Templars more as bankers and property managers than soldiers of the Cross.

It was my first extended time in Lubeck, the city that was to become my home. I came to love both the city and its people. The people were industrious, intelligent and prosperous.

Commerce, banking and shipping were respected professions. Indeed, the city's seal depicted a trading ship. Trade agreements were enforced fairly and uniformly within a loose confederation of Baltic towns. As an Imperial Free City both Lubeck and its commerce were protected from interference by king and lesser feudal lords. Graft and corruption as we'd encountered in Nantes was not tolerated. Yet Lubeck and its council had excellent relations with the Holy Roman Empire.

In the Baltic free cities wealth came from trade, the creation and exchange of goods. Not from strength of arms or inherited feudal power over people born to work the land. The art and science of double entry bookkeeping, the use of Arabic instead of the old Roman number systems, and new methods of mathematical calculation that moved beyond the abacus had spread from Italy throughout Europe. There was an energy, an excitement, the world was changing and the people of Lubeck were determined to play a major part.

I felt that energy and excitement and confidence. Experience in financial matters, the Templars' second skill, was respected. I believed I had the skills to be part of Lubeck's future. It took most of that year but I gradually came to realize something personally significant was taking place. My purpose in life was changing.

I'd been trained as a warrior of Christ with the purpose of taking back the Holy Lands in the eastern Mediterranean, the Levant. That purpose had defined my life. I felt that purpose slipping away but did not yet know what was to replace it. Lubeck was for me and many other Templars a place of transformation, of metamorphosis.

The city of Lubeck was also beautiful, even in full winter. Built on Bucu island in the Trave river the town was a natural fortress opening into a natural harbor. The stone architecture spoke of a solid, intelligent, and determined people, people of purpose and ability founded in faith. The Catholic Church was an important part of Lubeck. The four beautiful cathedrals, Marienkirche, Dom zu Lubeck, Jakobikirche, and the market cathedral, were all well-attended and supported by prosperous merchants, all devout Catholics.

When in town I attended Mass in one of the Lubeck churches but tried to rotate amongst them. I wasn't ready to attend just one. I was still a Templar at heart but there were no Templar services to attend. One Sunday morning I attended Mass in the Marienkirche and happened to meet Herr De Vries with his family. I remember it because it was the first time I met his older daughter, Catherine, and her husband, a respected Hamburg banker. They were visiting her parents at the time.

As Europe recovered from the difficult winter Philip and Clement were active again. Rumors and news from France, in the Spring of 1309, indicated several of the Diocesan Commissions established by Clement the prior August had started their work. Predictably the Commissions were not uniform either in the speed with which they pursued their assignments or in their adherence to procedure and canon law. Diocesan commissions were to investigate but a separate province council would have final judgment as to each accused Templar. By design it was an awkward, slow, confusing process.

Bishop Marigny presided over the Commission for the Sens dioceses which included Paris and Corbeil where de Molay had been held following his arrest. Marigny actively supported Philip and chose to put a wide interpretation on the Commission's jurisdiction to interrogate individual Templars found within its jurisdiction and ignored all interpretations to the contrary, including Clement's.

Throughout France, including Sens, the usual outcome in the two phases of the process was predictable. If a Templar confessed to misdeeds in his interrogation before a diocesan commission, the provincial council absolved the man and accepted him back to the Church in the judgment phase. Those who did not confess were imprisoned. The course of the proceedings became well-known and most men found it convenient to simply confess and be absolved and reconciled.

Clement had made it clear the diocesan commissions lacked jurisdiction to try the Order itself. He gave that jurisdiction to various Papal Commissions. Those commissions varied greatly in their enthusiasm for the assignment and most were happy to let the Papal Commission in Paris take the lead.

Clement reserved for himself, personally, jurisdiction to try de Molay and the other Templar leaders.

De Molay and others had confessed to several religious irregularities such as hearing confessions and granting absolution, or giving last rites to fellow Templars before or after a battle when a priest was not available. These actions were acknowledged as sins or offenses against the Church over which the Church, not the King, had plenary powers to punish or forgive. Clement had absolved de Molay on all offenses.

De Molay and others also confessed to having knowledge that other matters, commonly considered unnatural perversions, had taken place in some Templar initiations. But de Molay and the others steadfastly denied ever participating in such practices. These were not sins or offenses against the Church but were illegal practices and therefore within the King's authority to prosecute. Philip alleged Boniface had committed the same offenses and threatened the Church with a public trial. Now he used the charges against the Templar Order.

De Molay had told Clement of the problem before the arrests and we still had every expectation Clement would fulfill his promise to assist the Order in removing Templars who had committed such acts. The Order would continue, perhaps stronger for the cleansing.

It was, as de Molay had said, a brilliant strategy. Divide jurisdictional authority over the Order as opposed to authority over individual Templars. Separate the determination of guilt and the passing of sentence. Scatter jurisdiction amongst the many dioceses and provinces depending upon the geographical location of the Templars being tried. In all matters he had clearly separated the authority to investigate from the power to pass judgment.

By adopting such a strategy Clement had done what he could to avoid concentrating power. No single commission or trial had jurisdiction over all Templars, the Order itself, and all alleged offenses. Some innocent Templars would undoubtedly suffer but many more would be saved. In the end, the most wicked would be removed but the Order and most all of the Templars would survive.

The year 1309 dragged on. De Molay had set our course, trust in Clement and in God. We had to let his strategy play out. Matthew sent me a note after one of our meetings. I'd voiced my impatience and favored more direct action. His note was not in French or Latin, it was in German, *beharren mit geduld*, persevere with patience. It became a common greeting and parting for Hans, Dieter and myself.

My efforts shifted to commercial affairs, usually arranging financial and insurance transactions for Lubeck merchants. We kept as current as we could with the events in France but information was always late and sketchy.

That July, Clement confirmed Henry's election as King of the Romans. In return Henry swore an oath to protect

Clement but it wasn't clear what Henry meant. We waited to see if Henry would act on his oath.

In August the most important Papal Commission, with jurisdiction over the activity of the Templar Order in Paris, began its work. Its first act was to invite Templars to appear on November 12 to defend the Order, then adjourned to wait. Predictably, no Templars appeared when the Commission reconvened on November 12. The invitation had all the signs of a trap.

Later that month when the Paris Commission interrogated de Molay he requested assistance, professing that he was untrained in legal matters, civil or canon. Two days later Nogaret paid an unexpected visit during a second interrogation session and de Molay, in his weakened condition, refused to defend the Order and asked to appear before Clement. Clement had ordered that he alone was permitted to judge de Molay, and de Molay trusted Clement with the Order and his life.

In the struggle between Philip and Clement the year of our Lord 1309 ended with little changed. Pieces had been moved, time had passed, but neither Philip nor Clement had gained a clear advantage. Clement had a set-piece strategy, legalistic proceedings based on divided jurisdictions and divided authority. De Molay and the Templars had no choice but to accept Clement's chosen course. Philip's strategy was dynamic and bold. We were about to find out just how bold and how devious.

If 1309 had been quiet 1310 was not.

When news that no one had appeared before the Papal Commission on November 12 to defend the Order finally reached the other European states the response was predictable. If the Templars would not defend their Order and if de Molay was physically unable to address the Commission then Philip would prevail by default. That could not be permitted.

In February and March close to six hundred Templars quietly slipped back into Paris. In spite of the numbers, neither Philip nor Marigny knew of their presence. The Paris Commission was shocked when the six hundred appeared before the Paris Commission to defend the Order. The public rallied behind the brave Templars. Philip was outraged. Marginy was embarrassed. The six hundred were taken into custody and held in Corbeil.

The Paris Commission called de Molay once more and again he refused to defend the Order and requested he be permitted to appear before Clement. It would be his last appearance until the very end, four years later. The other leaders followed de Molay's lead and refused, or were physically unable, to speak in defense of the Order. The five had been held in Corbeil outside Paris, tortured and kept on bread and water. After their appearance at the Paris Commission they were moved again. No one knew where.

Philip wasn't deterred. He had an ally in Bishop Marigny and Marigny controlled the Sens commission. Both Paris and the Corbeil were within the Sens dioceses. Philip still held the six hundred Templars at the Corbeil and had each of them interrogated before the Sens Diocesan Commission.

When the six hundred Templars were interrogated by the Paris Papal Commission most all defended the Order and denied they had ever heard of the alleged irregularities in the initiation rites until after the arrests.

Most, however, had previously confessed to knowledge of the alleged irregularities before a diocesan council. Those who had confessed had been absolved and reconciled by their provincial council. This was to be a critical point of Canon law.

Philip sprung his trap. Philip and Marigny charged each man as a relapsed heretic. If a Templar had confessed to irregularities in his prior interrogation or knowledge of such irregularities before a diocesan council but later denied that confession as part of his defense of the Order before the Paris Papal Commission there could be no doubt. Under Canon law he was by definition a relapsed heretic. And by Canon law the sentence for a relapsed heretic was death by burning at the stake.

In late April Philip ordered Bishop Marigny to burn four Templars as relapsed heretics. The Bishop enthusiastically complied. The six hundred Templars were herded into the Sens courtyard to watch as four of their members were burnt at the stake.

The brutal murder of four Templars failed to put an end to the Templar resistance. A few weeks later, in May of 1310, Philip and Marigny had the remaining Templars held at Corbeil watch as another fifty-four Templars were burnt at the stake as relapsed heretics.

After that there were few defenders of the Order, to do so would result in a death sentence. It also made it clear why de Molay and the other leaders had refused to defend the Order after their prior confessions. Philip would declare them to be relapsed heretics and under the color of Canon law they would be burned at the stake. Philip and Marigny had side-stepped Clement's jurisdictional strategy and reverted to the ancient laws regarding relapsed heretics.

Philip made it clear to the world, he was clever and he was ruthless. He would stop at nothing to obtain his desired ends. Neither Clement nor Henry, the Emperor of the Holy Roman Empire, could publically condone, much less openly support, relapsed heretics. It also made it evident that Clement could not control his bishops in the north of France.

Marigny subsequently had his diocesan council try two other Templar leaders who tried to defend the Order. Both were found guilty. One subsequently escaped with the assistance of Herr Stagg's organization. The other was imprisoned. We do not know his fate.

As the year 1310 came to an end there was little to encourage Templars. De Molay had put his trust and his life and that of the Order in Clement's hands. Clement's jurisdictional gambit had failed. By intrigue, force, and outright murder Philip had outmaneuvered him.

There was little to encourage us that 1311 would be any better for the imprisoned Templars. The Templar Order was slipping away. Our purpose to free the Holy Lands was losing public support every year. Our leadership was imprisoned and without energy or financial resources. A great many Templars were dead at the hands of Philip or the Church. Templar knights and brothers of every rank who had managed to survive were either scattered throughout Europe or held in a French prison.

The Paris Papal Commission ended in early June. It had done its work to Philip's satisfaction.

Early in 1311 Clement struck a devil's bargain with Philip. Philip agreed to end the trial against Pope Boniface. In return Clement granted absolution of Nogaret and the others who had abducted Boniface in Anagni, then beaten him to death. To save Boniface's reputation and avoid embarrassment of the Catholic Church, Clement gave absolution to the very men who had murdered Pope Boniface. The allegations against Boniface weren't disproven or even retracted. In the public's eyes Clement's absolution of Boniface's killers only confirmed the allegations against the deceased Pope were true.

In return Clement received one significant benefit, he would finally be permitted to begin the Council of Vienne. Clement planned to open the Council in mid-October, some three years after it was first announced. It was Clement's final opportunity to save the Order and its leaders.

We watched with dread that summer, waiting to see what Philip would do.

CHAPTER XV
Gisors

Less than a week after the Paris Commission's report reached Lubeck I was at the Lubeck docks concluding a transaction with a Danzig merchant when Alleric stepped down the gang plank of one of our transport ships. He waited until we finished then approached me. He was friendly but not smiling when he suggested we meet that evening. His demeanor, not his words, told me whatever he had to say was serious.

That evening the two of us had a private dinner in my quarters not far from Marienkirche. Dinner finished, the housekeeper, an old Templar no longer able to crew on our ships, cleared the table, poured us each a tankard of excellent red wine, left the half-full pitcher on the table and bid us a good evening.

Alleric came to the point. "Erik, I've talked with our friends in the other Baltic cities. It is our belief Vienne will be the end. Philip has the upper hand and Clement will not be able to preserve our sacred Order. Henry has his hands full with his own wars in Italy, he can't start a new war with Philip. Philip has the support of the barons, that's been clear since the Estates General in Tours three years ago. Clement has no allies.

"It's very possible Philip will take both his army and de Molay to Vienne. Philip would find it a great and useful victory to have Clement personally condemn de Molay and the others as relapsed heretics in the presence of the entire Council, and publicly condemn and abolish the Order. Have

Clement order de Molay and the others be publicly burnt as relapsed heretics."

I recalled de Molay had retracted his initial confession on at least one occasion. I nodded and said nothing. So far I agreed with his assessment.

"You met de Molay in Chinon, talked with him."

I nodded.

"The last we heard from him was March of 1310. Over a year ago."

I could see where this was going and didn't move or say a word. I had no idea why Alleric wanted me to return to France. A rescue perhaps?

"Our sources tell us he's now at the Chateau du Gisors, between Paris and Rouen.'

I didn't ask how he came to believe de Molay was in Gisors. It was a good bet Herr Stagg's organization was involved in obtaining that information.

"There's been new development. After the first arrests in 1307 many of our Templar brothers settled in Portugal with the Templars of Tomar under the protection of Portugal's king, Denis I. You may have heard one of the four fleets in La Rochelle harbor sailed for Portugal. Through our emissary to Portugal, Denis has now made it known that all Templars are welcome.

"The Emirate of Granada in southern Spain, Andalusia as it's known, dreams of rebuilding the Caliphate of Granada in all Spain and Portugal. Denis, rightfully in my opinion, fears a resurgence of the Islamic armies on the Iberian peninsula now that the Holy Lands are firmly in Muslim control. Denis' Christian reconquista of the entire peninsula will take years and he needs trained men-at-arms to build his army."

As he spoke, without realizing it I was up pacing the floor. Excited isn't a strong enough word. This would be a rebirth of our Order, a renewal of our sacred purpose. I'd come to love Lubeck and the Baltic commerce but this was what? A call from God? The words *'Deus Vult'* filled my head. I was, without thinking, repeatedly clenching and unclenching my fists. I could feel the hilt of my sword, the heft of it. *Deus Vult.* It was a call for the Army of Christ I'd pledged my life to. I could fight as a Templar once again. All the frustration, all the anger, could finally be answered with action. I felt an excitement I had not felt for years.

"You want de Molay to lead the Templars to Portugal. Leave France and Philip forever."

"Yes. A new Crusade, without Philip and if necessary without Clement."

I slowly regained some sense of calm but could not sit. "I must think. Dinner again? Here, tomorrow evening?."

"Yes. Try to sleep, Erik. I'll see you tomorrow at Vespers bells."

I sought the comfort of prayer and God's guidance that night as I hadn't in many years, then slept well until morning bells woke me. I was at peace, my duty was clear. Prayer and God's will showed the way.

That evening I told Alleric of my decision, "I will find de Molay. He must see now his old strategy has not worked. Clement has failed us and him. Worse, Clement has failed God. De Molay will see the Order's future now lies with Denis in Portugal. The threat of an Islamic resurgence is real to the Catholic people of both Spain and Portugal, they will support us."

"France has forgotten the Muslim invasion," Alleric said. "It's been free of the Caliphate since Martel defeated the Muslim armies at Tours almost six hundred years ago. Islam isn't a threat Philip personally fears. But perhaps with Denis and Clement's help we can make Philip and the people of

France realize the mullahs and sultans wish to come north again. And it would be better to let Denis stop them before they reach Philip's lands. To do that Denis will need the Templars. Perhaps we and Clement, with the help of his loyal bishops and priests, can convince the French people to demand Philip send the Templars to stop this new Islamic threat."

Alleric and I talked late into that evening and the next. It became clear Alleric, Wilhelm and Matthew had spent a great deal of time and thought on this matter.

The following week Alleric had the same conversation with Hans and Dieter. He met with each of us alone. Alleric explained he did not want any of us to feel pressured into going simply because the others agreed to go.

In early July, 1311 Hans, Dieter and I were back in Le Havre but not as wandering, unemployed men of the sea. We were confident enough to transform ourselves into modestly prosperous Lubeck merchants with goods from the Baltic to sell in towns along the Seine as far as Paris. Lubeck had become a highly respected city with a reputation throughout Europe. Just being recognized as a Lubeck merchant was enough to open the doors of merchants in other cities.

Since our successful return from Chinon and Nantes we had established banking connections in La Havre, and other French cities, through the House of de Veron. References from Monsieur LeFeete, the crown's well-known, well-connected, and dependably corrupt trade representative in Nantes, had been of great help with letters of introductions to other equally corrupt port representatives who controlled and set taxes on imports and exports.

I took a certain pleasure in using the corrupt French commercial practices to aid the Templar cause. Every corrupt transaction weakened Philip's government and reduced trade.

Every arbitrary act undercut the people's confidence in Philip's representatives.

Every added tax, regulation, fee or bribe added to the cost his people paid for the goods they wanted. And reduced the proceeds received for the goods sold. All of it built a undercurrent of distrust in Philip's reign, a cynicism that grew over time.

Alleric required that we stop briefly at Nantes before making our way to Le Havre but gave us no reason other than on a specified date we were to pick up a man and drop off three others. Nantes is south of Le Havre and would delay our journey to Gisors. Alleric must have had his reasons and I suspected it all had something to do with Herr Stagg's organization. We were told not to ask questions, the less we knew the better. Dropping off the three men in the dead of night is easy and involves very little risk to anyone but we were instructed to meet the man at the Fille Par La Mer.

On the designated date in Nantes the three of us stopped at the Fille Par La Mer for a tankard. Hans stayed outside as our lookout while Dieter and I went in to meet the mysterious man we were to take with us.

As Dieter and I were taking out time with the first tankard a worried looking man, a sailor by his clothes, edged into the room as if apologizing for his presence and trying not to be noticed. His tattered clothes, unruly hair and beard, and distinct limp gave him the appearance of a man down on his luck and beyond his best years. Mostly he looked only at the floor as if afraid of falling but frequently glanced over his shoulder at the door. He clumsily took a seat at a small table in the farthest corner from the door and placed his wooden tankard before him on the table.

It wasn't until he looked around the room as if looking for someone to wait on him that we saw the patch over his left eye. I wanted a look at his tankard to be sure it was our man. He had just taken his seat when three tuffs came through the tavern door, stopped and looked around the room. When they caught sight of the man in the far corner they spread out and started his way. Although the poor man saw them coming, his bad leg made escape impossible. He was cornered.

One of the three men shouted at the injured man, "Got you now, you weaselly bastard. Thought you could get away, did you? Well, I'll break that damn leg now."

As the man was being dragged towards the door I saw his tankard on the table and quickly made my way across the room for a look at it. Even before I reached it I could see a beautifully carved fleur de lis and motioned to Dieter to follow the men.

The room was full of men drinking, laughing, gaming. All noisily ignoring what was happening so I shouted, "Hey, leave the poor bastard alone. He ain't hurting anyone."

It got everyone's attention. Several in the crowd must have thought Dieter and I intended to come to the injured man's defense and rose to join in what promised to be a good brawl. With that the mood in the room changed from curiosity to anger. Three tuffs were dragging their lone, defenseless quarry to the door.

The injured man called out, "Herr Stagg."

The largest of the three men turned to the crowd and announced in a booming voice, "Hear now. Quiet down and let us do our business. This man is wanted. He's a traitor and a criminal, as is any man who interferes with his arrest."

There was a great deal of mumbling and cursing but I expect there were several men in the tavern with outstanding warrants and a great many more who wanted no part of a brawl with the authorities. No one seemed to know the man, so no one interfered. It was easier to continue their carouse and curse the law.

The man was being dragged out the door at the same time Hans was trying to make his way in. In the jostling the leader roughly pushed Hans aside and yelled at him, "Out of the way, scum."

On the street outside we watched the three men drag the man behind a building. The three of us trotted to the corner where the four men had turned and could hear the sounds of a beating.

The same booming voice we'd heard in the tavern yelled, "You Templar bastards. Queers all of you. Where're the others? Philip wants to know where your Herr Stagg and the others are."

Each pause was punctuated by the sound of fist on flesh, followed by groans.

Misericordes in hand we rushed the men. We came out of the shadows without warning. I don't think they realized what was happening until the agony of a blade in the guts reached their brains. It was short work.

We robbed the three to make it look like they were murdered in a robbery. By then the man was unconscious so Dieter picked him up, threw him over his shoulder, and we made our way back to the safety of our ship. We knew his recovery would take time but he would be well taken care of in Lubeck when the ship returned home. The experience was another reminder of Philip and Nogaret's determination to wipeout the Templars. It seemed they had agents everywhere.

Our preparations in Le Havre took the better part of a week. Transferring our cargo from cog to barge was the easiest task and as one would expect de Verons' representative in Le Havre was both polite and efficient, requiring only a single day to complete our financial arrangements. Philip's port representative in Le Havre, however, required a full two days to inspect our goods, negotiate his own fee, set the appropriate tax for Philip's share, and complete the documents necessary to satisfy all the officials we might encounter between Le Havre and Paris with a side journey to Gisors.

While Hans and I dealt with banking arrangements and port authorities, Dieter and our crew were busy with other matters. He purchased a fine Seine barge, some forty-five feet in length with two lateen sails and a shallow draft. We needed a craft wide enough to be stable and carry a sizable cargo but narrow enough to be rowed efficiently by our crew of fourteen Templars.

We expected and needed a financially successful voyage with our cargo of silver and copper from the north Baltic lands, furs and skins from the Rus wild lands, fine Flemish fabrics, and whale and walrus ivory from Scotland and the northern islands,.

Our crew of Templars was an advantage in some ways, all were entirely trustworthy. But not entirely helpful, most were in their late thirties and early forties. It was an unfortunate fact. Since the fall of Acre in 1291, a generation before, few young men were inclined to join the Order. After the October 1307 arrests there had been none at all. Most of the younger Templars had not made their way to the Baltic but had sought refuge elsewhere in Europe.

Mid-day as our barge pulled to the Saint Adela dock, I looked forward to seeing our old friends and the opportunity to hear their views of events since our last visit. The tavern hadn't changed, smoke curled from the single chimney, the beautifully carved sign above the door had been recently painted, the quoits court beneath the old elm was in excellent condition, and the two wagon roads leading to the dock appeared to be well used. Near the dock two wagons loaded with firewood and a small quantity of harvest goods waited for the Seine barge to Rouen and Paris.

I felt very much at peace in Saint Adela. These were good people who wanted to live in peace, indifferent for the most part to the politics of greater Europe. These were people Templars protected. I didn't feel hunted in Saint Adela as I had in Paris, Chinon and Nantes. I felt removed from Philip's hatred.

I was confident our Order had a new mission, keep the Iberian peninsula free of Islam's rule and safe for Christendom. Templars would be permitted to leave France in return for the forgiveness of the debt Philip owed us, the transfer our lands to Philip, and our sacred promise never to return to France. I wondered how Philip or Clement could find fault with that.

If Philip released the Templars to Denis, and if Clement blessed our new cause, we had no further need of either. Clement would, I believed, bless both our association with our new sovereign, Denis, and our new cause.

I was confident de Molay would agree. I just needed to find him, meet with him and tell him the good news. We could leave France with a clean conscience, our enterprises in the Baltic had generated sufficient revenue to repay all the sums people had placed with the Templars and lost when improperly loaned to Philip. We'd already made good on all of it.

I stepped into the tavern with a light heart, Hans and Dieter close behind. Four young men, all laughing, sat around a table. I recognized Gaidar and Luc but not the other two. Guidar was holding a baby.

The man standing behind the long, wooden bar stopped his laughter, cocked his head, and took a long look at the three of us.

I stopped and grinned at Gaspard as he stepped from behind the bar, wiped his hands on his apron and called out, "Michelle, put on some eggs and plenty of bacon. Boys, pull up a table for our old friends, fellow sons of Rollo."

Michelle, with her same lovely smile, appeared from the kitchen. "Oh boys, it's so good to see you."

As she hugged each of us a new face appeared from the kitchen, pretty smile, blonde hair. As she stepped forward it was clear she was very pregnant.

Gaidar rose, baby in one arm, and waved with the other arm to the pregnant girl. "Elsie, come out and meet the three men I told you about."

At the same time a man I didn't recognize stepped through the door, looked around first at Gaspard, then at Gaidar. "Is that the barge to Rouen?"

Gaidar laughed. "No, father. It won't be here for another hour or so. It's our old friends, the ones who saved us in Rouen."

Gaidar's father stepped up, looked me squarely in the eyes, vigorously shook my hand, grasped my right elbow with his other hand, then as he turned to Hans he said, "Well then, you're all friends of mine. I'm Robert. Gaidar and Ulf are my boys. Thank God you were there to help in their time of need."

"Where's Ulf?" I asked.

Robert grinned. "Oh, he's visiting a young girl down the valley. He's seen how happy his brother is and he's jealous. Wants a wife of his own."

Michelle said, "Elsie and I are going back to the kitchen now. You all look so thin. Enjoy your ale but if you tell these boys what you've been up to you'll just have to repeat it for the two of us so wait until your food is ready then we'll all hear your story."

With that she looked out the open window. "My what a fine barge. Is that yours?"

I nodded. "We've got trade goods for Rouen and Paris, and Gisors, too."

"My, haven't you prospered," Michelle said with a smile. "Well, tell your crew to come in. Such wealthy merchants must feed their men. Gaspard will help with the cooking. Luc will handle the ale and wine. Gaidar will introduce his two friends, then you can fetch your crew. Elsie and I will get the food started."

I stood there looking dumb founded.

Michelle laughed as she said, "And you'll pay the bill."

With a grin Gaspard shrugged as he got up to follow Michelle into the kitchen. I interpreted his grin as, "What can I do? She's so beautiful. And it looks like you can afford to pay the bill."

I nodded, grinned, put my leather purse on the table and took a long drink of ale.

One of Luc's young friends watched the whole exchange then asked, "Going to Gisors. How will you get there?"

"La Roche-Guyon and L'Epte road. Is there a better way?"

He shrugged. "Might be. Have you hired wagons?"

"No. We'd planned to hire them in La-Roche. Do you know someone?"

"Yes, I do but that's not the best way. This time of year it's faster and easier to use L'Epte not the road. Flat bottom skiffs and draft horses, one on each side of the river works very well. So it's better to start at Vernon. It's a small town west of La Roche."

He leaned over the table and reached out to shake my hand. "My name is Rolf but my friends call me Le Loup."

Rolf put his arm on the younger man next to him. "This is my brother, Giles. Our father farms land north of here but we don't own it. That's our wagon next to Gaidar's. I'm on my way to Rouen with the next barge. Giles will stay with our father."

Rolf looked at his brother who was obviously not happy he could not go to Rouen, "Maybe next time, Giles. Father needs your help now."

Giles frowned but nodded. He seemed to understand.

I looked at Rolf, about Luc's age, stronger, a thick head of black hair, and a little taller. He wasn't grinning about the nick name but I saw nothing that would explain such a name. "Le Loup, uh. Like the wolf? You from Gisors?"

Rolf smiled. "Yes, and no. Yes, like the wolf. No, I'm not from Gisors. But I've been there many times. I know the area. Have you been there before?"

"No. We could use a capable guide."

I hadn't decided whether I liked Le Loup or not. He seemed bright and ambitious but perhaps too cocky. Maybe he'd over estimated his own abilities.

Luc apparently saw my doubt, and chuckled as he interrupted, "We call him Le Loup because he's always looking for a way to make money. The way a wolf looks for food. And he knows the area as well as any of us. He'll get you there and back, in good shape."

Both Dieter and Hans gave me an almost imperceptible nod of agreement.

"Well, Le Loup, do you know where we can hire two skiffs, four draft horses and four reliable men to assist us? The men must be from the immediate area, Vernon, La Roche, Guyon or Gisors."

"I do. But we haven't settled on the fee."

"We're not used to being cheap and won't start now. I believe your fee will be on the high end of reasonable. We can tolerate that, if your services are all I expect them to be. Do we have an understanding?"

Rolf's eyes were on mine when he nodded and added, "Yes, how long will you be in Rouen?"

"Four days, if all goes well."

"Good. I'll take less than a day to sell our goods. After I'm done in Rouen I'll continue on to Vernon to make all the arrangements, then meet you back in Rouen. I'll let you know what the fees are then. Half to be paid in Rouen and the balance after I get you back to Vernon from Gisors."

"Excellent. We'll be staying at the Two Maces in Rouen."

I watched Rolf and Giles as our crew ate. Giles said little, mostly smiled and nodded. Rolf stayed close to his brother and I had the impression Giles not only depended on Rolf, he was dependent on him. I wondered how Giles would do if Rolf was with us.

I took Luc aside. "Giles seems to depend on his brother. Will he be alright if Rolf comes with us to Gisors?"

Luc nodded. "We all look out for Giles. He's a nice kid but slow. Their mother died a couple years ago and their father drinks, a lot. Not mean but, well, he depends on Rolf, too. Gaspard and Ulf will take care of him, get him home. He can always stay here. Mom makes sure he and Rolf have enough to eat."

Rouen was as busy as I remembered, it took several hours for our turn at the docks. While Dieter managed the barge and the unloading of our goods Hans and I paid a visit to Rouen's trade commissioner to present our documents from Le Havre and pay fees required for the sale of imported goods within the city. Then we made arrangements with the market manager for a large stall with very good town traffic. We also hired three local barkers to advertise our goods throughout the town. With Dieter's supervision, our disciplined crew, and a few local laborers so as to not offend the market manager, the entire process didn't take long. By the time we heard the Vespers bell we were ready for business the next morning.

In between all the business matters that needed attention Hans, Dieter and I stopped at the Two Maces and took rooms for the time we expected to be in town. Andre was running the inn. Henri was not well and spent most days in his bed. When I asked about Milun, Andre assured me our old friend would be in for his usual tankard that evening, probably in the company of one or two other men from the castle.

Andre made a point of adding, "Milun's fine but the others have a hearty dislike of Templars. So I make a point to never tell them what the Two Maces above the door stand for."

We had quite a reunion that evening. Milun was in with two others from the chateau. Their uniforms were identical but the similarities ended there. Both men worked in the Rouen chateau's donjon. Milun still worked in the administrative office.

The man Milun introduced as Mateo was as large as Jacques Bonnet. He was a very rough looking man, missing three front teeth and proudly displaying a nasty scar above his right ear. Both the scar and missing teeth, he bragged, came from a Flemish ax. The other man, Alain, was just plain fat and from the looks of him not too bright. He also had a few missing teeth but offered no explanation for their loss.

We talked of Jacques and Greta. Both were happy and well when Milun had seen them in Paris just two months before. Milun said his friend Marc Lafevre, we did not see him while we were in Paris, was no longer at Notre Dame. He was working at Corbeil now. When Milun explained he'd heard the Sens bishop had need of experienced military men Mateo and Alain burst out in laughter.

I gave them a quizzical look and Mateo responded with a wide-eyed grin. "Templars, Bishop Marigny likes to burn a few every now and then."

Alain watched Mateo's expression then mimicked it, rubbed his hands together as he added, "Yeah! Likes to burn 'em."

Eventually the conversation got around to our intended visit to Gisors. All three men were well acquainted with the town. Milun explained he always stayed in the Chateau's military barracks when in Gisors but recommended we stay at L'auberge de Gisors. It was close to both the Chateau and the market square. He liked their fare better than what was served at the Chateau mess hall.

"Milun's right," Mateo assured us. "The Chateau food is terrible but Gisors is a great town. There's more to Gisors than the Chateau and L'auberge. Gisors women are warm and their wine is excellent. And when they have prisoners who must be interrogated. I'm allowed to be present."

Alain grinned. "Yeah! Warm wine. Women and interrogations." Alain nodded enthusiastically. "I like Gisors."

Mateo gave his companion a disgusted glance and shook his head.

"Have you been to many? Interrogations," I asked.

Mateo nodded and took a drink. "Yes, yes. Quite a few. Mostly Templars."

Alain nodded. "Me, too. Mostly."

Dieter leaned closer, eyes wide with feigned curiosity. "Templars, they have Templars there?"

Mateo nodded. "Yes. I've seen them myself. Even their leader, what's his name?"

"De Molay?" Milun answered.

"That's it, de Molay."

"What's he like?" Hans asked.

Mateo snorted. "Old, weak. They don't bother interrogating him anymore. He's already confessed to enough. I hear Philip wants him dead. But not just yet."

Mateo took a another drink. "The old man just talks to himself. Rambles on in Latin."

Alain watched Mateo then took a drink and added, "He's afraid of me. Afraid to look at me. When I'm around he just shakes his head, turns away and mutters to himself in Latin."

Mateo shrugged. "Well, sometimes they allow a priest or a monk to minister to them. Philip says even prisoners should be allowed communion, and confession, too. From what I hear the Templars have a lot to confess."

"We do that, too," Milun added. "The friars, Franciscans and Dominicans, any mendicant Order. We provide them shelter and food for a night and permit them to minister to our prisoners. Philip ordered it."

I recalled our efforts and deceptions to gain entrance to the Paris Enclos and my injuries. The thought occurred to me that maybe all we had to do was ask for shelter for the night and permission to minister to their prisoners.

"How long ago did Philip order that?" I asked.

Milun shrugged. "I don't recall when we got the order. Not long, why?"

"No reason really. I'd heard he had a problem with Clement and the Church."

Mateo nodded and laughed. "Oh, he's got a problem with 'em alright. But it makes him look good to the people. They call 'em Philip le Belle. He's such a kind, gentle king, see how he helps the poor. He even helps prisoners."

Throughout the evening Milun was strangely quiet. I thought he was embarrassed by his two companions. We made certain there was plenty to drink and eat that night, then invited the three of them to join us again the following evening. Mateo and Alain might provide information we would find useful.

I took my mid-day meal at the Two Maces the next day and had just sat down when Milun came through the door, saw where I was sitting and immediately joined me.

"I don't have much time, Erik. Last night was difficult. I apologize for Mateo and Alain. They're not really friends. We work together. I have to get along with 'em."

"Don't worry about that, I understand."

"I couldn't tell you last night but I'll be leaving the castle. Three months ago my officer was taken ill. I don't think he has long to live. The new man has his own people, men like Mateo and Alain."

I nodded. That explained a lot.

"I thought there might be room on your crew. I know the Seine and I've visited many of Philip's chateaus in the north of France. And I served with men in many of them. If you're selling goods in those towns I could be of help."

It was clear Milun could be helpful but he had no idea of our real purpose.

"Milun, we could use you, but not to row the barge. We've sold more goods today than anticipated and we still have three more days here. Then we're off to Gisors. If Gisors is as profitable then we won't go to on Paris. We'll buy goods in Gisors and in Vernon, then take them west to Le Havre to sell them. After that? Depends. Do you want to travel? God knows we travel more than half of each year."

"I have no future in Rouen and nothing holds me here. My parents died over the winter and my officer is dying. Every day he's worse. He's wasting away. You've prospered and you see new places. I still have quite a few good years. I've thought of buying an inn or a tavern, somewhere quiet. But I'm not ready yet. What do you say?"

"When we finish in Gisors, and Paris if necessary, we'll stop back in Rouen. You're welcome to join us then, if you still want to."

Late in the afternoon two days later I watched Rolf as he stepped off the west bound barge and made his way through the busy, noisy crowd and across the market square to our location. I couldn't help but laugh. Confident didn't express it. There were no apologies necessary as he moved easily without disrupting people and without letting them impede his own progress.

"Everything is ready for you," Rolf announced in a very matter of fact tone as he shook my hand and handed me a written bill.

"We'll be ready to go in the morning," I told him. "But tonight Dieter, Hans and I are having dinner at the Two Maces, can you join us?"

I looked at the bill. It was as I had expected. I nodded and added with a smile, "We'll have half for you at dinner tonight. We also want you to meet Milun this evening. I think he'll be joining us at some point. I believe the two of you would work well together."

Rolf smiled. "Of course, thank you. I look forward to seeing all of you."

On our first day in Rouen the three of us had arranged with Andre for modifications to the Two Maces. We told him of our experiences with several well-furnished, prosprous inns like Emdenhaus and Coeur de Lion and the gaming rooms we'd seen. Gaming rooms were becoming very popular in larger towns.

With Andre's approval and the help of our skilled carpenters and masons, and our financing, the improvements included a private meeting and dining room. It would not be as large or comfortable as the Emdenhaus or the Coeur de Lion but it would be more comfortable than any other Rouen inn. The two upper floors of the old inn would also be improved. During the day the meeting room could be used for meetings or private dinners. In the evenings it could serve as a gaming room. We were all confident the changes would draw merchant patrons and the country aristocracy to the Two Maces.

Unknown to Andre our improvements to the gaming room included a hidden opening to a narrow tunnel leading to a vertical passage way, much like a chimney. The passage was just large enough for a man to climb a ladder to a small room on the third floor. The little room had two double bunks and a crawl way to the roof. From the roof it was easy to get to the roof of any of the adjoining buildings. From there we would have access to an alley some distance from the Two Maces. If necessary we could hide for an indefinite time in the Two Maces, then escape across one of the roof tops and down one of several alley ways.

This was not difficult work for men trained and experienced in the building of complex fortifications but the work could not be completed before we left for Vernon so we hired ten local men for our barge. Our ten best carpenters and masons stayed in Rouen to finish the work while the rest of us went on to Gisors. By the time we returned the work would be completed, providing us a safe house in Rouen. And Andre's inn would have the best accommodations in Rouen and a new private room suitable for prosperous Rouen merchants as well as merchants and aristocrats passing through town on their way to Paris or Le Havre.

Dinner with Milun and Rolf went better than I had hoped. Our intention was nothing more than to introduce the two men but they got on very well. My personal view was that Rolf had unique skills and Milun, unique experience. And we might have need of both.

Dieter, Hans and I knew how difficult our task would be but there was no reason to burden either Milun or Rolf. Without being told, somehow both men seemed to understand we were involved in something more than commerce. Better they not know the true purpose of our journey, until and unless it became necessary.

We reached Vernon on the Seine's south bank three days later. We were met by an old dock master who greeted Rolf warmly and assured us everything was prepared as Rolf had required. Our barge was tied to a sturdy dock and our goods off loaded into two well-made skiffs.

I took Rolf aside. "I'm certain you've this planned well but Gisors is on the other side of the Seine and I don't see any horses."

Rolf grinned. "We take the skiffs up river to L'Epte. That's where we'll find the horses. I've arranged for your extra men to catch the next barge back to Rouen, it'll be along any time now. Those men over there in the shade of that oak are some of the men I hired. As you wanted they're all local. They know the river and have towed other craft up L'Epte to Gisors."

Directly across from a village Rolf called Port-Villez, we rowed the skiffs into L'Epte's shallow mouth. On each bank were two enormous draft horses and their handlers, one team for each skiff. Within minutes the tow ropes were attached and we and the skiffs were being towed up river. Where dense stands of trees and bushes lined the river on each side, which was most of the time, the horses and their handlers simply waded into the knee deep water and continued on.

From time to time the hired hand in a skiff would fend off a rock or tree limb but little human effort was required by anyone in the skiffs. It wasn't fast but with our heavy loads it was faster and more comfortable than an ox cart. We stopped for the night at the small village of Saint Clair sur Epte and reached Gisors shortly before noon the following day, early enough to settle in the rooms at L'auberge de Gisors Rolf had reserved for us.

Rolf walked Hans and me to the town's trade commissioner who smiled at Rolf, examined our certificates, set reasonable fees for the sale of our goods, then personally helped us make arrangements with the market manager for a stall. In the meantime four of the local men in our skiff crew circulated through the market hawking our goods. The men knew the town and the people of Gisors knew them. We were open for business the following morning.

That first evening the three of us had dinner with Rolf at L'auberge de Gisors and explained that Hans and I had business to attend to. It would take us two or three days. When our task was finished we would all move on either to Paris or back to Rouen.

Rolf nodded and said nothing.

Before dawn the next morning Hans and I slipped out of the inn, crossed town and took a room in one of the poorer districts on the outskirts of Gisors. By mid-morning we were once again Black Friars, mendicant monks on our way to Paris.

That afternoon we made our way through the busy market square towards the Chateau. As we passed our stall I intentionally brushed the arm of one of our crew. When he turned to see who had bumped into him I bowed my head, begged his forgiveness and made the sign of the cross. My face was hidden by the day's dirt and grime, my head covered by the hood of my habit.

He smiled as he said, "Forgive me, padre. May God be with you."

He hadn't recognized me. I was comfortable we fit our role.

An hour before Vespers bells we approached the front gates of the Chateau du Gisors and asked for a night's shelter.

The sergeant of the guard introduced himself as Sergeant Dumot. He seemed sympathetic to our request but told us he must first have his officer's approval before opening the gate for us. While we waited for the officer's decision I studied the Sergeant. He was middle aged and a little taller and heavier than Milun. He reminded me of a combination of Milun's meticulous attention to his uniform and appearance and Jacques Bonet's booming voice and brash joy of his surroundings

Once the officer approved our request, Sergeant Dumot motioned for his men to open the gate then waved us in with a grin.

Sergeant Dumot put his arm over my shoulders and said, "Welcome, Brothers. My own older brother, Hans, is of your Order. Come in, you're just in time. Vespers bells will ring soon and then there'll be hot food in the mess. I'll have one of my men find you a bed for the night, then take you to the mess for something to eat."

Hans grinned back. "Thank you. I'm Brother Hans and this is Brother Erik."

Dumot gave Hans a bear hug. "Brother Hans, what a coincidence. Welcome to the Chateau du Gisors. We'll talk in the morning. We're about to change the guard. Right now get settled, wash up from your day's work, then you must eat and get a good night's rest."

Sergeant Dumot assigned one of his young men, hardly more than a boy, to hunt down a space for us to bed down and escort us to the mess.

On our way to the mess I asked, "Do you have prisoners?"

"Oh, yes," he answered with a laugh. "We always have prisoners."

"Whom do we ask for permission to minister to them?"

"Just ask Sergeant Dumont in the morning. He'll get you permission. He likes mendicants. His brother's one, you know. He lets all the mendicants minister to the prisoners, just ask Sergeant Dumot."

"When does he come on duty?"

"With morning bells. He's very punctual. The guard changes with the morning bells and Vespers bells. You're fortunate to have come while he's still on duty."

I couldn't help but think this was easier than having my brains bashed in by a thief outside the Paris Enclos or cleaning waste buckets and eating slop in Chinon. On the other hand our experience in the Concierge was on the whole pleasant but unproductive. This visit, I hoped, would be productive without physical injury or suffering.

Hans and I rose before dawn for our morning prayers, then waited in the bailey for morning bells and Sergeant Dumot. At the first bell the officer in charge of the night watch stepped crisply out of the administrative offices followed by his sergeant of the night guard. Close behind him was the officer for the day watch and a half step behind him was Sergeant Dumot, smiling, beard neatly trimmed, uniform in perfect order, hair combed.

As Dumot approached, his men formed into two lines with their eyes on their Sergeant. Sergeant Dumot 's smile didn't really disappear but his demeanor changed. He clearly enjoyed his duties and took them seriously. In the morning shade of the tour we watched as he called his squad of thirty men into two smart lines for individual inspection. All were ready. It was hard to believe any of Dumot's men would not be ready for his inspection.

Satisfied his men were ready for duty Dumot turned smartly and saluted his officer who returned the salute and nodded to Dumot. Dumot called out orders for the flag of King Philip to be hauled to the peak.

With the formal ceremony completed, the Sergeant led his men in a column of twos for the changing of the guard at the dozen gates and guard enclosures along the fortresses outer wall. At each enclosure two men stepped forward to man the position and the two men relieved from their duty fell in to line behind the sergeant of the night guard.

Hans and I waited until the guard had been changed and the men were settled in their duties to Sergeant Dumot's satisfaction, then we stepped up and asked if we could minister to the prisoners.

He smiled broadly. "Yes, yes, by all means. They're being fed as we speak. Sergeant Moreau's in charge of the donjon. It will take a while so be patient. I'll let you know when you can go."

With that Dumot sent the same young man who helped us the day before to let Sergeant Moreau know our request. A short time later the man reported Sergeant Moreau would send one of his men to let Sergeant Dumot know when we could begin our ministries.

It was almost mid-morning when the young man escorted us up the steep hill to the inner donjon. Even with the circular walk it was an exhausting climb. An attack directly up the hill would leave the best of men too exhausted to be more than an easy target for a crossbow from the donjon's arrow slits. Any plans to rescue a prisoner here by force would fail.

Sergeant Moreau, arms crossed over his thick chest, smiled as he greeted us at the donjon's heavy, narrow door but said nothing. It would be foolish to think one might squeeze by him, he filled the door-way. As I came closer I saw he smiled with his mouth, not his eyes. It wasn't the smile of a friend, it was more in the nature of a challenge.

As I looked at the man my first thought was no one would enter his domain without his consent or a fierce battle. He stood two hands above me and must have weighted a quarter more than me, and all of it muscle.

Still winded, I smiled as I huffed out, "Greetings brother Moreau, er, I mean Sergeant Moreau. In the name of our dear Lord Jesus Christ, savior of the world, may we enter and minister to those poor souls held in the donjon?"

Sergeant Moreau nodded but his expression didn't change. "They've eaten so now's good but don't take all day about it. Charles, he's inside, will escort you to the cells."

With that he stepped aside just enough to let Hans and me slip by one at a time, if we turned sideways. Once inside I heard the door close, and the outside bar drop, and with it the light of day. Reflexively I made the sign of the cross. As my eyes became accustomed to what little light made its way through the arrow slits, I saw a man I assumed must be Charles by the door.

Charles, already accustomed to the half-light, led us to the frighteningly narrow, stone stairs that corkscrewed up the towers walls. We carefully followed him single file to the donjon's second level and its cells.

At the top of the stairs Charles pulled up an old three-legged stool, sat down with a thump and waved us toward the cells, me to the left, Hans to the right. At the first cell door I knocked softly but got no response except the sound of snoring. With my knock on the second door I heard a groan and knocked again, louder. The response was simply, "Go away. Leave me in peace."

I looked at Charles and shrugged, then moved on to the third door. As I leaned close to knock softly I heard the sound of a hymn, a Templar hymn of Christ's salvation. I knocked and the hymn stopped. "Yes?"

I chanted in Latin as softly as I could yet loudly enough to be heard within the cell, "I come from the East. Have you traveled?"

Within the cell someone shuffled closer to the door and chanted his answer in Latin, "Yes, in search of the light of Christ."

"*Deus Vult*," I responded.

I looked over at Charles. He was half asleep so I called to him, "This one's awake and wants to pray. Can you let me in, with God's blessing?"

Charles frowned but nodded and unlocked the cell door, then shut it behind me and locked it. With that he yelled, "Call when you're finished, I'll let you out."

The way he said it left the matter in doubt.

I turned to face the prisoner standing six feet from me and dropped the hood of my habit. In front of me was our Grand Master de Molay. He stepped closer, just a foot away, to examine my face, then smiled. "It's you."

He'd spoken in French and I shook my head. "In Latin."

He nodded and responded in Latin, "Have you come to vex me once again?"

"No. Our situation has changed. Please kneel, we're in prayer. I've come to minister to the prisoners."

The old man knelt, awkwardly, beside his cot. "Did you bring more of that wonderful venison?"

I handed him three slices. I pulled my hood over my head and knelt beside him as if in prayer. "Denis, King of Portugal, needs Templars, wants Templars. Granada's Caliphate is on the rise once more. Denis has offered us sanctuary and a new

Order. Our purpose would be to preserve Christian lands from the Islamic curse."

De Molay nodded as he slowly chewed the first slice of venison, then sat back against the cell wall, his head on his chest, his eyes closed, his breathing slow and deep. He didn't move or respond for a long time and I became concerned.

Finally, he looked up at me. "So we're defending Europe from the caliphates. What of the Holy Lands?"

"Neither the Pope nor any of the European kings, except Denis, not even the Emperor of the Holy Roman Empire have the stomach for a return to the Holy Lands. Perhaps later. But now we must preserve Christianity in Andalusia and the whole Iberian Peninsula. Pray God will provide another Charles Martel. Christianity needs a hammer. And we must rebuild our Order, then maybe we can retake the Levant."

In my mind I saw Denis as that Hammer, leading the Templars with de Molay's help, driving the Muslim Sultans, Caliphs and Mullahs from Portugal and Spain.

De Molay thought a moment. "Will Philip give us safe passage and will Clement bless and preserve our Order, and its independence?"

"We believe Clement will do what he can. Clement might threaten Philip with excommunication to preserve the Christians in Spain and Portugal. We're confident Clement will use this opportunity to dismiss all charges against the Order and against all Templars.

"Philip, on the other hand, has all our property and will do anything to keep it. He would fear we would eventually return to France stronger than ever. Nogaret will advise against it, he has defeated the Templars and won't willingly see us rise again."

"Nogaret, the Devil himself. What has Philip done since we last talked in Chinon? What has Clement done? I hear nothing."

De Molay slowly ate the rest of the venison as I told him of events since I last saw him, the back and forth of Philip's and Clement's moves, of what Henry, King of the Romans, had or had not done to aid our cause, and the coming Council of Vienne.

De Molay said nothing so after a long moment I said, "When we talked in Chinon you told me of the Holy Grail. I've thought of that many times. You've lost trust in Clement. All that has happened must test your faith, do you still possess the Grail?"

De Molay nodded with that worldly smile. "Yes, I still possess it. Erik, we must not test God. We must not demand that He act only in ways we understand. You once told me of the wonderful dog you and your father had. You told me how smart the dog was, how it seemed to understand how you felt, and how it would follow your commands."

I nodded as I recalled the dog and the recollection brought a smile.

De Molay continued, "Do you think your dog understood how and why your father built his forge, lit his fires, made horse shoes, or repaired a broken wagon wheel?"

"No," I responded.

"Yet the dog trusted you and your father. The dog did not demand you act in accordance with its ability to comprehend your actions. Isn't there a greater difference between you and God than there was between you and your dog?"

Again I nodded.

"Did your dog require that you act only in ways it understood? And if you didn't it would turn away from you or leave you or stop following your commands or lose faith that you would continue to feed and shelter it?"

"No."

"Then we must not require God act only in ways we understand."

He thought a moment, then smiled. "How is the Baltic?"

"Commerce and trade are growing. We've prospered. Enough to both repay all those whose money was given to our care and to help our brothers in need. Our enterprises provide enough to arm and provide for all the knights, sergeants, troops and equipment Denis will need."

"And what of the bishops and barons in the Baltic?"

"They leave us alone. We pay taxes to the barons and the lesser lords to support their troops and castles. And we tithe enough to build great cathedrals. So they leave us alone. We're the goose that lays the golden egg. We build wealth without war, without blood. And without cost to either."

"Do they know you're Templars?"

"If they do they say nothing of it."

De Molay listened intently, silently, as I described our victories over the svear pirates, our banking and insurance activities, escort services on land and at sea, and our shipping.

My explanation of our activities since the October arrests was interrupted by banging on the cell door. I rose and saw Charles peering through the cell's inner door.

Charles looked at me with his little squinty eyes and snapped, "Don't spend all your time with one prisoner. The others need your services, too. I can't eat till you're done. Your brother, I forget his name, he's already seen four prisoners."

As he unlocked the cell door I heard him mumble, "Damn Templars. More sins than they can confess all at one time."

As I left the cell I nodded. "You're right. He has a great many sins. May I minister to him tomorrow?"

From the look on his face it was clear Charles didn't want me back again.

Before he could answer I added, "It will take time to save his immortal soul. Our Lord Jesus Christ would be very angry if *you* let this man die with so many unanswered sins."

He stepped back, eyes darting from side to side as he considered what I'd said. The thought his refusal might affect his own immortal soul weighed heavy on him. He gave me a stern look. "If Sergeant Moreau says you can."

His look of relief said it all. He'd saved his own soul from a wrong decision and put the burden on Moreau's soul. God couldn't hold him responsible for following Moreau's orders. I was doubtful Sergeant Moreau had the same concern for his own soul and it might be more difficult to convince him I should be permitted another visit with the same prisoner.

I ministered to two others then to Charles' delight I told him I'd done as much as I could before the mid-day meal.

I met Sergeant Moreau at the donjon door. "Thank you, Sergeant. A man's soul must be saved if at all possible. I wasn't able to complete my ministry this morning and I promised to meet with some of the poor souls who live on the edge of town later today. May I come back tomorrow morning? Brother Hans and I had planned to leave for Paris in the morning but our work here isn't done yet."

Sergeant Moreau gave me a cold, hard look. "King Philip wants Clement's monks to do their work. We've been ordered not to interfere. Be here the same time tomorrow."

Sergeant Moreau and Charles, I never did learn his last name, were true to their word. I met with de Molay again without interference.

As we knelt in his cell de Molay asked, "What do you want from me? Any Templar is free to join Denis's crusade, his

Reconquista. No Templar requires my approval for such action. If there is doubt of this I will sign a proclamation."

I was perplexed. He seemed to have little interest in preserving our Order or helping Denis stop the Muslim threat. "We need your leadership. The people know you are the Templar leader. With you leading the Templars we would be a mighty force again. The French people would rally behind us and support Denis and his Reconquista."

"I've given this much thought," De Molay said. "I see no future for our sacred Order. There will be no more crusades in the Holy Land, not in our lifetimes. I once put my faith in Clement to vindicate our Order and help purge those Templars who dishonored it. But, sadly, Clement is not strong enough to withstand Philip's onslaught. Against men like Nogaret, Clement is weak."

I pressed, "If we swore allegiance to Denis and his Reconquista we might yet sway the people's support. Clement and his loyal bishops could rise to Denis' cause. Philip must yield to that."

De Molay slowly shook his head. "If Clement would. But he won't. He's already defeated. He has no faith in the people. Worse, he has no faith in God. And without faith in God to overcome such men as Philip and Nogaret there can be no victory. Clement has grown tired of the Templars. It's gone on for years and now he'd like us to go away and let him get on with other matters like consolidating his authority over the rebellious bishops in the north and in Italy."

I nodded. De Molay was right about Clement. And it had become clear the French barons and bishops all despised the Templars. We were a sore that would not heal. They, too, were tired of our fight with Philip.

"What will you do?" I asked in frustration.

"I will wait, patiently, for God's truth. *Deus Vult*. He has a plan. I do not yet know what it is. But it is clear I must not be willful. I will accept God's will."

De Molay was silent for a long time. He was at peace. De Molay smiled, a worldly smile, both sad and confident. "I am to wait for God's hand. God has already put you on your path. Our paths divide. Your way is a new way, a way I do not fully understand. Mine is to complete the past. I am confident both are part of God's plan. I think His plan for you and the others with you is in the Baltic not in France or the Mediterranean. The world has already changed. Have faith, *Deus Vult*.

"Only my mortal body is in the hands of Clement and Philip. My immortal soul is in God's hands. If I were to escape or even if I were released there is little I could do to change the course of my life. And even less that I could do to change the course of the Templar Order. So I wait for God's hand with faith and trust in Him."

It reminded me of a time years before. While in Cyprus on a raid along the coast near Latakia another young Templar, Jehan, told me he had seen his fate. He would be killed that night. I was to live and return to France but he could not see my fate beyond that. He was both sad and confident, and very much at peace. He wished me well. His sadness was for me, not for himself. My struggles, both victories and defeats, lay in front of me. His final victory, as he called it, was at hand. He fell that night, a crossbow bolt through his head.

"What would you have us do?"

"Those who would serve Denis' Reconquista should go to Portugal. Those who hope to serve in a future crusade of the Holy Lands should take the oath of the Hospitallers or the Teutonic Knights."

His eyes met mine. "And those who would build a new order for a new age, *novus ordo seclorum*, will go to the Baltic."

I stared at the cell's stone floor for a long time, uncertain what to say.

De Molay put his hand on my shoulder as if to comfort me. "Erik, Philip will check mate Clement in Vienne. Clement will be forced to dissolve our Order. Then all he can do is try to save what he can for the Hospitallers and that won't be much. Clement may want to help Denis but Philip and Nogaret will never permit us to reform as a military order.

"If I escape, or even try, Philip will tell the people and Clement that all Templars are a threat to him and the Church and to the French people. He will say we've become criminals as well as heretics and perverts. He will insist all imprisoned Templars immediately be put to death and the people will be afraid and force Clement to agree to Philip's commands.

"I must wait. Perhaps Philip will let Clement pass judgment on us individually. But the Order cannot survive. Philip will not allow it. Clement may be willing to let me and the other imprisoned Templars go free, that's the best possible outcome. But Philip will not permit even that."

"What do you mean, a new order?"

"Ah, yes, the new order. The two great orders in my lifetime have been the barons including the king, and the bishops including the pope. Ordinary people labor and die for one or both of those powers. They are manipulated and controlled by one or both of those forces."

I nodded. That certainly agreed with my own views.

"Wealth came from the land. And land and its wealth have been controlled by strength of arms or the powers of faith."

I agreed with that, too.

"You, the Templars in the Baltic, have become part of something new. Trade and commerce have expanded and we have facilitated it. We have managed wealth and its transfer. We have created, or at least promoted, the concept of an honest third party to manage financial matters. Trade and commerce can take place, safely and with confidence, over great distances and over months, even years. We've seen those involved in such trade and commerce grow in wealth.

"We didn't set out to do this. But you said it well, your efforts in the Baltic build wealth without war, without blood. The barons and bishops despise your commerce but they leave you alone. They will, of course, demand a share by way of taxation or tithe but they will depend on you to create the wealth they covet.

"That is a new power, a new force. The result will be a new order in our world."

I sat silently listening to de Molay. I'd never seen what we had done, were doing, in the way he described. He made it sound like a crusade, a righteous cause to free people from two old, corrupt, abusive orders. The barons and the bishops were corrupt. Philip and Clement were corrupt, each in their own ways. Barons fought barons. Bishops fought bishops. And they all fought each other. Only rarely did a baron or a bishop pay the ultimate price. Only rarely did ordinary people share in the wealth. That had been the fate of ordinary people.

"What of du Tour and the Templars who violated their oaths, those who corrupted our initiation rites? It was his corrupt loan and their perverse acts that provided Philip the means to destroy us."

De Molay shook his head. "They gave in to their own weakness, as all men do. Our Lord Jesus Christ taught us not to judge, lest we be judged. Let God deal with them. Trust His judgment, not men's, to be fair and just. Look to the future, not the past."

"What of Philip and Norgaret, Clement and the Marigny brothers? They murdered innocent men, our Templar brothers."

De Molay looked into my eyes. I could see there was no anger, just sadness, in his own. "Yes, they have. They are guilty of murder and they are, in time, subject to our retribution. God will deal with their souls."

De Molay stood and motioned to the cell door. "You must go now. It is not safe to stay longer. Tell the others you are all in my prayers. *Deus vult.*"

CHAPTER XVI
End of an Age

That evening in a quiet corner at L'auberge de Gisors, Hans, Dieter and I talked of de Molay's words. It was a somber evening.

Dieter summed up what we each thought, "We must return to Lubeck but I don't know what to tell Alleric and the others. The idea of a new order, that's what he called it?"

I nodded.

Dieter continued, "Maybe they'll understand. I'm sure I don't."

Hans smiled, then chuckled. "I think I do. I think he sees a counter balance to both king and pope. A way for ordinary men to be independent of kings and barons and of popes and bishops. Wealth creates power. And trade and commerce can make even an ordinary man wealthy."

"And ordinary men don't become barons much less kings," Dieter responded. "And ordinary men rarely become bishops much less popes."

That evening Rolf and the others closed up our market stall and packed our skiffs for the journey south. Early the next morning we were drifting down L'Epte to the Seine. There was no need for the horses so Rolf had sold them for us at a profit in Gisors. As the sun set that evening we reached the Seine and spent the night at Port Villez.

Rolf wasn't about to sell the two skiffs in Port Villez, they would bring more in Rouen. So we lashed them to the sides of our own barge. It worked well, with a broader beam the current carried us along quite well. We were on the Seine with the rising sun and made Rouen late the next day.

The following evening the three of us had dinner with Milun and Rolf in the Two Maces. Andre and Milun made certain Mateo and Alain didn't know of our meeting. Milun announced his decision to join us in Lubeck. I had the feeling he and Rolf somehow fit de Molay's vision of a new order, I just didn't know how.

Milun needed two days to complete his separation from the service and say good-bye to his old officer. I didn't envy him. He was leaving everything he'd known since he joined the army at age fourteen and now had little enough knowledge of what lay ahead. But he had no family, no ties to Rouen or France. The new officer didn't object to Milun's short notice, welcomed it according to Milun. The officer had his own men who'd served with him many years.

Milun had lived frugally all his life and had accumulated a sum I considered rather large. He had told me one time his plan, when he left the army, was to buy a small tavern or inn in the countryside. He certainly had enough for that.

I wondered what Rolf would do when we reached Saint Adela. Would he stay with his brother and family or continue on with us to Lubeck?

Luc was standing on Saint Adela's dock as the Rouen barge pulled away and we slipped into its place. He'd been helping Gaidar and Ulf load their goods when he'd seen our craft coming. As their barge passed us the two brothers waved and shouted their greetings.

Milun seemed to fit in well. His friendship with Rolf quickly spread to the other Templars in our crew. Milun was obviously enjoying his new life and was taken with the tavern. He smiled broadly and nodded enthusiastically as Gaspard proudly showed him around. Perhaps this was exactly what Milun had envisioned for himself.

We stayed the night so Rolf could visit Giles and his father. He needed to see for himself how they'd fared without him. When he returned the next morning he took me aside and explained he couldn't continue on with us, his father and brother needed him at home. Rolf didn't show any disappointment, just an acknowledgment that his duty for now was in Saint Adela. When I asked about his father Rolf shook his head and shrugged.

I assured him he and Giles were always welcome in Lubeck if circumstances changed.

We sold our barge in Le Havre and sailed for Hamburg with Captain DeGeer. We purchased horses for our journey to Lubeck and arrived late in September, 1311, almost four years after the arrests.

The next afternoon and evening Hans, Dieter and I met with Alleric and Wilhelm in Alleric's residence on Konigstrasse, not far from the Markt and Marienkirche.

After I related what de Molay had told me Alleric said, "He's had years to think about our situation and his own. How's his mental condition? Was he thinking clearly, was he coherent?"

"I saw and heard nothing that caused me to doubt his mental abilities. He was thoughtful, coherent as you say. He spoke logically. His words were well-formed and his thoughts sequential. He didn't jump from subject to subject."

"Was he dispirited?" Wilhelm asked.

"No. I felt he wanted to be realistic, to see things as they are, without judging whether it was morally good or bad. The same way he would evaluate a battle's progress and determine what action should be taken. He weighed the choices as best he could with the information available to him."

"How's his physical health?"

"He's thin, old, tired but at peace."

"Has he given up?" Alleric asked.

"No, I don't think he has. He outlined what I see as a rational course. As to his own fate he believes the outcome could go either way. I think he feels it is entirely in God's hands and out of our control and certainly out of his. He's comfortable with that, as a man who has fought well, done all in his power, and must accept the outcome with faith in God.

"Our work in the Baltic, he believes, is in accord with God's will but it is up to us and, therefore, within our control. He was very positive about what we're doing. De Molay believes the age of Crusades is past. Trade and commerce are the future."

"What's this new order for a new age he spoke of."

"It's a new idea but as I've thought it over I've become more comfortable with it. It shakes the old world orders I've lived in, a world controlled by the Church and the barons."

"What would your course be, Erik? Portugal, Hospitallers, Cypress, or this new order he spoke of."

"It would be here in Lubeck and the Baltic, the new order."

"Why wouldn't you join Denis in Portugal to drive the Muslims out? It's what we trained for."

"I'm not a young man, none of us are. Denis needs trained men, young men. And equipment, weapons, the best there are. All that takes wealth. How much does Denis have? Enough? I doubt it. But we can create wealth, wealth to pay for the men and equipment he'll need.

"Almost six hundred years ago Charles Martel knew he had to have wealth to form and train his army. He asked the Church for help but the Church, at first, refused. It finally gave in after it threatened Martel with excommunication. Clement doesn't have either the wealth or the stomach to threaten Philip to support Denis.

"Denis has the will and with our financial support he can drive the Muslims from Iberia. Make it safe for Christendom."

The Council of Vienne began in October of 1311, four years after the 1307 arrests. With that the end came quickly. A month later, Philip personally led his army to Vienne. He had the Council surrounded. It was "check" and "checkmate" would follow. Clement couldn't flee and was running out of options. On March 22, 1312 he had no alternative but to issue a Papal Bull dissolving the Templar Order. As of March 22, 1312 the Poor Fellow-Soldiers of Christ and of the Temple of Solomon ceased to exist.

At the same time he officially pronounced the Templars not guilty. It was to be his final effort to save Templar lives.

A few months later, in another futile effort to stand up to the King, Clement ordered all Templar lands transferred to the Hospitallers. What good did it do? None at all. The following year the Hospitallers agreed to pay Philip compensation and transferred the lands to Philip. Clement had accomplished nothing.

Our Order had been dying since the arrests in October 1307. No men had taken the Templar oaths after that date. Clements dissolution of the Order had a profound effect on all of us who had taken the Templar oaths before that date, including me. We were no longer Templars and no longer bound by oaths of poverty, chastity and obedience.

Personally, the transition was almost overwhelming. I had been a young man, barely more than a boy, when I took the oaths. I'd never owned property and had no prospect of ever owning more than the clothes on my back and tools of my trade, so the oath of poverty had little meaning.

I'd been obedient to my father. He'd told me to join the Order, so I did without questions. The older Templars, Matthew, Wilhelm and Alleric, had raised me in the seclusion of the Order. I had never been willful so obedience to those who fed and taught me was logical. In battle one must be obedient, lives and the outcome depended on it. So the oath of obedience was close to self-preservation.

There was no longer a reason for an oath of chastity. In a military organization with vows of poverty and obedience and a vow to fight for Christ there'd been little distraction by women. Now there was no military service, no oath of poverty, no oath of obedience.

At age thirty I'd experienced a great deal. I'd fought in battles, killed men, and seen friends die. I'd traveled. I'd learned how to become wealthy and I'd experienced the comforts it can bring. I'd learned I had judgment, not just will. I could decide for myself what course to take in life. I'd seen women and realized I was deeply attracted to them, physically, spiritually and simply the joy and comfort of their presence.

Clement had released me from my oaths. The freedom that came with release from their restrictions opened my eyes and my spirit to a new world. I could become a man of the world, prosperous, independent and with a woman as my partner. And I could have children of my own. Perhaps most surprising, I found I very much wanted children

Early in 1311 there had been another, unrelated tragedy. Herr de Vries' daughter, Catherine, lost her husband to a plague in Hamburg. Shortly after his death Catherine and her young child, Katherine, returned to Lubeck to live with her parents, Herr and Frau de Vries.

Freed of their oaths the Templars in the Baltic sold what had previously been considered by us as Templar property. In the summer of 1312 I found myself relatively wealthy, free to run my own business affairs, free to join in Lubeck's social life, and very interested in seeing more of Catherine.

Over the years Herr de Vries and I had become very good friends and shared several business interests. Perhaps he'd always suspected I was a Templar and realized that with the termination of the Order I was no longer bound by Templar oaths. Whatever it was I don't know but beginning in the summer of 1312 I was a frequent visitor and dinner guest at the de Vries residence.

After the dissolution of the Templar Order, Clement had but one option, attempt a stalemate on the one remaining issue he'd steadfastly reserved as his personal jurisdiction, the guilt of individual Templar leaders. In a desperate move Clement ordered that anyone who rose to speak on the guilt of an individual Templar without his permission would be excommunicated.

By year's end 1312, as in a chess game, Philip controlled the board. Philip held de Molay and the other Templar leaders in Gisors, north of the Seine. Other Templars were held in Corbeil outside Paris by Bishop Marigny and guarded by Philip's troops. Emperor Henry was fully occupied with his Italian campaigns. Clement was in the south of France, terrified of venturing north of Vienne. Philip was free to move and he did.

In February 1313 Philip assembled his barons in Lyon and with their support renewed his claims of heresy and sodomy against the long dead Pope, Boniface VIII. There was nothing to support the allegations of heresy. Clement V and his Church had no real interest in the issue of sodomy but the people of France did. If Clement let the trial continue he risked losing public support for himself and the Church. Clement was compelled to defend the dead Pope or strike another bargain with Philip in return for Philip's agreement to once again dismiss the charges.

Nogaret died suddenly in April of 1313. His death seemed a stroke of luck and for awhile we hoped the loss of Philip's most dependable henchman would stop Philip. But it didn't.

On August 24 Henry VII Emperor died, murdered by a disgruntled relative. With the Holy Roman Empire in the turmoil of succession there was no longer any constraint on Philip, he was free to work his will regarding the Templars and the Pope.

Henry hadn't been an effective ally but with his death it wasn't long until Clement folded to Philip's demands and washed his hands of the Templar affair. Clement had insisted that he alone judge the guilt or innocence of the four remaining Templar leaders but in December of 1313 he gave up even that position. He created a Council of Bishops to judge the Templar leaders. The Council included Merigny the Archbishop of Sens, the same man who had burned more than fifty Templars. Significantly Clement provided the Council would hold its sessions in Paris.

Clement had no choice. Philip would not permit de Molay to be tried in Avignon. If Clement wanted to try de Molay he would have to go to Chinon and that was north of the Seine. If Clement went to Paris or any castle or town controlled by Philip his own life would be in peril. Philip had already murdered two popes. In the end Clement chose to stay in Avignon, safely out of Philip's reach.

When news reached the Baltic towns that Clement had turned the trials over to a Council of Bishops, Matthew and Alleric decided Dieter, Hans and I must return to Paris. We could predict the trial's verdict but not the sentence. The public's reaction to the verdict might determine the sentence.

In the unlikely event de Molay or the other leaders were released we must be there to help them quickly leave France.

We suggested Milun join us, he had contacts that might be helpful. Alleric agreed. When we told Milun our plans and the reason for our journey, his response was direct. "It beats a long, cold winter in Lubeck. When are we leaving?"

Winter storms made travel by sea impossibly dangerous. Even major rivers were frozen over and impassable by boat. Horses were our only possibility but doubled our travel time. It would be a long, cold month or more, an arduous journey. We made our way south from village to village, camping in the open country side when we could not find a country inn or tavern. The Meuse was frozen over and we were caught in a terrible blizzard for three miserable days but when we reached Chateau Thierry on the Marne our fortunes changed, barges were running all the way to Paris.

We arrived in Paris in early March and took a room in the Trois Moines with its access to the Seine markets and every rumor in the great city. Dieter and I spent our time talking with merchants along the Seine. Hans and Milun spent their time in taverns and inns from Boulogne to the Marne. Between the four of us we heard a variety of rumors and speculations. Most believed the Templars would be found guilty. The question was what sentenced would be imposed.

On March 16th the Paris bishops announced that their judgment would be made public two days later at noon on the 18th in front of the Concierge on the Ile de Cite. The taverns and markets were wild with anticipation, people were betting on the outcome, fights broke out as people took sides. All Paris was focused on the coming announcement.

Many people remembered the old glories of the Crusades. Even the Templars' loss at Acre was recalled with gentleness. Most people believed or at least hoped the Templars would be released. After all, the argument went, the Pope had already abolished the Order and without the Order the remaining Templars were just harmless, old men.

Salacious accusations captured the public interest and many people were focused on the sodomy charges. The debate was about the appropriate punishment. Those who were most angered tended to believe the practice had become universal within the Order and the only way to end it was to lock all Templars in prison or kill them. Others felt the practice was limited to a few miscreants and the matter could be dealt with by expulsion, the way the Church dealt with priests who strayed. God knows the Church had its share of those dark practitioners.

Very few were concerned with allegations of denying Christ and spiting on the Cross. The Pope had already forgiven the offenders, absolved them of their sins. That was enough, that and any penitence the Pope required. After all, even Peter had denied Christ three times. If Peter could be forgiven then the Templars could, too.

Through it all, those who supported Philip argued guilt was clear, the men had confessed. But most people believed torture had been used and the confessions were invalid.

The morning of the 18th we were among the first on the Concierge's plaza, Hans and I together on one side, Dieter and Milun on the other. We mingled with the growing and excited crowd waiting to hear the bishops' pronouncement. Judging by the betting odds almost everyone anticipated the four men would be found guilty. The betting on the subsequent sentences, life imprisonment or death, was based more on emotion than judgment.

About noon Marigny and two other bishops led the four bound Templar leaders to the balcony overlooking the plaza. Lined up behind the bishops and the prisoners were a dozen soldiers. Between the balcony and the crowd was a long phalanx of Marigny's soldiers, three men deep. It was evident whom the Bishops feared most.

When Marigny announced the Council's judgment of guilt there was brief turmoil in the plaza, the judgment had been expected or at least anticipated. Marigny let the crowd calm down then announced the sentence, life imprisonment. That was followed by a mixture of cheers and gibes that was headed towards violence until de Molay stepped forward.

When everyone realized de Molay wanted to address them the crowd fell absolutely silent, waiting to hear from the old Templar knight.

De Molay, in a firm voice all the crowd could hear, asked that he be allowed to address the people. Marigny looked surprised, uncertain how to react, but the crowd demanded that de Molay and the others be permitted to speak. Marigny relented and de Molay took another step forward and in the same resolute voice all could hear, he renounced his confessions.

De Charney stepped forward and stood next to de Molay. With the same firm conviction de Charney renounced his confessions. The other two Templar leaders remained silent.

The people went wild. Fights broke out as the four Templars were quickly taken away. The crowd attacked the line of bishop's soldiers. Hans and I made our way back to the Trois Moines. Later that afternoon Dieter and Milun arrived with news Philip had pronounced de Molay and de Charney relapsed heretics and ordered they be burnt on the Ile de Juifs at sunset that night.

Ile de Juifs is a small island at the northwest end of the Ile de Cite, not far from the King's palace. Crowds, angry mobs, assembled along both banks of the Seine to watch. Hans and I hired a boat to take us as close to the Ile as the guards would permit. Dieter and Milun did the same. Both boats were able to drop anchor not far from the banks of the Ile and the four of us saw and heard the entire terrible thing.

After de Molay was lashed to the death stake and the kindling and timbers were made ready De Molay proclaimed to the crowd that he would stand before God and Christ that very night and accept Their judgment with confidence his soul was innocent of all charges. In the same firm voice all could hear, he predicted that before a year passed both Clement and Philip would stand before God and Christ for Their judgment.

With that the guards lit the pyre. The timber must have been soaked in pig fat for it rapidly burst into full blaze. Almost immediately and without uttering a sound De Molay disappeared in the smoke and flames. For a moment I believed he'd been taken by angels.

De Charney followed to the same fate. When the matter was done and the guards had left, the four of us slipped ashore and collected ashes and relics of both men. The ashes and relics were later taken to Visby.

Milun told us he'd seen many brave men die in battle, with dignity and honor. But he'd never seen one as brave as de Molay and de Charney. I felt the same.

Following the deaths of de Molay and de Charney the other two Templars were taken out of Paris. Later we heard they were held in Gisors. We made no further effort to aid them.

De Molay's death was, I believed at the time, the end of the Templar era.

The day after de Molay's murder we said our good-byes to Greta and Jacques and took the Le Havre barge west. There was nothing to keep us in Paris. I think of Greta and Jacques often but I do not miss Paris.

We stopped to see our friends in Saint Adela but said nothing of the real reason we'd been in Paris. It was easier to say we'd been in Paris on business, considering exporting furs from Russia and amber from the Baltic.

Rolf's father had died that winter. Neither Rolf nor Giles were farmers by nature and their lord had moved them off the land to make room for another family, one that wanted to farm. Giles and Rolf were living in a small hut the brothers built during the winter, in back of Gaspard and Michelle's tavern.

Giles did odd jobs for the couple in return for room and board. Rolf worked on the Seine barges running goods up and down the Seine and made a fair sum buying and selling trade goods. Rolf realized their future in Saint Adela and along the Seine was limited. We, really Milun, convinced Rolf to join us in Lubeck.

News of de Molay's death traveled with the Seine barges. Rolf and the others heard it before we left Saint Adela. When Rolf asked I simply told him we had been there when de Molay was murdered. If Rolf suspected we were Templars he didn't show it but he knew we hadn't taken the Seine to Paris. I certain he suspected the real reason we'd been in Paris had something to do with de Molay but he didn't ask.

On our journey to Lubeck no one spoke of de Molay's death or the Pope or King Philip. But it was always on my mind. De Molay had told me retribution was due. Just before he died in the smoke and flames de Molay had proclaimed retribution was due within a year of his own death.

In Lubeck Rolf put his talents to work. He worked hard and enjoyed all of it. In the energy and excitement of the Baltic trade he seemed to grow in knowledge, confidence and bearing. By nature he didn't seem to need more than a few hours sleep and when he wasn't sleeping he was learning accounting, the rules of Lubeck law, the names and natures of the other Lubeck merchants, tradesmen and bankers. And he was happy. He had always been an optimist. Other people sought his company in the taverns, along the docks, in the counting houses, and at social events.

Rolf had managed to pick up a working knowledge of a half dozen languages and dialects while working on the Seine, usually the language of the boat crews and docks. In Lubeck he had the opportunity to use all of it with the local warehousemen and tradesmen. It didn't take him long to transition into the language of the more prosperous merchants and bankers and he was welcome in their businesses and in their homes on social occasions. As word spread that his nick name along the Seine was Le Loup a dozen or more young ladies, all from prominent families, vied for his attentions.

Milun was by nature more reserved but he knew military ways and needs. Working with businesses that manufactured weapons and other military necessities he sold and shipped a great quantity of the goods barons and bishops needed for their personal armies.

Business went on as usual. Over the next few months negotiations of agreements took me to Rostock, Emden, Hamburg, and lands far south of the Baltic coast. I was frequently able to take Milun with me. With his quick mind for calculations and his experience with military personalities and equipment he proved a valuable associate.

Milun was also adept at gathering information in taverns. In the service of the French crown he'd seen much of northern France and parts of the Flemish countryside. He'd fought with and against men from all over Europe and seemed to know something of each part. In a tavern he fit in. His reserved, disciplined nature stood out and other men with military experience felt comfortable with him. Over a tankard or two he could bring out information otherwise unavailable to the rest of us.

Milun could pick up rumors and inside information as well as any one I knew. With his help we learned of commercial enterprises and political activities throughout Europe and passed on the information to Alleric after each journey. Although Milun had not been a Templar our trust and confidence in him had grown to the point that he might as well have been a lifelong Templar.

One evening I met with Wilhelm in Visby. Over dinner Wilhelm asked if I trusted Milun and his judgment.

I responded, "Yes, I do. And he keeps his confidences when many others don't. Why do you ask?"

"With the end of the Templar Order two years ago we, Matthew, Alleric and I, realized we must find a way to know who is trustworthy and capable, and who is not. All the old Templars will eventually die so we've considered creating a new Order, an Order of laymen, good men, honest men. When we travel to a new city or town or even to a different country we need to know who we can trust and confide in without risking life and fortune. Perhaps Milun would be such a man.

"An Order of men who are known for their integrity would facilitate commerce and trade. And keep us safe from the barons and bishops. Something like a guild but not limited to those of a certain trade, rather limited to those of intelligence and high moral character."

That was a new idea to me but later as I thought about it I realized it made sense. The Baltic cities and towns were a confederation of sorts based on the Lubeck law. Under the rules governing our trade and commerce members had confidence they would be treated fairly. I'd also experienced corruption in France and in ports along the Atlantic and the Mediterranean. I'd seen how that corruption limited trade and wealth. I'd also seen how honest men like the de Veron brothers could be counted on to help solve a problem.

"Milun would be such a man. So would Rolf, the young man from Saint Adela. And Andre in Rouen. What would be the nature of this Order?"

"A secret order with rites designed to be certain the members were of sound mind as well as good moral character. There would be no vows of chastity or poverty. And none of obedience. A free man could use his abilities to provide for himself and his family."

I thought about it for a moment. "Who would lead them, how would their leaders be determined?"

"Each city or town would have one or more lodges. Each lodge would from time to time elect their own leaders."

At the end of our last session that year Opa looked at me and smiled. "Enkle, you've been patient. There is more I must tell you but it must wait until you are eighteen. Before my transition from the Templar Order could be complete there were matters that duty required I and the other Templars attend to. We will talk more of this and after your next birthday I will finally answer your question."

CHAPTER XVII
Eighteen 1358 AD

I expected dinner on my eighteenth birthday would be as it had in prior years, my father and grandfather and I with roast beef, pudding and my favorite wheat beer. I was wrong. Only the fare was as expected. When I came down for dinner I found three guests in addition to my father and grandfather.

One man I had met before, the Teutonic Knight.

"Erik," my father said with a warm smile, "Your grandfather and I want you to meet three old friends of ours, Brother Alfred of the Teutonic Knights, Mr. Schulz from Visby, and Herr Wolfe from Hamburg. You already know Brother Alfred. We were impressed you sought him out to learn of the Templars. Well done."

Brother Alfred, with a warm smile, shook my hand. "Happy birthday Erik. It's good to see you again. You've grown since we last talked. You are now eighteen, I understand. You look a little older. I'd judge closer to twenty. Your father tells me you are very active both in your studies and sporting contests, good for you. The world needs strong, young men."

I nodded. Apparently he had known who I was all the time. What I now realized was his size. I hadn't noticed it before. Probably because all men were bigger than I was at the time I first met him. He was taller than me and in his youth must have been an imposing man even for a knight. I would not have wanted to meet him on the field of battle unless he was on my side of the fight. Even now in his monk's robe he was big and, if his grip was an indication, still strong.

Mr. Schulz was a stern, weathered looking man or maybe it was due to years at sea. He was tall, not big like the knight. With his thick hair and beard he looked close to my father's age. His hand shake was firm and warm, his eyes were bright, and his voice a mellow baritone. "I've looked forward to this day, Erik, since you were born. Meeting the children and grandchildren of my friends has been, is, one of the joys of age. You must come to Visby and meet my sons, perhaps with your father on his next journey. They're a little older than you but not too much. You have much in common with them."

My father continued, "Herr Wolfe is originally from France. He was not a Templar but was of great help to all who were. Before he moved to Hamburg, Herr Wolfe was known as Le Loup. He is a past Master of the Hamburg Lodge."

I said little as we sat before the fireplace waiting for dinner. It was clear the five men knew each other well as they talked of business in the Baltic Hansa towns and a number of other cities they all seemed to be familiar with. There were references to the English victory the year before at Pointers and the life of the defeated French king, John II, at the English court, the latest news of the Golden Bull issued by Charles IV the Holy Roman Emperor, the civil war in Sweden, and the earthquake in Switzerland. How these events might affect business and trade was their central concern, not the impact upon the various crowns or the church.

Finally my father stood and proposed a toast. "To the Hansa and our League."

We all stood, and the others responded before taking a drink. "To the Hansa and the League,"

With that Mr. Schulz turned to me and with something close to a smile said, "Erik, this will make more sense if you knew that Brother Alfred's brother, Dieter, was a Templar.

Alfred and Dieter were part of Alleric's twenty with your Opa."

My father nodded, then added, "And Mr. Schulz's uncle, Wilhelm, was also a Templar with Opa and Alleric. Wilhelm was a little older than your Opa but younger than Alleric. He died in the Hamburg plagues several years ago. As your Opa may have told you Wilhelm was one of the founders of our Lodges and Mr. Schulz is past Master of the Visby Lodge."

Herr Wolfe nodded then, with a slight French accent, said, "It has been a long journey to reach this day. I have looked forward to it since you asked about your family's coat of arms."

At that moment Mr. Koch, our "houseman" as my father referred to him when talking to people outside of our family, interrupted to announce dinner was ready. To my surprise Brother Alfred turned to him, smiled and said, "It's good to see you again my old friend."

Mr. Koch grinned. "It is a joy to again be among such old friends. But dinner is ready. It's hot, so please continue at the table. Erik, you should know that your father is currently Master of the Lubeck Lodge where I'm a member."

Such familiarity outside our family came as a surprise to me. Mr. Koch was as old as my father. He was, I'd been told, the son of our previous cook who'd been with Opa since he moved to Lubeck. He was another fixture that I had never realized had a life before my own and apart from our home.

After serving dinner Mr. Koch returned and took a seat off to one side of the table. I thought he might have something else to say but he didn't.

Opa cleared his throat and said, "Before we begin, Erik, do you recall the promises you made when I first talked with you about the coat of arms?"

I nodded. "Yes. I made two promises. The first was that I tell my grandsons when they are sixteen and the second was that I not tell my brother any of what you have told me. I will keep the first and have kept and will continue to keep the second."

All five men nodded.

Opa continued, "As I've said many times, dates are important. The first date, October 13, 1307, was the date King Philip IV arrested the Templars. The second date, March 22, 1312, was the date Pope Clement abolished our Order. The third date was March 18, 1314, the day King Philip burned de Molay on the Isle de Juifs. You have learned what led to those terrible events. Soon you will learn what happened after de Molay was murdered. But before you do we must ask for yet another solemn promise."

I nodded but said nothing.

"What you will be told involves serious crimes, including murder and attempted murder at the highest levels. If you told anyone, all of us including your father and me, may be subject to persecution, even prosecution, by the Church, the barons, the king of France, and the Emperor. Do you understand?"

This was nothing like the other two promises. I looked at my grandfather a long moment. He was dead serious. I looked at each of the others, all had the same expression.

I nodded and looked at my father, then at Opa. Neither said a word and neither changed his expression. There was no understanding smile that communicated everything would be alright. I had the strong feeling that I was about to cross a line I could never re-cross. But if I crossed it I would be part of something very important.

"What is the promise?"

"That you will not disclose to anyone, except your grandsons, what you are about to hear. If you violate this oath you accept the punishment of banishment. Your grandsons will not be burdened by this promise. Everyone who might be prosecuted will have died by then. And few would seek to persecute either the Hansa League or the Lodges for events that happened so long ago."

Herr Wolfe said, "You have a future, Erik, as a member of our Hansa and, perhaps as a member of one of our lodges, whether you make this promise or not. I look forward to working with you, whether you make the promise or not. We hold a terrible secret that could harm some of us. And might even destroy the Hansa League and the Lodges. But we do not want that secret lost. The Templars created something very important and we want their families to know what became of the Templars. I can assure you the promise does not make you complicit in their acts and you cannot be blamed or prosecuted for the knowledge."

"Then I promise," I said firmly.

My father smiled. "Excellent. Opa will ask you again in the morning, to see if you have second thoughts about the oath."

Opa said with a warm smile, "It's been a long journey and we have much to celebrate. You have sworn your oath to all of us and we are witnesses. I will have a great deal to tell you in the coming weeks and I expect some of it will be shocking but this history must not be lost. It is all part of the new order for a new time as are the League and the Lodges. *Novus Ordo Seclorum* de Molay called it."

With that conversation returned to the events of the year. We finished dinner and talked of business in the Baltic and events in Europe.

The following morning when I met with Opa in the quiet of his apartments, he smiled and asked, "Are you comfortable with your new promise?"

I nodded and told him I was and reaffirmed it.

"Good, I'll begin with Nogaret. One of the world's truly evil men. If animate evil exists, and I believe it does, Nogaret was that."

Over the following four days I learned what Herr Wolfe had referred to as a terrible secret. I won't try to relate what was said day by day, I'll just relate the entirety of what Opa told me as accurately as I can.

In late March of 1312 Hans, Dieter and I met with Matthew, Alleric and Wilhelm. Over dinner we talked of business matters but when we finished and moved to more comfortable chairs in front of the fireplace our conversation changed. Matthew told us that two days before he'd learned Philip was on the march to Vienne to threaten Clement.

Alleric got to the matter he wanted to discuss. "Philip has forced our hand. We must change the situation."

Dieter looked up in surprise. "Do what?"

"Reduce Philip's strength. Remove de Nogaret."

"Remove? How?" I asked.

"Nogaret must be removed, he must be assassinated," Alleric responded with the same quiet tone.

I was stunned. Open, honorable, warfare on the fields of battle was one matter. Targeted assassination, another.

"What good would that do?" I asked.

"With good reason Clement is terrified of Nogaret. Nogaret physically beat Boniface so viciously he later died. And he poisoned the next Pope. Philip may have other men who would murder a pope but there aren't many who would risk their immortal soul in such a way. With Nogaret dead Clement may be willing to stand up to Philip and give de

Molay and the Templars a fair trial. And without Nogaret Philip may have second thoughts about his plans. We might have time to reform the Order and find a reasonable resolution of our differences with Philip and the Church."

"What will happen to de Molay?" Dieter asked. "And the others."

"It will be done in manner that cannot be traced to us," Wilhelm said. "Philip may suspect Nogaret was murdered but there will always be a question about the cause of death. We will continue our efforts to gain de Molay's release by negotiation. "

"Why are you telling us? Do you want us to do this?" I asked.

"No, you will not be involved. But you've put yourselves at risk and deserve to know our plans. If Nogaret's death changes the situation, as we believe it might, we may need you to help bring de Molay out. You should know the risks."

The evening ended on that somber thought.

Not long after that Alleric and I had a quiet dinner at my residence to celebrate the successful conclusion of an agreement insuring several shipments between the cities of Hamburg and Rostock. Our conversation eventually moved from commerce to Philip and the Templars. I asked Alleric if he'd thought any more of Nogaret.

Alleric frowned and shook his head. "Yes, I have. But, Erik, it's better you don't ask."

I heard nothing more of the matter and asked no questions.

About a year later, in late March of 1313, Alleric left on business. Saarbrucken in southern Germany, he said. Such trips were not unusual.

He returned in May. When I asked about his journey he said it had gone well enough. The way he answered left it clear that he didn't care to discuss it further.

Not long after that we heard Nogaret had died suddenly, unexpectedly, in April. It was reported he died with his tongue out, black and swollen. In the taverns there were rumors of poisoning. We waited for Philip's reaction to the death of his chief minister but saw none and heard none. Nogaret's death changed nothing. That was all I've heard of Nogaret's death.

You've heard of de Molay's murder and his prediction that Clement and Philip would follow within the year. Now I'll tell you of the events following de Molay's death.

In early June of 1314 word reached us that Clement was dead. I wondered how he died and whether Templars had been responsible. De Molay had announced retribution was due within a year. For Clement it took a month and two days.

Several years later I heard from my old acquaintance Claude-Jean in Roquemaure. He always claimed he had a great many close friends in Clement's inner circle. I confess I don't believe his entire account.

According to Claude-Jean, Clement was terrified of what he called 'de Molay's curse.' When Clement heard of de Molay's murder and his prophetic last words Clement left Avignon and went north to the Chateau Roquemaure where he locked himself in his chambers, stopped eating, and hid in his wardrobe during the day. According to Claude-Jean, Clement roamed his papal quarters through the night, afraid to sleep.

Others said he refused to leave his bed and summoned his physicians who bled him several times a day. He ate only mush and drank only beer, and jumped, cried out at any sudden sound. Whatever the truth of all that is I don't know. There seems to be agreement that each morning and each night he was given his last rites.

On April 20 Pope Clement died at the Chateau Roquemaure on the Rhone. That night Clement had surrounded himself with his physicians and his personal confessor. He prayed constantly, insisted on hourly confessions and absolutions. According to all sources, there was a violent thunderstorm and lightening struck the chateau donjon several times. On one such strike Clement called out to God to forgive him, then collapsed and died.

Some say the Templars murdered Clement. I can with confidence deny that categorically. God and Clement's conscience killed Clement.

Philip and the Marigny brothers are different matters.

CHAPTER XVIII
Retribution

Clement's death, for all appearances the fulfillment of de Molay's curse, caused a great deal of confusion and indecision not only to me but other Templars. I was certain Templars played no part in Clement's death. It was not our retribution, it was God's. I wondered whether we were to wait for God to strike Philip. Or were we to act and in acting serve God's purpose? Hans, Dieter and I spent many evenings on that question. I think most Templars did.

I learned later Matthew, Alleric and Wilhelm had the same question. Over that summer of 1314 their conversations shifted from whether to act to how to carry out the act. Killing a king is a complex matter if one wants to survive and leave no evidence of who did it.

In early August Hans, Dieter and I had dinner with Alleric, Matthew and Wilhelm in the Lubeckhafen's private dining room, very much like the one in the Emdenhaus. After diner we moved to the fireplace where chairs had been set so the six of us could enjoy the fire and talk easily.

Alleric sat back and looked at each of us. "You know Wilhelm and I have been out of town a great deal the last two months. Ever since de Molay and de Charney were murdered we've been meeting with our Templar brothers around the Baltic and parts of Germany.

"Erik told us of his last meeting with de Molay. You've all heard of de Molay's curse and Clement's death. We had no part in Clement's death but our council decided Philip will be next."

Dieter leaned forward in his chair, teeth clinched, eyes narrowed and nodded. "Good riddance to the devil's child."

"I don't have a problem with that," Hans said. "But why Philip? Why not Marigny, either of them, the Chamberlain or the Archbishop. Either one would be easier to kill."

"We think Philip is the logical target," Matthew answered, "rather than Archbishop Marigny or Chamberlain Marigny. All are responsible for the murder of Templars in the most horrible of ways, by fire.

"Archbishop Marigny's half-brother, Philip's Chamberlain, is also responsible for carrying out Philip's financial policy to debase the coinage. He's very unpopular with the barons as well as the French people. He's also responsible for his half-brother's appointment as Archbishop of Sens, the one who burned more than sixty Templars. We're certain that upon Philip's death his Chamberlain will be removed by Philip's successor. The barons and the people will demand it.

"With Philip, Clement and the Chamberlain dead or removed the Archbishop would soon suffer the same fate.

"If either Marigny died first, Philip and the surviving brother would rapidly move to kill anyone and everyone who might have any connection to the death, simply to preserve their own lives. Fate will deal with the Marigny brothers once Philip has been removed.

"Philip's sons or his brother. Charles of Valois, the same man who wanted to be Emperor of the Holy Roman Empire are the most likely successor to Philip's throne. They will be occupied with consolidation of their powers and devote little effort to find those responsible for Philip's death. After all, those who had done the deed would have cleared the way for his successor but pose no threat to the successor."

The logic of it was well thought out but I wondered how they planned to accomplish the murder of a king.

Wilhelm looked at us, then began, "Philip spends most of his time in Paris occupied with governing his country. He isn't vulnerable in Paris. When he's not in Paris he's usually inspecting his lands in the north of France or watching over several of his more questionable barons. On such occasions he takes a hundred soldiers and several of his trusted barons with him.

"Fortunately, he likes to hunt stag and boar. That's when he's most exposed. His favorite hunting grounds are in the forest of Halatte outside Criel, north of Paris and east of Gisors. We have reliable information, current information, concerning his schedule. He has a hunt planned in early November."

Wilhelm paused to let that sink in.

"How long will he be on this hunt?" Dieter asked.

"Three days, not counting days of travel, Alleric said. "But if winter sets in early the hunt will be cancelled."

Dieter asked, "Have you heard where he'll stay on this hunt?"

"He and his hunting party stay in the field"

"How many in his entourage?" I asked.

"Philip and three, perhaps four, of his favorite barons. And the required cooks, stable hands, horse handlers, hunt guides, servants. Total of fifty or so, maybe fewer."

"And guards?" Hans asked.

Wilhelm nodded. "Yes, we've been told there'll be guards. A hundred of his best men from the Paris garrison. All are loyal and well trained but they'll be kept some distance from the hunt so's not to scare the game."

"Do you have a plan how this will be carried out?" I asked.

Alleric nodded. "Yes, we do. But before we discuss that we'd like the three of you to think this over and decide if you're willing to do this. If you aren't we'll find others. No one will hold it against you if you decline. Obviously it's dangerous. If you're captured you will be tortured and killed. And if you're successful, well, murder by ambush is not the same as killing on a battle field. Before you decide you must ask yourself whether you can live with this."

"When do you need our decision?" I asked.

"In three days," Alleric answered.

The three of us went about our work as usual but each night we had dinner together. On the second evening we reached our decision. We would go to France.

The following day we met with the three men to tell them our decision. Each took the news as soberly as expected. There was no joy or excitement in such a mission, only the acceptance that it must be done and we were the ones who had the best chances of success.

I told Alleric, "We want to include both Rolf and Milun. They know the area and each has special skills and knowledge that would be useful."

Alleric nodded. "We thought you might suggest it. We'll include them in the plans if they agree."

The following afternoon the three of us met with Milun and Rolf in my quarters. After explaining our mission we made it clear they would be in a supportive role, well away from the actual killing. We needed reliable men who were familiar with that part of France to get us to the forest and home again.

We'd previously told Milun of our Templar history and he'd been present with us when de Molay was murdered. He knew of the curse and he knew Clement had died. Milun wasn't surprised when we told him of our intentions. He didn't hesitate.

We hadn't told Rolf of our Templar life but that day he told us he had surmised there had been something more than trade involved in our trips up and down the Seine and the Rhone, particularly in Gisors. He, too, agreed to help.

The following day Alleric and the three of us left Lubeck to train in the forests surrounding the country retreat of a wealthy Hamburg merchant. Over the next five days we practiced with our crossbows and stalked game through forests similar to those where Philip would be hunting.

We spent our evenings working out details of our mission and discussing recent developments in France. Philip had far more than the Templars on his mind. It was well-known in northern France that two of Philip's daughter-in-laws, Margaret and Blanche, had been accused of adultery with two brothers, Gautier and Philippe d'Aunay, both Norman knights from England. Apparently the assignations had taken place in the Tour de Nesle on the Seine across from the Louvre. Philip learned of the affair from his own daughter, Isabella, wife of Edward II of England.

Philip's Chamberlain, Marigny, managed the prosecutions. Predictably both knights were found guilty and sentenced to be executed. The executions in April of 1314, a month after de Molay's death, were uniquely horrible. The father of the two executed men, himself one of King Edward's important knights, swore Marigny had framed his two sons. The father vowed revenge on both Marigny and Philip.

The two women were found guilty and were banished, apparently to the satisfaction of their husbands. The fathers of the two women were important French nobles, Otto IV, Count of Burgundy and Robert II, Duke of Burgundy. Both fathers also believed the charges were false.

The father of the two executed knights and the fathers of the two banished women all believed the so called Tour de Nesle Affair was a plot by Philip and his daughter Isabella, wife of England's King Edward II, to pass the French throne to

Isabella's young son, Edward III, thereby consolidating the thrones of England and France.

The Scottish defeat of the English at Bannockburn in June seemed to add to the argument that Isabella and Philip had designs on the two thrones. Isabella's husband, Edward II, was seen as weak and Isabella was known as 'the She-Wolf of France.'

At first all that seemed an irrelevant distraction from our plans but as the political situation became more heated we realized it could be important to our mission. Philip had enemies other than the Templars, powerful enemies with both motives and means. If Philip were assassinated there would be a period of uncertainty as to who his successor would be and the successor would be fully occupied with retaining the crown. Any investigation would likely focus on someone other than the Templars.

Alleric and Wilhelm's plan was simple. We would be met outside Villers-Saint-Paul, a small town up river from Criel, where our weapons and equipment would be brought to us by our Halatte guide. Our guide would take us to the area Philip intended to hunt. We would not be told how the man obtained that information, we didn't need to know.

Alleric and Wilhelm were certain Philip would be alone. He enjoyed the single pursuit of stag and boar. And he had a temper so his friends and his troops were careful not to interfere.

We would each have a dozen bolts for our crossbows, six Norman and six Burgundian, each identifiable by its distinct characteristics. We would carry the standard crossbow used by the French army. When either we'd sent Philip to his reward or found it impossible to do so, we would make our escape down the Oise that flows along the forest's west boundary. Boats would be ready for us. At Conflans, where the Oise flows into the Seine, we would take one of the many Seine barges to Le Havre and board a ship bound for Amsterdam.

It was simple enough but I recalled another simple plan. Our plan to gain entrance to the Paris Enclos almost cost my life.

The five of us left in early September. From all appearances we were exactly what people expected, Lubeck merchants on routine business to arrange for the export of fine French wines to the Baltic cities. We made it known in Lubeck and the other towns and cities we visited that we expected to visit a dozen or more wineries along the Seine and it was not possible to provide a precise schedule of where we would be from day to day.

Seine barges took us from Le Havre to Rouen with a day's stop in Saint Adela to see our friends. In Rouen four of us stayed at the Two Maces for three days while Rolf went ahead to Port Villez to purchase horses for the ride to Gisors.

Andre's father, Henri, had died not long after we were last in Rouen but Andre continued to prosper with his new accommodations. He didn't mention the additional room or the passage ways. I wondered if he knew of them.

Andre had introduced his new gaming room to the city but without the women. Sometime ago, at our suggestion, he'd spent time at the Coeur de Lion to learn the trade and had brought Gilbert back with him to manage the gaming room much as Geoffroi did in Chinon. The Two Maces had become the social center of the merchant class and the country aristocracy between Le Havre and Paris.

The second evening, as we had dinner with Andre in his private dining room, I said, "Andre we're going to Gisors, and perhaps Paris, on business. Our business may bring us into conflict with Philip's supporters. If so they will come after us. If they catch us they will kill us and anyone who protects us."

Andre gave me a quizzical look but said nothing so I continued.

"After we've finished our business we may come back though Rouen, but perhaps not. If we do we may need a place to stay for a few days, maybe more. A safe place where we can't be found. If we're found anyone associated with us will be arrested, tortured and imprisoned. Perhaps murdered."

Andre nodded and waited silently for me to continue.

"We'd like to stay here. I doubt we can be found here."

Andre looked at us in disbelief. "You want to stay here?"

We all nodded.

"You'd be easy to find here. Many of Philip's knights and officials stay here. Even some of the nobility stay here."

"No one would know it, not even you. We'd like to show you something but first you must bar the door."

When we finished our tour of the hidden room and corridors it was clear Andre had no idea of their existence. Amazed would describe his reaction. It was close to impossible to find, and impossible to open, the entrance from the private dining room to the passage way leading to the hidden room unless one knew exactly where to look and how to unlock and swing the panel open. Once in the passageway, the panel could be silently swung back into place and barred to prevent anyone following.

The exit to the roof was as cleverly hidden and had not been disturbed. It was impossible to enter the passage from the roof unless one knew where the entrance was and how to open it.

Later as we sat before the fireplace discussing the room and passages Andre fell silent for a long moment then looked at each of us in turn. "What are you about that Philip's men should be after you?"

"Andre," I said, "it's better you not know. It's serious and dangerous for us and for anyone who helps us."

Dieter added, "If we come this way we may not all come together. And we may not come as merchants. One or more of us may be in the hidden room. Do not look for us. When it's safe we'll let you know we're here. That may be the first you know of our presence."

Hans nodded. "We could come as anyone. And we may be gone without you ever knowing we've been here."

"But we will not come unless you agree," I said.

"If you need me," Andre said. "I'll not turn you away."

Several days later, when we reached Port Villez, we crossed to the Seine's north bank where Rolf waited with saddle horses, and two pack mules loaded with food and gear. Our ride up to Gisors was easy, gated horses are fast and very comfortable. We stayed in L'auberge de Gisors, making it clear to everyone that we were in search of fine wines for export. After three days visiting local wineries we announced we were leaving to visit several wineries in the vicinity of Meru, a small village just a half-day's ride east of Gisors.

From Meru it was only another half-day's ride east to Criel. The five of us visited two local wineries in Meru. The next morning we continued a little north of due east towards an even smaller village, Villers-Saint-Paul on the Oise just up river of Creil. That night we camped in a woods on the river's west bank outside of Villers-Saint-Paul. And waited.

Late in the afternoon two days later four men leading two pack mules approached our camp. When one introduced them as 'men bound by an ancient oath' we knew they were the men we were waiting for.

Before anything more was said the man pointed to the five of us in turn, "Albert, Benjamin, Charles, Denis and Edward."

I happened to be Charles.

He then pointed to himself and in turn to his companions, "Foucon, Georges, Hector and Ignatius."

After the strange introduction the leader, Foucon, said with a grim smile, "Philip has set his camp in the Halatte."

I didn't say it but the thought crossed my mind, in two days Philip would be dead.

Foucon's men unloaded our clothing, weapons, packs and provisions from the mules and that evening Hans, Dieter and I were transformed from wine merchants to men of the forest.

In the morning Milun and Rolf, alias Denis and Edward, along with Georges, Hector and Ignatius would enter Creil from the west. They would stay an Oise inn for one night and make it known they were in the market for local wines. The next afternoon they would follow the Oise to Pontoise, a small town north of Conflans and present themselves as wine merchants.

If all went well people would say they'd seen five merchants come from Gisors to Meru. A few days later five wine merchants were seen in Pontoise and a day or two after that in Conflans where they boarded a Seine barge headed to Le Havre. No one knew us in any of the four towns and no one could say with knowledge it was not the same five men in each town. For all appearances all five had left the area before anything happened in the Halatte.

Faucon was our guide. Although hunting in the Halatte was illegal and he could be hung for poaching if caught, Faucon said he hunted the forest regularly and knew it well. He looked every bit a hunter, a little shorter than average, stocky, no fat, keen eyes, bushy dark hair, dark complexion, and hands that looked capable of strangling any game he encountered. He looked to be about my age but weathered by years in the field.

By mid-afternoon the following day the four of us were deep in the Halatte on a rise over looking a meadow of grasses standing between knee and waist high. Scattered through the meadow were a variety of bushes, some barely as tall as the grasses, others as tall as a man. In a few places the meadow looked marshy. How deep the water was I couldn't tell but Faucon told us this time of year it wasn't over ankle deep and usually only deep enough to wet your boots. It was an ideal environment for the game Philip would hunt.

Faucon pointed to a faint column of smoke south of us. "That's Philip's camp. Philip has three camps he uses in rotation. His men leave a terrible mess after a hunt, takes a year or more for the land to recover. They have no appreciation of nature. It wasn't difficult to predict which camp he'd use this year. Tomorrow or the next day he'll hunt this area. I think it will be tomorrow."

He pointed to the south end of the clearing. "At first light he'll come north on one of those two trails, there's no way to know which. Deer and the other game graze in the meadow at dusk and dawn. Usually, but not always, close to the trees."

"Where will his men be?" I asked.

"His companions, if they hunt tomorrow, will be well behind him. It's not unusual that his companions sleep late. They prefer to hunt at dusk then eat and drink late into the night. They sleep most of the day. Philip eats little, drinks less. He's asleep shortly after the sun sets and rises before dawn. Philip has a temper. If they scare his prey he'll be mad as hell. So he'll most likely be alone. He'll dismount somewhere back in the trees and approach the meadow on foot, bow ready, then study the meadow for game. If he sees game he'll move as close as he can before taking a shot. He's a capable hunter and an excellent shot with his long bow.

"If there's no game he'll return to his horse and ride north through the meadow to the next clearing."

"Where should we be?" Dieter asked.

Foucon pointed to three spots. "One over there on the west side of the meadow by that thicket, one on the east near that tree, and one will slip in behind Philip after he leaves his horse, to block his retreat. The rest is up to the three of you.

"There'll be a quarter moon tonight but it will set before midnight. With these clouds there won't be much light. You'll need to be in place before dawn so find your places tonight and wait there alone, no fires. Take water but no food. Take your heavy cloaks, it'll be a cold night.

"When you've finished your work return to the river where we crossed. There will be two skiffs for you, take both. You won't see me but I'll be across the river watching. Someone must report what happened. If you're not pursued then make your way down river, don't hurry, drift with the current. There'll be fishing poles in the skiffs, do a little fishing on your way.

"If you're pursued make for the river's west bank. I may be able to help you escape but I can't promise.

"If you're successful throw one of your hats in the river. I'll know what it means."

Foucon gave us a skeptical look as he slowly shook his head. "It would be better if you didn't miss. There may not be another chance."

"And you? You're not coming with us?" I asked.

"No. I will meet up with my three friends tomorrow. We have farms and families to care for. They'll leave Pontoise with your two friends. Outside of town my three friends will head north. Your friends will wait for you on the trail to Conflans. I need to go now to make final arrangements for the skiffs."

He looked at the three of us but didn't smile. "May God be with you."

It seemed a strange request of God, that He help our efforts to assassinate a king but I just nodded.

I never learned who made the arrangements with Foucon and his friends. I never asked. I judged it a good bet Herr Stagg and his organization was somehow involved. I never saw Foucon or his three companions again and I often wonder what became of them.

After Foucon left we drew lots for the three locations. I was in the trees on the west side of the meadow. Hans in the woods on the east side. Dieter at the south end. Each man carefully selected his hiding place then signaled to the others so each would know where the others would be in the morning.

Each of us camped alone that night without a fire. Northern France can be terribly cold in early November and I wrapped the heavy wool cloak around me and waited for dawn, hoping Philip would come in the morning, early. Another day and another night alone, eating cold food in the forest without a fire was not something I wanted.

Foucon was right, even the birds weren't singing when I spotted a hunter in the trees at the south end of clearing. He was patiently studying the meadow, looking at something in the meadow I couldn't see. I wondered if he could see me but there was no indication he did. He must have seen something in the meadow and began to move very slowly, crouched over, arrow knocked, bow kept low.

I'd never seen Philip before, only drawings of him. The man in the meadow was dressed as a hunter in drab clothing not as a king in furs and bright robes. Foucon had told us Philip was a capable hunter and this was the time and the place we expected Philip. He'd also said the only distinguishing mark would be the royal coat of arms over his left chest, an azure shield with three gold fleurs de lis topped by a gold crown.

The man in the meadow was stalking something. Whatever it was I couldn't see without standing up but if I did he would see me. For some reason he wasn't working his way along the tree line. He was coming one careful step after another, very slowly, straight up the middle of the meadow where the grass and bushes were thickest.

With each step he was farther from his horse and safety. With every step he was closer to Hans and to me. With a few more steps I'd have a clear shot, a long shot but a shot. So would Hans. I couldn't see either Hans or Dieter but I knew where they were and I knew they were watching the man with the same thought I had, whoever this man is, he's a dead man.

The hunter took another three steps then stopped and studied the meadow ahead and to both sides, as if unsure. At one point he turned to search the surrounding meadow and I caught a glimpse of the brightly colored coat of arms on his left chest.

Out of the tall grass and bushes to the man's right a massive boar charged straight at the man. At first I thought it was a bear but the hoarse, guttural squeal was unmistakable. My first reaction was to distract the animal, my crossbow was up, involuntarily I took aim at the beast.The boar hit the man waist high and tossed him into the air as it charged past. Through a cloud of grass, mud, and bodies I could hear the man's screams and the boar's guttural squeals. The boar spun and charged back into the man as he stumbled, flailed and rolled in an attempt to escape. I had no shot, the man and beast were tumbling together. The boar backed off, hooves throwing clods of dirt, mud and grass high in the air, then charged a third time. The hunter was on all fours when the boar hit him in the ribs. He tumbled and rolled as the beast trampled him, stomping him, tusks shredding his legs, arms and stomach.

Then silence, how long I couldn't say. The animal was standing over the body, head butting it, testing for life. There was no life left in the man.

It was over. I slipped back into the forest and headed south to find Dieter. When I found him it was all I could do to speak. "Holy Mother of God. Did you see that?"

Dieter shook his head. "The bastard didn't have a chance. I've never seen a boar as big as that one."

Hans had the same idea I had and a moment later he appeared out of the forest shadows. "My God, the size of that thing. Philip never had a chance."

I looked at my two companions. "We've got to be certain it's Philip, and he's dead. Finish him if he isn't, it would be an act of mercy to put him out of his misery."

The three of us slowly worked our way through the forest on the meadow's east side ready to take to the trees if the boar appeared but it didn't. Through the branches of a tree near the thicket where Hans had been waiting we could see and hear half a dozen or more animals in the meadow. I've seen hogs and sows pushing and forcing their way to a feed trough, heard their squeals and grunts. That's what was happening. They were eating him.

We left Philip's body in the field and his horse tied where he'd left it. The saddle and tack all carried the royal crest. In time his men would find both horse and body. By then we would be far from the forest.

At the Oise we found the two skiffs. I took one, Dieter and Hans the other. Mid-river where I was sure Foucon would see I threw my hat in the river. Sometime later it was clear we were not pursued so we threw our crossbows and bolts in the river and began to fish as we drifted with the current. I was exhausted. Physically from lack of sleep and hot food. Emotionally by seeing the utter brutality of the killing and eating of Philip. Spiritually by the realization that the age of the Templars had finally reached its end. De Molay's curse had been fulfilled. But not by Templars.

That night we camped without a fire in a grove of trees somewhere along the Oise river. We talked in whispers, edgy at the slightest sound but finally slept from exhaustion.

Late the next day, on the trail from Pontoise to Conflans the three of us found Rolf and Milun. The three of us burned the clothing we'd worn in the forest and became wine merchants once more. The next morning we found rooms at a Conflan's inn, ate well and slowly calmed down. Tightened muscles relaxed, smiles returned, vision broadened. Nothing was said of the Halatte or Philip. The next day we caught the first Seine barge heading west. Thankfully, news of Philip's death had not yet reached the town.

Although we had no reason to believe we were suspected of causing Philip's death it was better we had no known connection with Andre or Gilbert. When we reached Rouen we waited until dark then slipped through the roof entrance to the Two Maces' hidden room. No one, not even Andre or Gilbert, knew we were there. We stayed in the Two Maces' hidden room at night and each morning before dawn we slipped out again, dressed as day labor, to work the Rouen docks until late afternoon.

With Philip's death there was no certainty as to his successor so we waited for news from Paris to reach Rouen. Rumors, fact or not, were the only way we could gage the public's reaction to the event and learn what might happen to the French crown.

After Clement's death there was uncertainty as to his successor. It still hadn't been resolved. A number of bishops and cardinals, in Italy and in France, were in fierce completion and a few in open warfare. Philip had been at the center of that storm. His support was critical and no one could be elected Clement's successor without Philip's support.

Succession to the throne of the Holy Roman Empire was also uncertain. After Henry's death there had been two separate elections to determine the new Emperor. One election had been controlled by the Hapsburgs, the other by the Luxemburgs. Two men now claimed the throne. The Hapsburgs and the Luxemburgs were preparing for war to determine the Empire's succession.

The Church, the Empire, and France were all without leadership. Europe was in chaos.

On the fourth day we heard the first rumors. Some said an unidentified member of the royal family had been seriously injured or killed in a hunting accident. Other rumors said whoever it was had died or was unconscious either from a brain seizure or after being thrown from his horse. None of the rumors mentioned either the Templars or mysterious wine merchants. And none mentioned a boar.

After work that evening the five of us made our way in the front door of the Two Maces. When we told Andre how long we'd been there all he did was laugh and pour each of us a tankard of ale. Then he took us to his private dining room and told us he had news we should hear.

"Late yesterday afternoon one of Philip's officers, from the Concierge in Paris, took rooms at the Rouen fortress for an indefinite stay. When he came in to eat, he also had quite a bit to drink. When I asked him what brought him to Rouen he said there had been a terrible accident on Philip's hunt. Someone, but he wasn't sure who, had been seriously injured, maybe killed. All Paris, he said, was consumed with speculation and rumors. Some said one of Philip's sons had been thrown from a horse. Others speculated it was Philip himself. Some said he was still alive, others said he was dead. Some said it was an accident, others said it was an assassination attempt. A few said it was a medical problem. No one knows for sure where Philip is."

Dieter reported, "I heard more rumors around the market. Pretty much the same as what Andre heard from the officer. Some say Philip is recovering at Fontainebleau."

I added, "I heard the father of the murdered knights tried to kill Philip, revenge for the murder of his two sons. And there's a struggle by Philip's three sons for the throne."

"All of that fits with what I've heard," Hans said. "Speculation is that Philip was thrown from his horse, hit his head and hasn't regained consciousness. His oldest son, Lewis, wants to take the throne until his father recovers but the father of Lewis' wife, one of those women who carried on with the Norman knights they castrated and hung, threatens a rebellion if Lewis does. Others say Philip's daughter, Isabella, and her husband Edward will try to unite the two thrones when they hear of this. Edward will mount an invasion in Normandy and march on Paris. He'll come up the Seine the way the Vikings did."

Rolf had been at the docks talking with the bargemen coming down from Paris. "I heard vague rumors that something had happened to one of the king's sons. But no one could say for certain what or which son. Most of the bargemen believe it was an assassination or an attempt. Some say it was the work of the Duke of Burgundy, others say it's the Count. Either way it was revenge for the treatment of the man's daughter."

Milun had spent his time with Mateo and Alain, filling them with meat pies and ale at a tavern on the other side of the market. "Mateo says the officer, the one Andre told us about, is here to be certain there's no attempt to overthrow Philip's family, the House of Capet. Paris wants to be certain the Rouen fortress remains loyal. Norman lords are always suspect when it comes to Edward and Isabella, and Rouen controls the Seine and access to Paris.

"He's certain there will be a sizable force arriving soon. Probably be here within a week to reinforce Rouen's fortress."

Over the next two days we continued to hear rumors, not much different from what we'd already heard. The most troubling rumor was that it was one of Philip's three sons who had been injured or killed. We knew whoever it was had been killed but the rumor it was one of Philip's sons could be true. Any of his sons could have been on the hunt and all of Philip's sons could rightfully wear the family and royal coat of arms. Significantly most rumors blamed the death or injury on a fall from a horse, something we knew to be false.

Dieter summed up our thoughts, "It must have been Philip. If it were one of his sons there would be no fear of a rebellion by Norman or Burgundian lords or an invasion by Edward and Isabella, and no reason for rumors the man might still be alive. They might not admit how the man died, that's understandable, but not the rest of it. If Philip still lived, even badly injured, we'd all know of it. He'd be on display in Paris just to quash the rumors and prevent his enemies from attacking."

I believed that with Philip dead a rebellion by the lords of Normandy together with an invading English army lead by Isabella and Edward was a very real possibility. The Holy Roman Empire was divided and not a threat to France or England. The other lords in France were not powerful enough to do more than demand greater independence from Philip's successor much as the English barons had done at Runnymede a hundred years before.

With Philip dead, Edward and Isabella in England allied with the Norman barons could overwhelm France. It would not be difficult if the barons in Burgundy joined them or even if they decided not to actively support Philip's sons. Isabella, after all, also had a legitimate claim to the French throne.

We debated whether to stay in France or return to Lubeck. There were good reasons for each.

It was important that we have confirmation that it was Philip who had died in the Halette and learn who was in control in Paris, who was creating the rumors, and what forces were at work. If Philip was dead his successor must be determined. We needed to know who was to be blamed for Philip's death.

On the other hand, Wilhelm, Alleric and Matthew must know the truth as we knew it and the reasons for our belief that it was Philip who had died in the Haslette. It was already late November and travel by sea would be difficult and soon impossible until spring. We decided Hans and Dieter would return to Lubeck. Rolf, Milun and I would stay in Rouen.

We hadn't forgotten the two Marigny's, Philip's Chamberlain and his half-brother the Archbishop of Sens. Together they'd murdered more than sixty Templars. In the current turmoil and chaos the Templars might have an opportunity to exact retribution. If Matthew, Alleric and Wilhelm were certain Philip was dead they might have plans for us.

The three of us stayed on at the Two Maces collecting rumors and trying to sort out what was happening in Paris. The additional troops Andre had heard were on their way to Rouen arrived not from Paris but from southern fortresses around Nantes, Tours and Le Mans. Those troops might be used to stop an uprising by the Norman lords and an English invasion.

Milun made a point of having lunch or dinner with Mateo once or twice each week. For a free meal and plenty of free ale Mateo gladly informed Milun of developments at the Rouen fortress and rumors of what was happening in Gisors. Significantly, the troops in Gisors and other northern castles had not been moved to Paris. They'd been moved to Fontainebleau south of Paris where they formed an arc to the south and east of Fontainebleau.

Milun believed it was to protect someone in Fontainebleau from an attack by the forces of Burgundy. The question was who was in Fontainebleau and needed protection.

Rolf worked the Seine barges from Saint Adela to Paris. Bargemen took a great interest in royal intrigues and the personal failings of the aristocracy. The route also gave him time with his brother in Saint Adela although our friends in Saint Adela were mystified as to why such an ambitious young man would waste his time on the barges. When asked he just answered that he was working with Dieter and Hans to arrange for the export of wine and other fine goods.

I spent my time with the Rouen merchants, gaming at the Two Maces and enjoying Rouen's social life. Most of the prosperous merchants had contacts all along the Seine and in Paris. Several had friends and business connections with merchants and bankers in Burgundy, Le Havre, Chinon, Tours, Nantes and as far south as Avignon and the Mediterranean. They knew the Rhone and the Loire trade almost as well as they knew the Seine trade.

With all of us willing to listen to anyone with news or rumors over the next months we developed a clearer picture of the situation. Philip was dead. The official story was that he died from a fall from his horse while hunting in the Halatte. Philip's oldest son, Louis X, aided by his uncle, Charles of Valois, had been chosen as his father's successor.

Under pressure from his uncle, Louis arrested Enguerrand Marigny, Philip's Chamberlain. Charles and Enguerrand had been court enemies for years and Charles had the final victory. About six months later Enguerrand was executed.

Phillipe de Marigny, Archbishop of Sens, disappeared shortly after the arrest of his half-brother and protector. No one claimed knowledge of his fate or whereabouts. I suspected Charles and Louis had him murdered. Dieter and Hans believed Thomas Weir and Herr Stagg's organization were somehow involved. In the end it didn't matter.

In a single stroke a wild boar had changed the fate of France and brought the retribution de Molay had called for. Was it the act of a thoughtless beast or was it God? I'll leave that up to you to decide.

Louis was fully occupied with consolidation of his throne. Jealous siblings, rebellious barons, and a demanding uncle were enough to deal with. There was no investigation into Philip's death. The evidence seemed conclusive.

There was little more we could accomplish in Rouen. In March when the weather began to clear Milun, Rolf and I made our way to Saint Adela and then to Le Havre and Lubeck.

In Lubeck I began my new life, not as a Templar but as an ordinary man. Catherine and I were married shortly after my return. A year later your father, Matthew Jacques Munger, was born. Two years later your aunt Michelle was born. You already know the family history since then.

When Opa finished I sat quietly for a long time thinking about all he'd told me. When I finally looked over at the old man he, too, was lost in thought.

I waited until he coughed and reached for his incense then I spoke, "Thank you. Now I understand the need for the oaths. But you haven't yet told me about the seven fleurs de lis on our coat of arms, a German coat of arms."

The old man smiled. "You're right, Erik. It's time to answer the question you asked years ago. The coat of arms was granted to our family by the Lubeck Council. All members of the Council were men of commerce united by the Lubeck law, now the Hansa League law. I had very little to say about the matter of the coat of arms but the Council talked with many of my Templar brothers and other members of our Hansa League.

"Under heraldry custom, military custom, the bend is from left to right. Templars were a military order. The fleur de lis, as you know, is widely used in France. Because I was born in Normandy the fleur de lis is appropriate. The Council specified seven fleurs de lis to represent the seven Hansa cities with which our family trades. The red belt above the shield represents our military service both as Templars and as protectors of the Hansa trade in the years after the arrests. The hawk rising is the new order de Molay spoke of."

It made sense to me but not yet complete so I asked, "Why the silver, argent, field on both sides of the black bend? And the colors black and gold?"

"The black field through which the fleurs de lis pass represents the evils and difficulties through which all men must travel, taking care not to miss step. Argent, silver, represents honor we must strive to preserve through life.

"The fleurs de lis and hawk are gold representing the power of commerce that frees a man to rise by his own strengths, on his own wings. The face of the gold florin is decorated with the Florentine fleur de lis and has been the standard for our European commerce and banking sine it was first struck over a hundred years ago. That alone was sufficient to warrant its use on our coat of arms."

I nodded. Again it made sense, in heraldic terms. But I thought he might have a more personal interpretation. "You've told me how the Lubeck Council specified the arms. How do you see it?"

"Well, there are other interpretations. Since I married your grandmother I see the seven fleurs de lis in a more personal way. Each of us begins our adult lives alone, that's the middle fleur de lis. We meet someone and become two, two that beget another. So there is in life a natural progression that reminds us all that we are not the first and we are not the last. We must always look to the future and those who come after us. And not forget the past and those who came before us. They are gold because there is no greater wealth than family.

"It also reminds me of the family I had before the Templars, my father and mother and my four siblings who died before me. I hope to see them once more, if our Lord permits.

"Remember, Erik, I am a Templar and a member of the Lodge. I firmly believe in and trust in God. The argent surrounding the black bend reminds me of the twenty-third psalm. As we walk through the dark path of evil and troubles in this life His grace surrounds us and comforts us. We should fear no evil but act with confidence in Him.

"The red belt of war reminds me of my brother Templars who died in battle to gain and preserve our rights and ability to prosper in our endeavors.

"The hawk, ah, the golden hawk. The hawk reminds me of our family's opportunity to rise above circumstances and difficulties, those of the past and those of the future. It is a reminder to you and all future generations that opportunity comes not from the old orders of Church and King but from the new order of trade and commerce, *novus ordo seclorum*, and your own strengths. But you must persevere with patience."

I thought of what he'd told me and smiled. It made sense.

CPSIA information can be obtained
at www.ICGtesting.com
Printed in the USA
FSHW011952150319
56427FS

9 780578 455877